as

simple

as

snow

G. P. PUTNAM'S SONS

New York

as

simple

as

snow

GREGORY GALLOWAY

G. P. PUTNAM'S SONS
Publishers Since 1838
Published by Penguin Group (USA) Inc., 375 Hudson Street, New York, NY 10014, USA •
Penguin Group (Canada), 10 Alcorn Avenue, Toronto, Ontario, Canada M4V 3B2 (a division
of Pearson Penguin Canada Inc.) • Penguin Books Ltd, 80 Strand, London WC2R 0RL,
England • Penguin Ireland, 25 St Stephen's Green, Dublin 2, Ireland (a division of Penguin
Books Ltd) • Penguin Group (Australia), 250 Camberwell Road, Camberwell, Victoria 3124,
Australia (a division of Pearson Australia Group Pty Ltd) • Penguin Books India Pvt Ltd,
11 Community Centre, Panchsheel Park, New Delhi – 110 017, India • Penguin Group (NZ),
Cnr Airborne and Rosedale Roads, Albany, Auckland 1310, New Zealand (a division of Pearson
New Zealand Ltd) • Penguin Books (South Africa) (Pty) Ltd, 24 Sturdee Avenue,
Rosebank, Johannesburg 2196, South Africa • Penguin Books Ltd, Registered Offices:
80 Strand, London WC2R 0RL, England

This is a work of fiction. Names, characters, places, and incidents
either are the product of the author's imagination or are used fictitiously,
and any resemblance to actual persons, living or dead, businesses,
companies, events, or locales is entirely coincidental.

Lines from "A Season in Hell" are reprinted from *Arthur Rimbaud: Complete
Works*, translated and copyright © 1967, 1970, 1971, 1972, 1975 by Paul Schmidt.
Reprinted by permission of HarperCollins Publishers Inc.

Library of Congress Cataloging-in-Publication Data

Galloway, Gregory.
As simple as snow / Gregory Galloway.
p.   cm.
ISBN 0-399-15231-8
1. High school students—Fiction.   2. Missing persons—Fiction.
3. Teenage boys—Fiction.   I. Title.
PS3607.A419A8   2005   2004044500
813'.6—dc22

Printed in the United States of America
1   3   5   7   9   10   8   6   4   2

This book is printed on acid-free paper. ∞

BOOK DESIGN BY AMANDA DEWEY

That, mermaid-like, unto the floor she slid,
One half appeared, the other half was hid.

CHRISTOPHER MARLOWE, *Hero and Leander*

as

simple

as

snow

good-bye to everyone

Anna Cayne had moved here in August, just before our sophomore year in high school, but by February she had, one by one, killed everyone in town. She didn't do it all by herself—I helped with a few, including my best friend— but still, it was no small accomplishment, even if it was a small town.

She captured all of these lives and deaths in fourteen black-jacketed composition notebooks. By the time she had finished, there were more than 1,500 obituaries, on just under 2,800 handwritten pages. The lives she wrote about were real, all true, but the deaths were fictions she invented, an average of around eight a day. "I'm not predict-

ing the future," she said, "but it's only a matter of time before everyone catches up to me."

She had known things about people, or had discovered
them—the secrets and private information that showed up
in her notebooks were things that people who had spent
their entire lives in our town didn't know. The funny thing
is, during the months when the bodies were piling up in
the imagination of Anna Cayne, I don't think a single person actually died in town; it was the longest drought for the
funeral home that anyone could remember.

The obituaries were private; her friends and a few other
people knew that Anna was working on them, but besides
me, I don't believe anyone else was allowed to read them.
She must have started the project on her very first day in
town, the day I saw her sitting on the front lawn of her new
home, writing in one of her notebooks as the rest of us
stood with her parents, watching their belongings parade
from the long yellow truck into the house. And after she
had written the last page almost seven months later, she
was gone.

Maybe.

She left behind little more than suggestions, hints, and
suspicions. But there were enough of them to make you
go crazy trying to figure out what it all meant. But you have
to try.

. . .

I have to change some things—some names, some events—and then there are things that happened that I didn't see, didn't experience, and that I'll never know. There's stuff I've tried to piece together and stuff I've tried to leave alone—I had to rely mostly on what I remember and what I could find.

There are a few newspaper accounts of some of the events, some TV coverage, and there's the police report (which I wasn't allowed to see), but none of those is really helpful. They all focus on the superficial details, and miss the real story of what happened. They've got their own version of the world to sell. Besides, they only tell what they've been told anyway, and very few of them talked to the person who knows the most about it—me.

This is what I know happened, or think happened. I fell in love with a girl, and then she left, and later she tried to come back, or I thought she did, and I went after her. It should have been simple but in the end it could not have been more complicated, and maybe that was the whole point to begin with, but if love is true and still leaves you lonely, what good does it do? I started going over everything again, thinking I might find a way to her, wherever she was, or at least figure out what to do with all the things she left behind.

"You have your whole life ahead of you," my mother told me, "don't spend all your time in the past." It's good advice, I know it is, but the past has its own ideas. It can follow you around with a life of its own, casting a long shadow.

spooky   girlfriend

She was born in a thunderstorm. I don't know if that's true, but somebody once wrote that about her and it seems to fit. She swirled into and out of my life, quickly changing everything, a dark question mark disappearing into a darker hole. Her name was Anna Cayne. "It's supposed to be 'Coyne,'" she told me in maybe the second conversation I had with her, "and there's a couple of theories of how it got to be spelled with an *a*. One is that some of the family was involved in some sort of criminal activity a long time ago, hundreds of years—murder, kidnapping, that sort of thing— and that the more respectable relatives changed the spelling of their name to distance themselves from the bad ones. Another version has it that it was the criminals who changed their name to Cayne, so it would be harder to find them once they left their old lives behind." I told her that I'd heard the same thing about my family, since my last name was also available in an *o* and an *a* version.

"You'd think that if they really wanted to distance themselves from each other, they'd change more than just one letter," I said.

"Well, it's a bit mysterious," she said, maybe a little put-off by the fact that her story wasn't as unique as she thought.

She and her parents had moved into town, which in itself was an odd occurrence, since not too many people moved into town; they almost all moved out. But there were the Caynes, watching the movers unload the truck and put their boxed belongings in the white two-story three-bedroom house on Twixt Road, just before it intersected with Town Street, which ran down by the river. The neighbors watched too, slowly pulled out of their houses and down the street, attracted to the yellow moving truck as if it were a huge magnet. They came by and introduced themselves and stood with the Caynes like spectators at a parade, a ball game, or some great historical event worthy of a rapt, attentive crowd.

My friend Carl Hathorne and I rode our bikes over and stood with the large group that had formed. We didn't really care about the truck or what came out of it; we didn't really care about the parents and what they looked like. We'd already heard that the Caynes had an only child, a girl our age. We wanted to see the girl.

We were disappointed; she was not what we had expected, and far from what we had hoped for. She came out of the house wearing a pair of headphones over her short, straight blond hair, the cord snaked into the pocket of a short black jacket. It was the kind of jacket someone would pump gas in, worn on a hot, humid day when it was, with complete certainty, the only jacket being worn in town. Under the jacket she had a black shirt, which, I found out later, was long-sleeved. She never wore short sleeves. She was also wearing a pair of jeans and heavy boots—black. She wore thick black eyeliner and a black expression. She sat down in the grass and started writing in a black notebook. I didn't give her much thought that day, but once I got to know her I often wondered whether she had been completely different the day before we first saw her, whether she had dressed in normal clothes, with a more inviting appearance and expression. Except for two notable exceptions, I never witnessed any other incarnation; she was always in her Goth gear, black and blonde and brooding.

"It's a freak show," Carl said. "Let's go back to your house."

I lived about a mile and a half north of the Caynes, in a house that was very similar to theirs. We lived on Valley View Road, but you couldn't see a valley from it. We were actually at the bottom of a hill, where we saw only hills, in all directions.

It was a long walk to the Caynes', if you stayed on the streets, but you could save some time if you cut through Mrs. Owens's yard and then across the vacant lot where the Boothe house had burned down two years before. Then, when you got to Talus Road, you cut through the Bordens'. You could get there in about fifteen minutes. I would do it lots of times.

All of this would become important.

Her given name was Anna, but she insisted on being called Anastasia. We had that in common. I wanted everyone to use my full first name. It wasn't out of vanity; I was named after my mother's brother, who had died young—just thirteen—and I had always been called by the full name because he had been. I never liked my name much, it never really seemed mine, a sort of hand-me-down from someone who never got enough use out of it, but what can you do? Only famous people have had their names changed, or else somebody has to give you a nickname, and no one was going to do that for me. Or you have to be someone like Anna, and just take the name for yourself.

"I love your name," Anna said. "It's almost a perfect double dactyl."

"A what?"

"Higgledy-piggledy. That's a perfect double dactyl. Two three-syllable words with the stresses on the first syllables. Your first name and your last name have the same number of syllables and almost the same sounds—they mirror each other, or are parallel or parallax or something."

"Okay." I was ready to be done with it. If she hadn't said "higgledy-piggledy," I might have told her about my dead uncle and how he had died under strange circumstances and maybe she was on to something, maybe there was a connection between the two of us. Maybe he was the parallel, although we shared only the same first name. We could have gone into all of that, but I didn't really want to continue with any conversation where "higgledy-piggledy" was used, and especially when I was being compared with it.

"You should pay attention to things like that. It's your name—you'll always have that. It means something. The mirror thing is worth thinking about. Or is it repetition? It's a double nature, anyway. The first and then the next being similar. Maybe you had a twin you don't know about. Maybe there's a ghost following you around. Or maybe it has something to do with parallel lines. You know, they meet at infinity. That's interesting. But maybe it has nothing to do with you. I don't know you well enough to figure it out yet."

"Okay. How about your name? What does it mean?"

"You'll have to figure that out for yourself."

She was always spooky. Her friends were worse. They strolled silently through the school in their funeral clothes and black lipstick and eyeliner and gun-black hair. There were seven Marilyn Manson types in school ("One for every day of the week," Carl had said, "as if one wasn't enough"), three of them in our sophomore class. There were two seniors and two juniors and no freshmen. We hoped they were a species headed for extinction.

They stuck out like badly bruised thumbs and we thought they were pretentious and full of shit. They were rarely alone, a traveling convention of mourners, except for her. I would see her sitting off by herself in class, eating alone in the cafeteria, or just standing on her own in the hallway between classes. It's what I disliked most about her at first, I thought she was even more pretentious and bolder than her friends, and then it became one of the things I liked most about her. Sometimes it works out that way, I guess, and sometimes the other way.

Our school, good old Hamilton High, was three stories tall, a long rectangle situated east-west on top of a low hill, with an entrance on each of the shorter sides. There is some debate about whom the school was named after. Almost everyone assumed it was after the adulterous Alexander Hamilton (as Anna liked to call him), who was shot dead by Aaron Burr in a duel on the banks of the Hudson River, for spreading lies and rumors about Burr. There had been Hamiltons around town years ago, but no one had ever found anything they had done to be noteworthy or exceptional enough to name a building after any of them, but there were people who still believed the school was named after some of these other Hamiltons. My mother was one of those people, she contended that the town would never name a building, especially a school, after such an immoral man. "He's on the ten-dollar bill, Mom," I said.

"What the federal government decides is suitable has nothing to do with us," she said. It was the most political statement I ever heard my mother make.

Everybody stood around in the hallways before class, and every group had its own spot. The bandoids were always in the basement, the arty types hung around Mr. Devon's classroom, the jocks were on the first floor by the west entrance, down the hall from the 4-H'ers, the geeks hung out at the eastern end of the second floor, the speech and debate team was on the western end ("I don't do a lot of business on the second floor," Carl always said). Carl traveled from floor to floor, and it never mattered where I was. Anna and the rest of the ghouls were always on the third floor, a dark cloud hanging there. Sometimes walking to school I would look up and see them, crow-black and still, perched high in the morning sky. And after school they walked together into the nearby woods. They were said to do all sorts of things there: They took drugs and had sex and performed rituals involving animal sacrifices. They cast spells there, placing curses on people in town, and plotted whom to torment and inflict pain and suffering on. Some people in school avoided the woods, but I never had a problem. Carl and I had come across trees with strange markings cut into them, and a circle of upside-down crosses, but we never knew whether these things had been left by the Goths themselves or by somebody else trying to add to their reputation. It all seemed so silly—but what was more idiotic, a group of high schoolers standing around chanting a bunch of mumbo jumbo, or the rest of the school thinking this type of stuff actually happened, and that it might really work?

There were tons of rumors about them. They were burnouts and vegans. They had pierced their bodies in strange places and had tattoos of runes and symbols and foreign languages all over. They were Satan worshippers, witches. They performed strange occult rituals involving decapitating animals and drinking blood. There were rumors that the guys in the group had taken the girls as their wives, and that they all shared them with one another. They engaged in bondage and torture and self-mutilation. They had sex with corpses. They were all gay. If you believed everything, they were tattooed Satan-worshipping Goth Mormon homosexual S&M piercing necrophiliac drug-using vegetarians. It was a small school, and they must have known what was being said about them all the time behind their

black backs, but they never responded. They were mysterious and odd and no one liked them.

I would have gone on ignoring Anna Cayne forever, except for the fact that she spoke to me first. If I had known
that she was coming my way, I would have done everything
in my power to avoid her. She wasn't the person you wanted
to be seen with. She wasn't someone you thought would
talk to you first either. She sneaked up on me. It was the
end of September and I was in the library stacks, wasting
the rest of my lunch hour, trying out a new theory, a suggestion one of my teachers had given me. I had taken *On
the Road* by Jack Kerouac from the shelf and turned around,
and there she was, standing quietly a few feet away, calmly
staring at me.

"Burroughs is better," she said.

"I don't know about that." I looked at the book in my
hand and then looked past her. It should have indicated to
her that I wanted to get by to check out the Kerouac. She
didn't pay any attention. She stood her ground and gave me
a slight smile. She had more to tell me.

"He shot his wife, you know."

"I know," I said. I didn't know. I didn't even know
whether she was talking about Burroughs or Kerouac. I was
just hoping that she would stop talking and let me get away
from her as quickly as possible.

"They were playing William Tell. They were drinking
at a friend's apartment, and Burroughs pulls out a gun

and turns to his wife and says, 'It's time for the old William Tell act,' and she puts a glass on her head, and then he shoots her."

"Really?" I said. Then she told me the whole story about William Burroughs and how he was the grandson of the inventor of the adding machine and how he was friends with Kerouac and is in *On the Road* as "Old Bull Lee" and his wife is "Jane" and how even killing his wife didn't do anything to curb his fascination with guns and that he used to make paintings with cans of paint and a shotgun. The words streamed out of her; she could have been making it all up, for all I knew, but I actually wanted to hear more.

"Did he go to prison?"

"It happened in Mexico," she said, as if that was all the explanation I needed.

There was an awkward pause; I wanted her to continue, but she had finished. I panicked and said, "I suppose you're looking for Stephen King," and moved to let her go around me and deeper into the stacks. She looked at me as if I were an idiot. I could feel an embarrassed blush fill my face and I was afraid that she might turn and leave. A couple of minutes before, I had wanted desperately to get away from her, and now I was hoping that she would stay and pay more attention to me.

She stayed. "He's only written two books worth reading," she said.

There wasn't a pause, but a full stop, and I stood waiting for her to speak. If I hadn't asked her to name the books, she never would have divulged her opinion. She had an intriguing way of speaking. Her sentences were icebergs, with just the tip of her thought coming out of her mouth, and the rest kept up in her head, which I was starting to think was more and more beautiful the longer I looked at her.

"*Carrie* and *The Shining*," she finally said.

"I've read *The Shining*," I said, happy to have something in common.

"One to go," she said. "And then you can be done with Mr. King."

She was looking for H. P. Lovecraft, whom I had never heard of. He wrote horror stories, she said, in the early 1900s. She read anything, but she especially liked books (fiction and nonfiction) about the supernatural. She continued to move through the stacks, and I followed her. She was done talking, so I watched her scan the rows and rows of books, selecting authors and titles I would probably have never heard of, like Yukio Mishima, James Baldwin, and *All the Little Live Things*, until she had an armful. I went to the front desk and checked out both the King and the Kerouac while she simply walked out with hers and waited for me by the door. "I'll return them when I'm finished," she said. I had the feeling that she did that sort of thing all the time. The rules didn't apply. I had to get to class, but I wanted to keep following her, I wanted her to talk to me more. By the time I had thought of saying something else to her she was disappearing down the hall.

i d o n ' t w a n t t o b o r e
y o u , b u t . . .

This is what you should know about me: I'm bland. I'm milk. Worse, I'm water. Worse yet, I'm a water glass—at least water can change shape or become some other form, like ice or vapor. Instead, I'm bland and rigid and everyone can look right through me and see that there's nothing. I've got nothing. I'm walking wallpaper. I almost wish I had a broken nose, or a cauliflower ear, or a scar across my face, something that you would remember. If there were something on the outside to grab some girl's attention, she might see that I was a good person, a quality person. Most girls just look once and don't see me, and move on.

When I was a freshman I tried imitating the cool guys in class. I went out and bought the same clothes that they wore and tried to wear them the way they did, but I ended up looking like an idiot. Something was missing. The clothes were cool, but I wasn't. There was nothing to be done; I was stuck with who I was. Everyone seemed to have something on me. The geeks had their own look, same with the Goths, the jocks. They all had some way that connected them with someone else. Even the retarded kids had better style than I did.

"Wear what makes you feel comfortable," Carl told me. "If you're comfortable, people will be comfortable around you." It was easy for him; he knew what he was doing. But

I took his advice and started wearing jeans or khakis and a plain shirt and sweater. Anna called it the "harmboy" look, somewhere between hip and farmboy, she said. I liked Abercrombie & Fitch clothes, but I hated the fact that their name was on everything. They put it on the pockets and sleeves and tails of their shirts, and the backs of the pants. I didn't want to go around advertising some company, so I took off the labels on the shirts and pants and sweaters my mother bought for me. Most of them came off all right, you just took a small pair of scissors and cut the thread in the back, and the thing unraveled and the label pulled right off (if my mom bought me anything with the name printed on it, I would either wear it underneath something or not wear it all), but removing some labels left holes in the sleeves or at the bottom of the shirt. That was my only defining characteristic: a few holes here and there. I wore some Carhartts once in a while, which no one else wore except the shit-kicking farm kids. "Bussers," we called them. Bryce Druitt had been a bus rider, and he was also a Goth. He was the only Goth on the bus, which might explain why he was such an ass. He had a chip on his shoulder about something, although he shouldn't have. He wasn't really a farm kid, though; he lived over near Hydesville, about fifteen minutes away. That was the only other town where they rode the bus to our school. The rest of them were farm kids. Bryce was a senior, which meant that he no longer rode the bus. He drove.

Bryce Druitt had started as a jock. He played football and ran cross-country, and was one of the best basketball players in the school. He started on the varsity team when he was a freshman (that was the only team the school had; we didn't have enough players for another squad), and helped lead them to the second round of the state championship. The funny thing about that was that the old court in the high school, built in the 1940s, no longer met the minimum state requirements and so our team had to play every game of the season on the road. A new gymnasium was built at the end of the season. It was a big ugly metal building plopped down between the school and the football field. It had a cramped, dingy weight room, and a small balcony that was never used for anything. But it had a great basketball court, and bleachers that folded up into the walls so you could fit almost the whole town in the metal box for meetings and dances and whatever else people could think of, but they never thought of anything, so the place was always empty, except for games. Everyone was looking forward to the next season. Everyone was looking forward to seeing Bryce, a year older, a year better. He was a strong, tall blond athlete who had secured himself in the school's elite and who had everyone's admiration.

When football practice started at the end of summer, Bryce didn't show up, and when school started he had a shaved head and was dressed all in black. He wasn't the first, but he was the one they cared about.

Bryce Druitt was a world away from me—he lived in another town, he drove, he was a Goth, and he was a senior. We never should have had anything to do with each other, and I wish he wasn't in this story at all.

locker

To be honest, I wasn't much of a reader before I met Anna. I was in the library only to see if I could meet someone. This was advice that was given to me by our coach and art teacher, Mr. Devon. "It's a good way to meet girls," he told me as I handed in my helmet and uniform and pads. "It gives you something to talk about with them, you know, breaks the ice a little. You have to think about it, though. Don't just grab the first book you see, or the books everybody else is reading. You want to stand out from the crowd." Mr. Devon always seemed to be hanging out with some girl in the hallway between classes, or after school, so I figured he knew what he was talking about. Besides, I didn't really have anything to lose. I thought about where to go in the library and what books to try out. I didn't want to get stuck with any nonfiction—that seemed like too much work—and I wasn't going near poetry or any of that romantic stuff. That left fiction (or encyclopedias and other reference books, if I wanted to attract a very particular, peculiar girl, the kind you didn't need a book to attract in the first place). I finally decided to go after books that I would actually want to read and that would attract a certain type of girl, somebody interesting and smart, or who at least thought I was smart. I ended up picking Jack Kerouac because I knew that few other people in my class would even know who he was and I guess because he was kind of like someone I hoped to be. He was a cool guy for a while in the 1950s, a James Dean type, and maybe I thought that some of that would rub off on me if girls saw me with his book. If I could be more like Jack Kerouac, then maybe I wouldn't need to hang out in the library to meet girls. For me, it worked the first time out. I guess Mr. Devon didn't think that football was going to do the trick for me.

I was too light, for one thing, but I was fast and had good hands, so he put me in at wide receiver. I didn't start or anything like that, but I saw some action and wasn't entirely horrible. We lost every game anyway, so you had to be completely worthless not to play. I had maybe a dozen or so passes thrown to me, even caught one for a touchdown, but it was called back on a penalty. Then in practice after the fifth game of the season I broke the index finger on my left hand. Even my injury lacked any sort of glamour or interest. I had caught a pass in the flat, maybe ten yards from the line of scrimmage, and was tackled by three or four guys, and somebody stepped on my hand as they were getting up from the pile and my finger snapped like a twig. It didn't hurt, but it swelled up immediately and turned blue and purple. The assistant coach, Mr. Ham (he was an enormous guy, so no one ever made fun of his name, not even behind his back), walked me back to the locker room like I had a broken skull or something. He even offered to call my parents for me. I told him that I used the phone with my right hand, which got a laugh out of him at least.

My mom picked me up and drove me to the hospital. They took X rays and a day or two later told us what we already knew. The season was going to be over before the broken finger could heal, and my parents wanted me to quit, and I didn't try to talk them out of it, and Mr. Devon didn't try to talk me out of it, and that was that. It might have been different if I had been a starter. I imagined myself pulling down a game-winning pass with one good hand and the other heavily taped. Of course that didn't happen. "Put some weight on and study the playbook and we'll see about next season," Mr. Devon told me after I had cleared out my locker.

The morning after she had talked to me in the library, Anna was waiting by my locker. At least I like to think that she was waiting there—she might have just been standing near it with some of her friends. They were grouped together as they always were, only this time in a different spot. I saw her as I started to open the lock, and gave her a quick nod when she saw me. She left her friends and came over.

"Did you finish Kerouac yet?" she said.

I laughed. "No."

"You'd better get a move on, we've got a lot to accomplish."

"Like what?"

"You'll see," she said. "Maybe."

I opened my locker and found a note she had left for me. "Dear HP—There's a whole world all around more interesting, wonderful, terrifying, mysterious, amazing than any novel ever written. Pay attention. Take a chance. Dare life. Love, craft."

Over the following months, she would always call me different names in her notes and letters, and never sign anything with her own name. Sometimes the references were obvious, and sometimes I didn't know what the hell she was trying to tell me. This one seemed obvious. She had been looking for H. P. Lovecraft in the library, but then I started thinking about it more, thinking too much perhaps. Could both the HP and the pun at the end refer to the same thing? It would mean that the postcard was addressed to and written by the same person, so I began to think that the HP didn't refer to Lovecraft at all, but was short for "higgledy-piggledy." I didn't like that so much. Maybe she was making fun of me, or trying to humiliate me. That moment made all the difference; two paths were clearly marked: Turn my back on Anna's difficult attention and continue with my life, or respond to her, follow her, and watch the world I thought I knew reveal things I had never imagined. Of course, at the time I was unaware of any of this. I just followed whatever instinct I had. I wasn't sure if I liked Anna. Although I thought she was beautiful and sexy and all that, she was scary, mysterious. I knew there could be trouble. I think I knew it even then.

I threw the note away, but by the time I reached home I regretted it.

1 october

She had left a postcard in my locker. The front was a photograph of some old Mexican guy, who, I discovered, was Pancho Villa. On the back was written: "Lora—Good-by— if you hear of my being stood up against a Mexican stone wall and shot to rags please know that I think that a pretty good way to depart this life. It beats old age, disease, or falling down the cellar stairs. To be a Gringo in Mexico— ah, that is euthanasia! A. Bierce." This was Goth flirting, this was Anna Cayne. This one was a keeper. I taped it to my bedroom wall; it was the first of many to go there. Each one was a little puzzle, and now I know that each was a piece of a larger puzzle too. It was a game, and I spent most of that night trying to think of some clever comeback, but she had me at a disadvantage. She was smarter. I spent the rest of that night thinking about her.

4 october

I had wanted to ask her out after we talked in the library, but it didn't seem to make any sense. What would the rest of the school think? I would be linked with the Goths and further alienated from everyone. Of course I was alienated already. On Friday I saw her in the hall before class and went up to her.

"I finished," I said.

"Finished what?"

"Both books. Both. Kerouac and King."

"Good for you," she said. She was cold and distant, quickly walking away from me. I had to follow her.

"I was thinking that maybe you could help me pick out something else."

"Sorry," she said. "You're on your own." She stopped and looked straight at me. Her eyes seemed to be looking at something behind me, gazing straight through me and then off into the distance. "I've got to go to class."

That was almost the end of it. But I was getting my coat from my locker at the end of the day when she came up to me. She was in a hurry. "Here," she said. She handed me two slim paperbacks: *This Way for the Gas, Ladies and Gentlemen* by Tadeusz Borowski and *The Street of Crocodiles* by Bruno Schulz. "Read these," she said.

"More dead guys?" I said.

"No one can disappoint you when they're dead."

I took the books and started to walk away.

"Where are you going?"

"I don't know. Home, I guess."

"I'll walk with you." We left school and she said she wanted to walk down by the river. "Are you in a hurry to get home?"

"Never," I said.

The Furniss River was about a half-mile east of the school. It cut through town and ran south, bending around until it flowed eastward for about a mile before it snaked south again. It was a small river, no more than a quarter of a mile across, but it was deep and had a strong current, especially in the spring and fall. Two bridges crossed the river, one at the south end of town and one that ran into Main Street just north of the middle of town. Main Street, which defined the business district, was only five blocks long and consisted of two restaurants (The Oaks and Burke's), three bars, a post office, a public library, a liquor store, two pottery stores, a used-book store and a video store, a bait-and-tackle store, a canoe and kayak rental shop, a small grocery that was almost worthless (you were better off going to Gurney's gas station at the south end of town—at least they never ran out of milk and other staples), and an art gallery where local artists sold their stuff.

A dirt hiking path followed the river along the western side from one edge of town to the other, and we walked south along that. We could see a few fishermen packing up their gear before it turned dark.

"Do you ever walk down here at night?" she said.

"No."

"You should. It's quiet, with just the sound of the river and the wind. It's calming. Sometimes I come down here when I can't sleep, and I just sit and listen. I've fallen asleep on the banks before, and then had to hurry home in the morning before my parents found out. You should come here sometime late at night."

"I'd probably fall in," I said.

"Can I ask you something? Something kind of personal?"

"It depends," I said.

"When you came up to me earlier today, were you going to ask me out?"

"What?"

"Were you going to ask me to the game tonight?"

I couldn't even get a response out, just an open-mouthed, slack-jawed silence.

"Never mind," she said. "Let me try this again. Would you go to the game with me?"

"Why?"

"Well, that's for you to figure out," she said. "But let me tell you something. I thought that you were going to ask me out earlier, and that's why I acted like a jerk. I'm sorry. I wasn't ready, and then when I realized what you were doing, it freaked me out. I'm not used to people paying attention to me, I mean like that, so I had to figure it out first. I had to buy some time."

"And?"

"And I would be very happy if you would ask me to the game tonight."

"Would you go to the game with me, tonight?" I said.

"Yes," she said, and then she leaned over and gave me a very quick kiss on the mouth.

I went home and ate my dinner in as few bites as humanly possible and then walked over to Anna's. Her mom drove us to the game. Mrs. Cayne looked nothing like her daughter. While Anna had a round face with a small nose, her mother was almost gaunt, with a sharp, prominent nose. Her hair was crazy and frizzy and went everywhere before it finally collapsed below her shoulders. She looked slightly deranged or dangerous. In fact, she looked kind of like the Wicked Witch in *The Wizard of Oz*. I half expected monkeys to fly into the car and grab me and take me to some cage somewhere.

She was a paralegal, or a legal aide, something legal.

We were sitting in the bleachers, near the top, in the second-to-last row, where Anna always sat. None of her friends had arrived yet. It was just the two of us. I was nervous. By Monday everyone in school would know. I felt that everyone was staring at us, but that was impossible. They were all looking at the field. No one cared, but I still felt awkward, sitting with my stupid blue and gold school jacket, and she was dressed all in black. My parents had bought me the jacket when I made the football team. "You need it so you can wear your letter," my mother said. Only now I wasn't going to get a letter. I just had the jacket. I wished I could be down at the bench, at least there the jacket would make sense, and people would see me with the splint on my finger. I was nervous. All of a sudden, I didn't know what to say.

"You haven't said anything about my finger." I kind of held up the splint toward her.

"What did you want me to say, 'Way to go, dumbass'?"

"Most people say something," I said.

"Most people say the obvious."

She had teased me from the first time she spoke to me, and I liked it. A bright glint would appear in her eyes, a sense of enjoyment and a clue not to take her seriously. Her mouth took on a hint of a smile, and her voice was not as deadpan as she probably would have wanted. It was a game, flirtatious and fleeting, a way to pass the time and test each other's agility.

"I didn't know if you knew about it."

"Don't flatter yourself, but I did know about it."

"Believe me, I'm not flattered," I said. I asked her if she had been to any of the games before.

"All of them," she said. I already knew the answer. We used to talk about them on the bench, the vampires huddled together at the top of the stands. They never cheered; they just sat and watched, like menacing birds on a wire.

"Why?"

The glint evaporated and her eyes turned dark and hard. "What you don't know about what you don't know about." She shook her head. I had been scolded. Then she started to laugh.

"Have you ever seen the movie *Strangers on a Train*?"

"No."

"There's this scene where the character Bruno is at a tennis match and everyone is watching the ball go back and forth across the net, their heads moving right to left, right to left, but Bruno's head is perfectly still, because he's staring right at one of the players. You can see the entire stadium watching the ball, and there's Bruno, the only one perfectly still, staring."

"Why's he the only one?"

"You'll have to watch it to find out," she said. "Come on, let's go make some Brunos." She jumped up and grabbed me by the hand, and we walked down the steps to sit in the front row. Now everyone was watching.

"What's it feel like to be the center of attention?" she said.

"Let's go back up where we were."

"Relax. Enjoy the game."

I looked back up into the stands. No one seemed to be staring, until you got to the place where we had been sitting. All of Anna's friends were there, looking right at me.

"They don't look happy."

She laughed again. "Do they ever? Forget it. Pay some attention to me for a change. It's a date, remember?"

At halftime I went to get us something to drink at the concession stand behind the bleachers. "You'll be here when I get back?" I said.

"I won't make any promises."

I waited on line and wondered how many people had noticed Anna and me together. No one said anything to me and no one appeared to be paying any more attention to me at all. It was a little disappointing. I bought a box of popcorn and a couple of large cups of soda. It was hard to carry everything with the splint on my finger, and I was sure that something was going to spill before I could make it to my seat.

When I got to the walkway above our section, I noticed

that Bryce Druitt was sitting next to Anna, in my spot. I wanted to wait and watch them. I couldn't see his face, but Anna was looking at him with concentration and affection; it was an intimate look that made me suddenly jealous. I also became aware that the rest of the Goths were watching me as I stood in the walkway, so I moved down the steps toward my seat.

Bryce stood up and passed me on the steps without saying a word to me, but I could hear a few of the parents in the stands speak to him. "We could use you out there, son." "It's a shame you're not playing." Things like that.

Anna took a cup of soda from me and I sat down. "Bryce wants us to go sit with them," she said, "but I told him to get his own date."

notes

I wasn't popular, but I didn't think I was unpopular. I didn't think anyone even paid that much attention to me. I was never in anyone's thoughts or opinions, at least that's what I had believed. Anna changed all of that. We became something of a scandal, the talk of the school.

We both got notes in our lockers on the same day, the Tuesday after the football game. It was the same message for both of us: Stay away from each other. "What are you thinking?" That's how my note started. It was handwritten on lined notebook paper. It was sloppy, as if written by a child, or someone using the wrong hand. "Stay away from that witch. You don't know what trouble you are in for. What do you know about her? She will fuck you up. Take it from someone who knows."

"This is for your own good. Stay away from that geek. You can't trust him. He's a liar. He will hurt you." That's what her note said. It was typed on plain white paper.

I had an idea who had written both of them, but I wanted to find out for sure.

"Don't worry about it," Anna said. "I get notes all the time. Just ignore it, and it will take care of itself."

She didn't wait for me after school. I was walking home when I saw her in the passenger seat of Bryce's car.

At school the next morning all the talk was about Bryce Druitt. He had been in a serious accident the night before, slamming his Intrigue into the side of the northern bridge. They said that the car bounced off the bridge and spun down the bank, and almost went into the river. Bryce was taken to the hospital. Luckily he had only a broken leg. I didn't particularly care about Bryce before, but I wouldn't have wished that on him, not then anyway.

Anna was having a hard time maintaining her usual calm, almost trembling when I saw her.

"What was he doing?"

"I don't know," she said. "Somebody said he'd been drinking, but I don't know what he was doing over here. He hardly ever comes over here at night."

"He's going to be all right. That's what they say, that he's going to be all right."

"That's what they say."

I noticed that a bruise was visible underneath the makeup on her left cheek. "What happened there?"

Her hand sprang up to hide the spot. "I got punched," she said.

"Who did that?"

"Never mind. I took care of it. I told you I would take care of it."

"You said it would take care of itself. Was it Bryce?"

"Why would you say that?"

"I saw you with him after school yesterday."

"It wasn't Bryce," she said. "He gave me a ride home after. He was helping me. You won't be getting any more of those notes."

"Who was it?"

"Don't worry about it."

"Do they have a bruise they're hiding this morning?"

"I didn't punch anyone," she said. "But they got the message. Don't worry, I can take care of myself." She gave me a hug and hurried off to class.

the   house   of   cayne

It's funny how strangers can pass in front of you every day and all you see is a flat shadow, a vague outline, not noticing any of the details. They move in a gray crowd, always looking the same and acting the same, simple caricatures of who they really are, but once you get to know them, you notice the specific, tiniest things, you pay attention to the intricacies of their personalities, their habits and particular ways of walking and talking, the subtle changes in their appearance and dress.

It was that way with me and Anna. I had once thought of her only as a generic figure, one of a set of identical ghouls, but now I began to notice the smallest changes about her, the things that made her unique. I used to think that she wore the same black dress and same black pullover sweater every day. I thought that she wore the same black boots, but she really had three different pairs of Doc Martens, the six-eyelet, eight-eyelet, and ten-eyelet versions ("What's wrong with fourteen?" I had to ask her later). She also had a pair of the three-eyelet Gibson shoe, but you almost never saw her in shoes.

I noticed how her hair would curl just under her chin on some days, and how other times it would curl away from her face. I wondered if it did this naturally or if she woke up each morning and had to decide which way she would curl it.

Even her eyes were constantly changing. They could be clear, bright blue and then suddenly darken and become almost gray. At times they would flicker with light, and I would swear that I could see them changing, with white clouds passing across her pupils, and the next second they would look like ice. She would stare at me or at some point far beyond me, or at nothing, with her eyes locked and still, not tick-tocking back and forth but dead calm, and the blues would darken and become as vacant and useless as empty swimming pools. I began to take note of her mood and the color and texture of her eyes to see whether there was some sort of correlation, some sort of code that I could use to better understand her. If there was a code, I didn't have enough time to break it.

As time went by, I began to notice things that were strange and unsettling. The first was harmless; they all might have been. She had a cut on the left side of her lower lip, and when I asked her about it she responded that she couldn't remember how she had gotten it. "Maybe I bit myself in my sleep," she said. A few days later I noticed bruises on the back of her neck, on both sides, as though someone had choked her. She couldn't remember how she had gotten those either. "Maybe from a necklace I was wearing," she said. She always shrugged them off and acted as if they weren't anything, like the bruise she had the morning after Bryce's accident. They matter more now, looking back.

There were some things I did question her about, however, things she couldn't easily shrug off. She always wore long sleeves, no matter what the weather, and the first time I saw her bare arms I noticed a number of small cuts on her left forearm. There must have been twenty or thirty, some fading and healing, others scabbed over, and some fresh, still red and swollen. "I'm trying to quit smoking," she said. "I started cutting my arm every time I wanted a cigarette, to associate the pain with smoking." She looked down at her arm. "Unfortunately, I think it's worked the wrong way. I'm starting to associate the pleasure of smoking with cutting. Now instead of thinking that smoking will hurt me, I think that cutting will feel good, you know, like a cigarette should." She laughed. "I just have to be smarter than my own mind."

I also discovered that she had a tattoo. At least I think she did. It wasn't always there. This was another game, perhaps. Whatever it was, the mark was on her hip. It was a wheel, and the spokes inside the wheel turned into sharp spikes as they came out of the wheel. There was writing on each of the spokes, but I could never tell what they said. "I don't know what they are either," Anna said. I didn't believe her.

"Why did you get the tattoo, then?"

"It's a family thing. My parents have the same one. In the same place. It's a tradition." I didn't believe that either. Not entirely.

"What does it mean?"

"It has something to do with the fact that we're all witches." She looked at me, reading my face and eyes to see if I had believed her. She started laughing.

"Is any of that true?" I said.

"My parents have the tattoo. I don't really know what it means. I think it's kind of cool, though, don't you?"

I did.

The next time I saw her bare hip, the tattoo was gone, and I began to doubt everything she had told me about it. To be fair, I saw it only a couple of times in good light, so maybe it was there all the time but I didn't notice. You'd think you'd notice a thing like the impermanence of a tattoo, though. Maybe it was a fake, and she kept removing it and applying it, hoping I would say something. I never said anything. I just waited for that little spiked wheel with the strange writing to come and go.

A week or so after the football game, and after a few days of walking around together after school, Anna invited me to her house. Her room was nothing like I had imagined. I guess I had in my mind that she lived in a crypt or a coffin, a dungeon or a cave, something spare and black and dark. It wasn't that at all. It was more like a guy's room. There was stuff everywhere. There were piles of books, biographies on Ambrose Bierce and Houdini, art books of the works of Jackson Pollock and Ray Johnson, fiction by Kate Chopin, David Hartwell, Robert Bloch, and a ragged copy of *Gray's Anatomy* set off by itself. There were books of poetry—Shelley, Hart Crane, Frank O'Hara, Frank Stanford, Federico García Lorca, and Sylvia Plath—and a stack of nonfiction I didn't even comprehend, titles like *The Psychology of a Rumor, Alan Turing: The Enigma, Secret Signals,* and stuff by Albert Camus. I'd seen some of these books before, in my brother's room after he'd started college. "What kind of grades do you get?" I blurted out. She laughed. "Straight D's." At least I had that on her. I'd been on the honor roll every semester so far.

I also noticed that there was a paperback copy of the Lovecraft book she had grabbed when we first talked in the library. It was on her bed, open with the front and back of the book exposed. "Why did you bother to take that out of the library?" I said.

She looked at the book and blushed slightly. "I can't keep any of this stuff straight. I need to get better organized. Do you want to start on that for me?"

I looked around and saw that it was a hopeless case.

There were discs everywhere, and even vinyl records. Music by Tim Buckley, Nick Drake, Gram Parsons, Buddy Holly, Patsy Cline, Bix Beiderbecke, Chet Baker, Robert Johnson, Mozart. (I don't know if these were the exact objects on that first visit, but they were definitely things strewn around her room during the time we spent to-gether.) There must have been twenty or thirty discs poorly stacked on the floor, and more than fifty records spread around like a dropped deck of cards. About the only thing I recognized was a Nirvana disc, everything else was obscure to me, country and jazz and classical. There were posters and postcards covering the walls, mostly of people I'd never heard of, like Isadora Duncan and Robert Schumann and a scarred, engaging, mysterious man named Louis Kahn, or people I'd heard of but never knew what they looked like, like Anne Sexton and Amelia Earhart, but whoever they were, they were everywhere, their dead faces plastered on the walls and their eyes calmly watching me. Houdini was bound in chains in a large picture above her computer, Natalie Wood smiled from the closet door, and James Dean stood on a frozen farm pond above the bed, looking at his reflection in the ice.

"Do you have anything from our lifetime?" I asked. She

pushed the door to her room closed to reveal some long-haired guy with a beard staring sternly at me from the back of the door. He looked like Charles Manson, but it said "Dennis Wilson" above his head and "Pacific Ocean Blue" just under that. "Why do you have this here?" I said.

"It's some old poster of my dad's. I like it—he's cute," she replied. Everything was old. She liked old things. She didn't believe in reincarnation or anything like that, but sometimes she felt that she might have been born in the wrong time. She didn't feel much connection with the world, she felt connected only to things in the past. That's what she told me, but later.

Her bed was a girl's bed, with a flowery comforter and an old stuffed bear on the pillow. "It was my mother's," she said. "Hold him, he's soft."

I was at a loss for words, so I just held on to the bear and looked around again. There was another book on her bed, *Arshile Gorky: Paintings and Drawings.* I put the bear back on the bed and looked at the book. Stuck into the pages was a large folder, and I opened the book to it. The painting re-produced on the left-hand page was a number of black patches connected with black lines on a gray background.

Anna quickly took the book from me. "It's a painting about losing his earlier paintings and books in a fire," she said, and put the book back on the bed.

"Gorky. It's a funny name."

"It's not his real name," she said. "He just invented it."

"He's not alive, I bet."

"Dead."

I knelt on the floor and looked at the scattered albums. "Did you buy all these?"

"My father used to work in a record store in college. He must have a thousand albums."

She seemed to enjoy my exploration of her room, sifting through the artifacts she had carelessly assembled.

We heard the front door open. "That's going to be my dad," she said. "There's something I have to tell you about him. He doesn't have any hair." A second later her father appeared in the doorway.

She was right, he didn't have any hair, but I had thought she meant he was bald. He didn't have *any* hair. He didn't have any eyebrows or eyelashes or whiskers, nothing. He was as smooth as an egg, and shaped like one as well. He was a small man, no more than five and a half feet. He looked meek, with his small black expensive-looking eyeglasses and conservative blue suit and white shirt. But his appearance was deceptive. His large, fleshy hand extended toward me as we were introduced, and when I shook it I could tell he was strong. He squeezed my hand hard and kept exerting more pressure. It was one of those fatherly gestures, I guess, like telling me not to mess with his daughter. I tried to give him the best "You can trust me" or "Don't worry" shake back, but I'm sure he interpreted it as "We'd be in bed right now if you hadn't come home." He gave me a stern look with those bald eyes, distorted slightly by the lenses of his glasses. I got the message: He could hurt me.

Anna later told me that he worked out every day. He didn't lift weights, but ran and jumped rope and boxed. He was younger than my father by about ten years, but he was maybe in the best shape of his life and getting stronger, while my own father was riding around in his golf cart and softening into a marshmallow.

He talked for a couple of minutes and then left the room, saying, "Please keep this door open, Anastasia, at least while you have guests." The door swung open and the hairy Dennis Wilson disappeared.

Mr. Cayne was a loan officer at the bank. "He used to be a repo man," Anna told me. "So don't mess with him, or me." She said that he had once gone to repossess a car and had just started it and was ready to drive off, when the owner flung open the door and grabbed the steering wheel. Mr. Cayne grabbed the guy's wrist and told him to let go of the wheel. He didn't, and Mr. Cayne began to squeeze. "My father broke his wrist and pulled his arm out of the socket," she said.

"He told you this?"

"I found out about it," she said. "Just a word to the wise—be nice to me." She reclined on the bed. I walked over to her, but remained standing.

An old Bible rested on the nightstand next to her bed; it might have been the last thing I expected to find in her room. I picked it up and marveled at it. "You read this?" I said.

"Look around you, I read everything," she said. "Don't read too much into it."

I opened the Bible to Ecclesiastes, where a bookmark

was placed. One passage was underlined: "And I gave my heart to know wisdom, and to know madness and folly; I perceived that this also is vexation of the spirit. For in much wisdom is much grief; and he that increaseth knowledge increaseth sorrow."

She watched me read the passage and then took the book from me and tossed it on the bed. "It's an old copy," she said. "I didn't do that."

Anna told me that she was an only child, just like me. Okay, that last part isn't true, technically. I have a brother and a sister, but they are ten and twelve years older than I am, respectively, and they have been long gone for most of my life, so I'm basically an only child. Both of them left home when they turned eighteen, and my sister hasn't been back at all. My brother, Paul, went to Princeton and would come home for the holidays, but now he's married and has three adopted kids and lives in Baton Rouge, Louisiana, and we hardly ever see them. "Why would anyone want to go to someplace called Baton Rouge?" my father said the few times my mother asked if he wanted to go. She's gone a couple of times, but the last time she tried to go, her flight was canceled and she didn't know what to do, so she just sat in the airport. After my brother called to see which flight she had taken, my father drove out to the airport to pick her up. She hasn't expressed any desire to go to Baton Rouge again.

My sister, Joan, left for California the week after she

graduated from high school, and we haven't heard from her since. She had a lot in common with Dad; she also liked to retreat to remote places, and now she has virtually disappeared.

There was also a daughter between my brother and me, seven years older than me, but she died. She lived to be nine days old. Her name was Denise and she's buried in the cemetery south of town. My brother told me they used to go out there once or twice a year—the whole family—but I've been there only once and that was a long time ago. I wonder what my parents were like before.

Once, when I was younger, I accidentally broke something of my brother's, a model plane or something, and he started screaming at me that I would never have been born if Denise had still been around. I don't know if that's true or not, but try getting the idea out of your head. Sometimes I wish that she had lived and that I wasn't around.

parents, idiots, and incompetents

My father's an accountant. He's a numbers guy, not a people person. That's an understatement. I imagine he inhabits his spreadsheets as if they are other countries, places where he is the silent master of his silent subjects. Maybe that's why he likes numbers—they can be tamed, domesticated, they are pliable, dutiful, and quiet.

My father started his business with his best friend right after college, and they make a nice, comfortable living in our small town. They are no longer friends, but they still work together. My father is a quiet, solitary person anyway. If he's home, he's in his den. It's a small room at the back of the house on the first floor. It's just off the dining room, so he can get up from the table and retreat immediately into his dark, wood-paneled cave. In fact, he always sits at the table with his legs out to the side, ready to bolt to the den. I've been in there only a few times. Entry is by invitation only, and my father rarely invites anyone.

A bookcase covers one entire wall, filled mostly with books on golf, pictures of golf, and a few trophies my father has earned. He still plays, but he's starting to lose interest even in that. I'm sure it's because he has to play with other people; if he could be the only person on the course, I bet he'd play all the time. His world is slowly being reduced to his office and his den, and no one thinks that this is odd.

My father went to Brown University. He played football there, and he now has the appearance of a former lineman who has gone soft. He has a paunch, a sagging gut that hangs over his belt, dragging his whole body with it. His body looks slack and fleshy, although he isn't a fat man; he just sags, in either contentment or resignation.

You might think that our respective football experiences might have provided some sort of father-son bonding, but they did not. He came to a game or two of mine, but offered no comment afterward. He didn't offer any advice either, take me into our yard and give me any pointers or practice.

He didn't even tell me any anecdotes about his own days on the field. I have no idea if he was a good player or terrible. I've seen photographs of him in his uniform, looking large and trim, peering out of his mask, staring steadily into the camera, but there's no story to go with these images. He didn't even show me the pictures; my mother did. He remains as silent in life as in the photographs, and my mother is horrible remembering the details of their college days anyway. Even when I broke my finger he had little to say, no words of encouragement or sadness, only a matter-of-fact comment. "Football's a tough sport." No shit, Dad.

My mother was a professional incompetent. My father one day came up with the idea that she should work, that we would live better, more comfortably, if she contributed to the household income. My mother agreed, with little resistance. She wanted to get out of the house, and was eager to see if she could make her way in the working world. She soon discovered, however, that she had no talent, no aptitude, no training, and no skills. She attempted numerous jobs, mainly of the clerical, receptionist, office-assistant variety, but was fired from all of them. She couldn't type, couldn't file or work a computer, and was helpless with a phone that had more than one line. She was a detriment and a liability to any company or organization. Her friends joked that she had even been fired as a volunteer at the local library. I don't know whether this was true, but my mother turned bright red every time the subject was mentioned.

For a time, my father was convinced that her employers held her to too high a standard, or didn't take enough time to train her properly, or were bad managers with unclear expectations. Or they were simply idiots. My mother agreed. Together, they would show those idiots a thing or two about work and how things should be done. So my father hired her as his own assistant, or more accurately, as an assistant to his assistant. Of course, by now my father had forgotten about the initial reason for wanting my mother to work. He was now paying her, so there was really no extra money coming into the house. It was now a moral issue, family honor, and a matter of worth. "What the hell," he said at dinner when it was all decided. "How horrible can it be?"

It was horrible.

From the few hours of interaction I witnessed on weeknights, between the time they got home and the time my father retreated to his den, they fought, argued, bickered, and baited each other, constantly. Mistakes, misunderstandings, miscommunications, and all other unresolved issues of the day would surface surprisingly and suddenly. "What were you thinking?" my father would blurt out, and they would be off, thrashing through a thread of my mother's fuck-ups. She couldn't do anything correctly, it seemed, and often admitted as much, although she defended herself frequently, blaming an assortment of circumstances. Some of it would have been laughable, if their arguments hadn't descended into anger and resentment, and if either of them had had a sense of perspective, objectivity, or humor. After my father had bawled her out for mangling yet another phone message she had handed him, she would yell,

"I wrote it exactly as they told me." "They're changing their story." "They're liars."

My father is a stubborn man, and because of that stubbornness, blind confidence in his abilities as a manager and mentor, or the strength of his desire to see that his wife did not become the laughingstock of the work force, he stuck with her for more than a year. Finally they gave up. I don't know who raised the white flag first, but one morning my father left for work and my mother stayed at the kitchen table, dressed in her robe and drinking coffee. Her days as a member of the working class had come to an end.

Now she is incompetent for free. She is almost as ineffective as a homemaker, housewife, whatever you call it, as she was in the corporate world. If she has trouble with anything around the house, she is more than likely to leave it for my father to deal with when he gets home. Once, when she had trouble opening a can of chicken broth, it waited on the kitchen counter for my father to open when he got home so she could start cooking dinner. This of course meant that dinner wasn't waiting for Dad when he walked through the doorway, which meant that his disappearing act into the den was also delayed. This was fine when my mother was working, but unacceptable when she is home all day. He was not happy. "Solve the problem," he screamed. "Solve the problem by yourself." I don't know how many cans of soup the neighbors opened after that, but dinner is always ready on time.

The greatest, most obvious, talent my mother displays is her ability to straighten. She has a vision in her head of how she wants the cloth napkins and placemats arranged on the dining room table, and she spends time over days, weeks even, adjusting them until they are in proper alignment. She labors over the drapes, forcing the pleats and folds of the fabric to align to her will. Before I had my own phone, I would sometimes use the one near the bed in my parents' room, and my mother would always yell at me because I had disrupted the comforter or pillows, or who knows what else. We were running late one time and she stopped on her way out of the house to adjust the coats hanging on the wall pegs near the back door, and I joked that if my head were cracked open and I needed to get to the hospital, she would still stop to straighten things before we left. She didn't think that was funny.

I always tried to avoid going home immediately after school, because there would always be something for me to do, something to straighten or something to be yelled at for having unstraightened, or some problem or mishap to solve for my mother. She is a woman who needs someone to take care of her, but it isn't going to be me.

I shouldn't give the impression that my mother is utterly useless. She cleans around the house (although my father complains that she smears everything: she smears the windows, she smears the countertops, she smears the furniture), and more often than not she has breakfast ready by seven-thirty so my father can eat and get out of the house, and dinner ready at six thirty-five, a few minutes after he has entered the house from another day of not talking to his business partner, so he can quickly sit down at the table and not talk to his marriage partner and son. Some nights all you hear is the sound of our forks scraping against the plates, with my father leading the pace as he shovels food into his mouth. My mother eats at an alarmingly slow pace, counterbalancing my father's inhalation. You see the fork move toward her mouth, carrying food, but her plate never seems to empty. She is left by herself every night, alone at the table, slowly finishing her meal. The only times my father and I stayed until the end of her eating were holidays, and that was long enough to last the whole year.

My mother isn't a terrible cook, although I remember my father sitting over a burned breakfast and muttering, "How can you screw up scrambled eggs?" She had a distinct propensity to make chicken breasts with cream-of-mushroom soup poured on top more than my father and I would have preferred, or more than anyone would prefer, I imagine. It had to be the world's easiest dish: you put the chicken in a casserole dish, pour the soup on, directly from the can, and then make some rice and a salad, and there's dinner. She also claimed to make an "exotic" dish, tuna curry. While the meal contained both tuna and curry, it wasn't in any way exotic, unless your idea of exotic is a can of tuna, a can of cream-of-mushroom soup (a family staple), a spoonful of curry powder, and some instant rice. It tasted about as good as it sounds. My father ate oyster crackers at every meal. He kept a plastic container filled with them, which he would bring out from his den and set to one side of his plate. He would shove a handful of the little unsalted hexagons into his mouth after every few bites.

Sometimes he would emerge from his den with cracker crumbs all over the front of his shirt or sweater, carrying his plastic bucket to the kitchen for a refill.

What my mother lacked in imagination, she made up for in presentation and arrangement. She served her dishes on platters lined with precisely arranged flowers or other garnish. She had elaborate tableware. When we had grape-fruit for breakfast (which was frequently—it's almost im-possible to screw that up), a small black box would appear on the table, containing spoons with one serrated edge, de-signed specifically for removing the sections of a halved grapefruit. After breakfast the box would disappear, and the next morning, if we were to have grapefruit again, it would return to the table, the spoons lined up in their case, ready and precise.

My mother is a big fan of precision, and tries her best to maintain it. Unfortunately, her own incompetence gets in the way. Dinner is served, except when a can won't open. That's the way she is: fine unless something goes wrong and that minor obstacle becomes a huge wall she can't scale. She becomes helpless whenever things don't go smoothly, or exactly as she imagined them.

school

Anna and I had two classes together, history and math. We never sat together. Mrs. Bell had assigned seats in math, but you could sit anywhere you wanted in history. Anna always sat up front, her chair pulled away from the rest of us. She frequently slept in class, or at least she appeared to be asleep. She would put her head down on her desk and close her eyes, yet nothing was ever lost on her. She seemed to know more about what was going on in class than anyone else did. If she was ever called on, she would answer the question without lifting her head or opening her eyes. Once in history class, Mr. Morrison became so frustrated by her "attitude" that he demanded she sit up and "pay attention." Anna sat up and began reciting Mr. Morrison's lesson on Martin Luther King, Jr., word for word from the beginning, providing an impressive demonstration that she'd been paying attention all along. She went on for a good three minutes before Mr. Morrison dismissed her with a wave of his hand and her blond head slowly descended into the black sleeve of her sweater. It was said that all of the Goths could do the same trick, but I don't believe it.

Anna and I spoke before and after school, and almost never once classes began, but we were in constant contact. She would leave notes and postcards in my locker, or send them along with one of her friends. I would open a textbook and there'd be a note from her, folded neatly and placed at the day's lesson. I suspected that she knew a number of magic tricks, could pick locks and get into my locker and leave things there without my knowledge. They weren't your usual notes. She would relate conversations she had overheard, interesting facts from class, stories from the newspaper, even other people's notes. "Found this near my locker this morning: 'I hate you. I never want to see you again. You said it wasn't true but I saw your car outside her house. You lie, and I can't take it anymore. I hate you. P.S. Call me later.'"

I was unprepared for her outpouring of energy and enthusiasm and attention, and at first it overwhelmed me. I thought that I would never be able to keep up with her, that she would be bored with me. Instead things became easier. Her energy was contagious and I wanted more of her attention. We talked on the phone, but she preferred to send text messages or, better yet, IM or e-mail, where she could reference websites and send me along a trail of other information. She was constantly changing her name on my buddy list, using people's initials and making me figure out who they were: A.B.C. (Anna Belle Cayne), E.A.P. (Edgar Allan Poe), J.T.R. (Jack the Ripper), E.M.H. (Ernest Miller Hemingway), A.A.F. (Abigail Anne Folger), G.A.H. (Gary Allen Hinman), E.W.H. (?).

After maybe five or six weeks, she stopped putting postcards in my locker and started sending them to me through the mail, along with letters and large envelopes filled with things she had found interesting, magazine and newspaper articles, or even random objects like a key ("I found this near your house. What do you think it opens?"), photographs ("Who are these people?"), and letters or notes she had found on the street or left behind in classrooms. It was a constant stream of stuff, and I didn't know if she wanted me to send her things in return. Much of what she sent me I puzzled over for a while and then discarded (the key, for instance, looked as if it went with luggage or a briefcase, and I wasn't going to sneak into every house in the neighborhood to find out which). I could identify some of the people in the photos, and she seemed pleased with what I could tell her. She didn't seem to really care whether I had a response to what she sent or not—her enjoyment appeared to come from sharing the item with me and sparking some train of thought. I never sent her anything; I stuck to the phone or the computer, but even then there was no way to keep up with all the things she sent me. Everything seemed to interest her, and it made me interested as well. Sometimes her interests uncovered things that were secretive and personal. She sent me a handwritten note she had found: "I need help with Carl," and in her handwriting asked, "What does this mean?"

carl

My friend Carl Hathorne was a drug dealer. "I don't care," Anna said when I told her, and then laughed. "It's always the popular ones you have to watch out for." Carl wasn't like a superstore, big-box pharmacy dealer, though. You couldn't buy whatever you wanted; he had a limited inventory. He sold whatever drugs he could easily get his hands on, which meant that he sold his younger brother's Ritalin, and he sold his older sister's Prozac, and his mother's Prozac too. He would sneak into their rooms and swipe a few pills and then sell them around school. It was an easy way for him to make money, and he started going to the junior high school and buying drugs off kids, mostly Ritalin, and then selling them to upperclassmen. He would buy the drugs for no more than a dollar a pill and sell them for anywhere between two and five dollars. He didn't sell drugs to anyone younger than a sophomore, but he had no qualms about paying nothing to the younger kids. I once mentioned that he was ripping off kids who didn't know the value of what they were selling, and he lectured me. "Value is relative," he said. "A quarter is a lot of money to some people, a quarter of a million is not to some other people." Carl is the only person I knew who talked about things like "supply chain," and "distribution models," and concepts like "lifetime value of a customer." I have no idea where he got this stuff— maybe he was born with it.

He made good money, but he never got greedy. He knew he had to be careful. There were too many ways to get caught. He could get caught by his family for stealing their drugs, he could get caught by the teachers or principal for selling the drugs, and he could get caught with more supply than demand, but that was hardly likely. There were too many kids who wanted drugs, even in our small school. I had asked him once if it was true that the Goths used drugs. "They've never bought anything from me," he said, but you couldn't take Carl at his word about that stuff. He was like a doctor protecting his patients' confidentiality. Everyone seemed to know (or suspect) that if you needed something, you went to Carl, yet no one seemed to know who ever actually went.

He had one prime attribute going for him: Everyone

liked him. Carl was the most popular person in our sophomore class; he might have been the most popular person in
the whole school. He treated everyone with respect and appeared to genuinely like people. And all the teachers liked
him, all his customers liked him, all his suppliers liked him.
"It's a service industry," he said. "It's just good business.
Where would I be without my suppliers and where would I
be without my customers?" He's the only person I knew who
talked about a moral code. "The Ten Commandments are
okay," he told me, "but Dale Carnegie's better."

Carl could usually be seen wearing a worn-out blue
blazer, every pocket stuffed with scraps of paper. They were
reminders of who owed him how much and when it was
owed, or whom he had to meet to collect from or transact
with. Everything was written in a cryptic code he had invented, some obscure shorthand that he could decipher in a
second, but that no one else would understand. Each pocket
even meant something; it was a whole system. "I'm on top
of it," Carl said. He certainly was. He carried *The Wall
Street Journal, Fortune,* the *Financial Times,* and *The Econ-
omist* around in his backpack. He kept notebooks, detailed
logs of all of his transactions. He would transfer the notes
on the scraps of paper into his notebooks, which were filled
with a different code. I sometimes wondered whether that's
why he and Anna got along—they each kept their own set
of strange notebooks, tracking the town in their own ways,
chronicling our lives from two different points of view.

Carl's notebooks never left his room. He locked them in a
gray two-drawer file cabinet beside his desk, and unlocked

the file cabinet and removed the ledgers only to record the scraps into the notebooks' orderly columns. "You've got to keep them balanced," he said. I asked him why he was so sensitive about them, since they were all in code anyway. "You have to do everything to protect your customers," he told me. "Besides, any code can be broken. It just takes time. It also makes me feel important." Carl was important, by the look of the number of notebooks he kept locked up. He showed me one once. Of course it made no sense to me, but he pointed to the column where he tracked the money he had collected. "A perfect record," he said. "I've never lost a penny." It could have been true, knowing Carl. He had a way with people. His notebooks aligned perfectly with the world. He was in control; the columns confirmed it. People asked, Carl gave. Carl offered, people accepted, on his terms. Everything was an agreement.

Carl's other constant was a blue Notre Dame visor, with the interlocking ND removed, so you could see only the darker blue shadow where the logo had been. He had bent the bill of the cap, but then blunted the left side (his left) so that it pointed skyward. "I had to have it trending up," he explained. His father wanted him to go to Notre Dame. "He's going to be disappointed," Carl said. "But that's all right, he's used to that." When he first said this, I thought that Carl was referring to other disappointments, not related to him, but now I'm not so sure.

Carl was practically the only friend I had, and we'd been friends almost since birth. He used to live a few blocks away and his mother looked after me during the time my mother was working. They moved to a different house, a mile outside town, but we still see each other at school and hang out whenever he's not taking care of business. Sometimes I think that Carl is my friend only because we've been friends for so long, that if we met for the first time tomorrow he would never be my friend.

I was worried about telling him about Anna and me, especially because of his reaction the first day we saw her. I told him about a week after the football game. By then he already knew. "Good for you," he said. "You're definitely one of the more interesting couples in school. Just don't let me catch you wearing makeup." Carl knew me better than that.

When we were younger, my mother used to pick Carl and me up after school, but that stopped when I was in the fourth grade. "You can walk home," she said. "It'll be good for you." Carl's mom picked us up sometimes, but that couldn't be relied on when she started having trouble at home, and then stopped altogether when they moved. Carl had business to take care of now anyway. I don't know what my mother had to take care of during the day. She talked on the phone with her friends, maybe, or ran over to Hilliker, about ten minutes away. She used to hang out with Mrs. Hathorne during the day, and frequently she would do things with Mr. and Mrs. Hathorne (my father rarely joined them, preferring the sanctuary of his den), but they stopped being friends. I thought it was Mr. Hathorne's fault.

He was a drunk, that was the start of it. Carl's father

wasn't one of those guys you had to go and drag out of the bar or anything like that. He would drink by himself. He would drive his car to the liquor store in Hilliker or Shale and then find some back road and park his car and drink until all the bottles were dry.

He sold cars in Hilliker, and his wife first suspected something when there was a noticeable decrease in his monthly paychecks. He wasn't making the commissions he used to. She would call the dealership and he wouldn't be around. Then he would come home late, smelling like alcohol. She told him that it was a problem. He said he would quit. He didn't.

He missed more work and finally was fired. Still he didn't quit drinking. Finally Mrs. Hathorne asked my mother to help. She must have been desperate. My mother took the initiative for once and called a bunch of his friends and family together, and a few of Mrs. Hathorne's friends too, and they held an intervention. They all told him that he had a problem and that he needed to get it taken care of for his sake, for his family's sake. A couple of days later he went down to Joplin and spent three weeks in rehab.

It was when he got back that Mrs. Hathorne stopped wanting anything to do with my mother. She stopped seeing a lot of her friends, as if they had been the cause of all the trouble. Or maybe she was embarrassed. Then the Hathornes moved north of town. It was only a few miles away, but it might as well have been the North Pole. Carl and I still hung out, but our parents never socialized anymore. You never saw Carl's mom.

Everyone saw Mr. Hathorne, though. After he got out of rehab, he spent his days down at Gurney's gas station. Gurney's was a full-service gas station; you had to go to the other end of town, to Downey's, for self-serve, and the gas was usually the same price. You would see him anytime you went by, sitting in a black plastic chair by the front counter, sipping on a big styrofoam cup of coffee. Every once in a while he might get up and clean someone's windows, but he never pumped gas. He wasn't working. Derek Gurney or his twin brother, Erick, did the work. Carl's dad sat and sipped.

Carl's mother waited before she said anything to her husband about going back to work. She gave him time to adjust to his sobriety. But Carl thought differently. "Why doesn't he just sit on the road with a sign around his neck that says, 'I'm a drunken out-of-work bum'?"

Carl's father sat at the gas station for a long time. It was the only place I saw him anymore. One day after school, in the middle of October, I guess, Anna and I were walking down along the river and Carl came out of the woods, holding his hand over his right eye. I was a little embarrassed to see him, since I'd been ignoring him since I started hanging out with Anna. It was nothing personal, it was just all Anna, all the time.

"Are you all right?" Anna asked him.

"I will be." He took his hand away and revealed a swollen mess.

"That's going to look good in the morning," I said.

"What happened?" Anna said.

He looked at her with his left eye and then at me. He didn't want to say. "Customer dissatisfaction."

"Do you want to go after the guy?" I asked.

"No, I'll take care of it later." He looked at my hand. I would have gone after the guy, even with my splint. I was about to say so, when Anna spoke.

"Put a raw potato on it. It's the best thing."

"How do you know that?" I said.

"It's an old witch's trick," she said. "I can also put a curse on the person who did it."

"That you can do," Carl said.

I invited them both over to my house. Carl didn't want to go to his own. And he didn't want to be seen around town with a swollen eye. That would be bad for business. So we walked to my house.

We went in through the garage and into the kitchen, which was a mistake. We should have gone in through the front door—that way we would have avoided my mother. I should have known better; I spent every afternoon avoiding her, and here I led Carl right in on her. When we walked into the kitchen, my mother and Carl's dad were sitting at the table, drinking coffee.

"Anna and Carl are going to hang out for a while," I said.

My mother was startled. She got up from the table but then sat down again. "Okay," she said. Carl's father didn't say anything. Carl didn't say anything. Then, without looking up, Mr. Hathorne said, "Tell him to get out of here before I blacken the other one." He hadn't even moved his head; he spoke directly to his coffee. My mother looked at Mr. Hathorne. We quickly went upstairs to my room.

"What do you think that's all about?" Carl said.

We didn't say anything about his eye. I don't see how Mr.

Hathorne could have beaten his son and then made it over to my house. I wasn't going to bring it up unless Carl did.

"What do you suppose he's doing here?" he said.

"Maybe he's been helping my mom out," I said. "She's always getting somebody to do her work for her."

"Maybe they finally kicked him out of the gas station," Anna said.

"Maybe she's trying to help him," I said.

"Maybe they're having an affair," Carl said.

Carl's dad was at the same table, drinking coffee, a few nights after that. It got so that Anna and I wanted to see if he was there, but we didn't want to go at the same time. It made us uncomfortable. Carl always asked if we had seen him. "You'd think that if something was going on they wouldn't just hang around drinking coffee after," Anna said. "You'd think she'd get him the hell out of there before anyone saw him."

"But maybe since we saw him that first time, they figured what the hell," I said.

"It's strange," Carl said.

It got stranger.

One night I came back later than usual from Anna's after school. I was late for dinner, which is usually a crime in my house, but that night no one said anything about it. I walked in the door and there were my parents, sitting at the ends of the table as usual, and there was Carl's father, sitting at the table with them, at my spot. He was even eating off my plate. I didn't know what to do, so I stood there in the kitchen with my coat on, looking at my place at the table.

"Where have you been?" my mother asked in almost a friendly tone.

"Over at Anna's. I lost track of time. I'm sorry."

"Well, get a plate and get some dinner while it's still warm," she told me.

Nothing more was said. I sat at the table across from Carl's dad.

After dinner I went up to my room and called Carl. "What happened at your house?" I asked.

"Nothing," he said.

"Your mom didn't say anything?"

"No."

"Well, guess what happened over here."

"I don't know."

"Your father ate over here. And my dad was here too."

"You're not serious."

"The three of them were sitting there as normal as can be."

"Your dad didn't do anything?"

"None of them did anything. We all ate dinner and then I came up here and called you. I think your dad left a few minutes ago." Carl said that he would call me if anything happened at his house, but he didn't call.

Carl's father sat at my place at the table for the next five or six nights, and then it was over, without a word or a warning. This episode had ended, and no one said anything about his being in our house.

my   h e a r t ,   p r e v i o u s l y

Anna Cayne wasn't my first girlfriend; I had dated Melissa Laughner in the spring of the same year. There was nothing wrong with Melissa Laughner. She was smart and nice and pretty, tall and thin, with straight brown hair. She wore glasses, sometimes, and she was quiet. Near the end of March her younger brother, Adam, had told Carl that she liked me, so I called her up one night and asked her if she wanted to go see a movie or something. She did. On the Friday of that week, her father drove us to Hilliker, where the nearest theater was, dropped us off, then picked us up when the movie was over. She said barely a word the whole time.

"I don't think she likes me," I told Carl on Monday.

"That's not what her brother says."

"Even after Friday?"

"He says she had a good time."

"Maybe he's just jerking me around."

"It's true," Carl said. "Everyone's out to get you."

I found Adam after school. "Carl says that your sister still likes me."

"Why shouldn't she?"

"I'm not so sure things went all that well," I said.

"She's just shy. You didn't tell her that I talked to Carl, did you?"

"No."

"I mean talked to him at all."

"No," I said.

"All right. Give Melissa another call. If you want to, I mean."

I don't know whether Adam talked to his sister or not, but she was a lot different the second time we went out. She even spoke. We started going out after that, hanging out after school and on the weekends. She would call me every night, and it was all right at first. Then I got bored, I guess. I don't really know what happened; I just knew that I didn't really like spending time with her anymore, no matter how much we kissed. I didn't feel a connection with her; nothing drew me toward her. Something about her made me want to be away from her whenever we were together. I take that back—there wasn't anything wrong with Melissa Laughner. There was something about *me* that made me want to be away from her. We would sit at my house and watch TV, and the time would barely move forward to when she would leave. I didn't know what to say around her, and the fact that she was quiet made me uncomfortable or uninterested, or both. It was easier to be alone, I thought. At that time I wanted to be alone, I guess. And then I was. More than I wanted.

I hardly knew how to get into a relationship, and I had no idea how to get out of one. I wanted to break up with Melissa, but I didn't know what to say or what to do. Everything dragged on for a few more months, and when the freshman spring dance was coming up, Carl and I devised a plan.

Melissa and I were supposed to go to the dance together,

of course, but I called her at the last minute on the night of the dance and told her that I was sick and couldn't make it. She said that she wasn't going to go either then, but I persuaded her to go. She could hang out with her friends and have a good time without me. She had to go to the dance. That was critical. Because when Carl saw her sitting at a table by herself he went over to her and said, "I'm sorry you guys broke up," then acted all surprised when she acted surprised. "I didn't know he was sick," Carl then lied. "He told me he was going to break up with you before the dance, so I figured . . ."

Melissa immediately went home and called me. "Carl said that you were going to break up with me before the dance tonight."

"I'm sorry about that, Melissa. I was going to, but then I got sick and I didn't want to do it over the phone." To tell the truth, that's exactly how I had wanted to do it. Carl had no problem breaking up for me. In fact, I think he enjoyed it. It was simply another transaction for him. I was a coward, I admit it. And I'd like to say that I felt bad, but the next day Carl and I were laughing about it.

"You should have seen her face," he said. "It was like I'd hit her in the head with a shovel. How often do you get to do that?"

Melissa didn't talk to me again for a long time. She went around and told people some shit about me, and a few more people in the world stopped talking to me. I didn't have that many friends to begin with, and now Melissa was subtracting a few more. She left notes in my locker telling me how terrible I was and how much she hated me. I ignored them. I don't know why I was all in a hurry to get away from her; it wasn't like I was suddenly doing something more exciting after we broke up. I would wander around town by myself, try to avoid going home to my mother, and watch Carl conduct his business. I couldn't go with him— that was bad for business, he said—so I would follow him around, spying from a safe distance. That's what I did now that I wasn't with Melissa—I spied on my best friend. It was always interesting to see who was buying what from Carl. It wasn't just the burnouts and the jocks, there were people who everybody thought were squeaky clean, good students. There were preachers' kids and teachers' kids, even adults, who would meet Carl behind some building or at some out-of-the-way spot, and he would hand them a small bag of something and take their money. When I got bored watching Carl, I would pretend to run into him and then walk around with him for a while. He was good, though he never talked business. He *was* business.

Melissa and I had a few classes together and we would pass each other in the halls almost every day at school, but she had stopped talking to me. We ignored each other to the point that I had almost forgotten about her. But when Anna and I found those notes in our lockers after the football game, I was certain that it was Melissa who had left them.

h a l l o w e e n

It had snowed the night before. I looked out my bedroom window and saw a good five inches on the ground, covering everything. The plows hadn't come by yet, and no one had driven on the street. A perfect blanket of white stretched as far as I could see. I wished that it would stay like that, but no sooner did I wish it than I heard the sound of a shovel scraping against concrete. My father was out in the driveway. He would need help. I pulled on my clothes and a pair of coveralls, laced up my boots, put on a cap and a pair of gloves, and went out to ruin the spotless snow.

"It's a lot of snow," I said. "Have you ever seen so much snow so early?"

"Don't get your hopes up," my father said. "There's school."

It was costume day. Everybody was supposed to wear one. Carl went as an executive. He wore a suit and tie and carried a briefcase. His visor was tucked away in his locker and his hair was combed and neat. During classes, he pretended to be on his cell phone the whole time.

Anna came dressed in a private school uniform: black shoes, white stockings, plaid skirt, white blouse, and a blue blazer with a crest on it. She didn't wear anything black (except her shoes), not even eyeliner. Everyone was shocked. I thought she was beautiful, but by then I thought she was beautiful all the time. On the crest, in tiny gold script, were the words "Satan's School for Girls." Only a few people paid attention to the details.

At first I didn't want to wear a costume, but in the end I went as a box of Velveeta. I should have gone as a pirate. I could have put on some junky clothes and a bandanna, and had a hook cover the splint on my finger. Instead, I got a big cardboard box and attached a pair of my father's old suspenders, so it would rest on my shoulders. I painted the box bright yellow, and had my mother help me with the logo. She made a stencil so I could paint the letters red. "Why do you want to go as a box of cheese?" she said. "It seemed like something easy," I told her. "And who else is going to wear anything like it?"

Billy Godley, a freshman, also came as a Velveeta box. And his costume looked a lot better than mine. I had made mine too big, and it got bent when I tried to fit it into the backseat of the car. It was snowing again when I got to school, and the heavy wet flakes spotted the paint and made some of the red run. The worst thing was that I couldn't sit down in class. The cardboard went from my shoulders to my ankles, and I had to either keep standing or take off the costume, and what was the point of that? Billy Godley had hinges in his costume, at the knees and waist, so at least he could sit on a chair, even if he couldn't fit into a desk.

Before last period I stopped by Mr. Devon's classroom to throw the thing in the trash.

"I like it," he said. "It's a statement."

"Billy Godley's got a better one," I said.

"Well, how many pirates did you see today?"

"About twenty."

"And what was their statement?"

"I don't know," I said. "I don't even know what mine was."

Mr. Devon motioned me to follow him into his office, where he pulled a book from one of his shelves. "Look at these," he said. "Brillo pads and soup cans. Not so different from cheese boxes, are they? And these are in museums and books."

"Maybe I should get that out of the trash, then," I said.

Mr. Devon laughed. "I wouldn't go that far."

A book on his desk caught my attention. *Arshile Gorky*. It was the same one I'd seen at Anna's. "Did Anna borrow that from you?" I asked.

"No," he said. "Anna. That's your friend, right?"

"Yeah. She had the same book."

"Oh, really? Maybe we should all get together and talk about art sometime."

"She'd probably like that," I said.

The book was a coincidence, I guess, and later Anna made it clear that she didn't want to have any conversation with Mr. Devon, let alone one about art. At least that's what she told me.

When the final bell rang and I went to my locker, I realized that I hadn't worn a coat. It was because of that stupid costume I'd had on in the morning. You would think that someone would have reminded me, been looking out for me. Isn't that what mothers are for? And of course she wasn't picking me up after school. Which meant that I had to walk home with no coat, no hat, and no gloves. I started out of school and walked slowly past parents parked in their cars, waiting for their sons and daughters, in hopes that someone would see my plight and offer some help.

"Hey, cheese loaf," I heard someone yell at me. I turned around. It was Anna. She was hurrying out the door. "Where's your pretty yellow wrapper?"

"Billy Godley is wearing it."

"Come on, you were a lot more believable as a box of cheese than he was."

"I'm sure I was."

"Where are you going now?"

"Home, I guess."

"Aren't you forgetting something?"

"I forgot it this morning."

"Do you want to wear mine?" It was a man's coat. An old black overcoat from the 1940s or 1950s. It probably would have fit me.

"That's okay," I said.

"You could wear my blazer," she said.

"I wouldn't want to misrepresent Satan's School."

"My mom's supposed to pick me up. Do you want us to give you a ride home?"

"That would be great."

"Who knows, maybe we can convince her to take you home after a while. Instead of right away, I mean."

"That would be even better."

Mrs. Cayne pulled into the circular drive in front of the school, and Anna went and spoke with her and then motioned me to the car. "Get in front," Anna said, "so you can be closer to the heat."

It was the first time that I had seen Anna's mother up close in the daytime. She looked crazier than ever. Her hair was particularly wild that day, and seemed magnetically drawn to the roof of the car. There was a pencil sticking out of the back of her hair, as if someone had jabbed it into her skull.

"So where's your costume?" Mrs. Cayne asked.

"I took it off late in the day," I said.

"Anna said you went as a block of cheese."

"Velveeta." I didn't want to correct her.

"That's interesting. Seems like a good idea for a costume."

"It seemed that way, but it wasn't really."

"Not very practical?"

"Exactly. Cheese doesn't offer a lot of range of motion."

Mrs. Cayne laughed. It has to be a good thing when you make your girlfriend's mom laugh. Especially when she's thinking that you're an idiot for (1) going to school dressed as a box of cheese and (2) forgetting your coat right after a snowstorm.

When we got to the Caynes', Mrs. Cayne offered me some candy. She had bowls of chocolates and M&M's and nuts all over the place. "I can't eat any of this stuff," she said. She always said that. You might think that she had so many bowls of stuff around the house because it was Halloween, but they were there every time I was at their house. And I always saw her eating it. She would never take more than one piece of candy out of a bowl, but when you have twenty bowls of stuff lying around, that adds up. And Mrs. Cayne always said the same thing: "I can't eat any of it. Help yourself."

I left Mrs. Cayne and her candy and went with Anna to her room. She closed the door and cleared a space on the floor for us to sit, pushing books and discs and papers into a heap under her desk. She dug around in a pile of discs and pulled out one with a dark cover, and white lines forming jagged mountains on the black. It looked like a cross between an X ray and a topographic map. "This was my dad's favorite band, when he was in college," she said, and put the CD in the player. She turned on her computer and showed me some fan sites. "The lead singer killed himself two days before they were starting their U.S. tour."

"It sounds like it," I said.

She gave me a disapproving look and moved on, jumping from site to site, subject to subject. We moved from the band to the city of Manchester to a site about London. "Have you ever been?" she asked.

"No. I haven't been anywhere."

"There's nothing wrong with here."

"Are you serious?"

"Sure. This is fine by me. You might want to try and see the world someday, though."

"And where have you been?"

"I've been lurking around in the dark," she said, "waiting for you."

She ejected the disc and fished around for another. The

cover was a black-and-white photograph of an antenna and wires. "My dad just played this for me yesterday," she said.

It wasn't music. People were reciting numbers in foreign languages, over and over, often barely discernible behind the static. A horn or a buzzer went off every few seconds. There were four discs of the stuff, recordings of radio broadcasts.

"What is it?"

"Nobody knows," she said. "It's been going on a long time, for more than twenty years. Some people think that they're coded messages, used by spies, the CIA, KGB, stuff like that."

There was a knock on the door. I quickly got off the bed. It was her father.

"Please keep the door open," he said. He looked at the stereo. "What do you think of this?"

"It's weird," I told him.

"Have you ever heard anything like it?"

"No."

"Are you staying for dinner?"

I looked at Anna and she nodded at me to accept. I did. "I just need to call my mom," I said.

"Well, after dinner, let's go listen to some more of this," he said. "But on the radio."

Mrs. Cayne was dressed in a princess costume when we came to sit at the table. She had her hair pulled back so that she could fit her funnel-shaped hat on her head, and I noticed for the only time a resemblance between her and her daughter.

"What does your mother do for Halloween?" Mrs. Cayne asked me.

"She likes to bake." This wasn't entirely a lie. My mother bought the cookie dough that comes in a tube, and all you do is crack it open, separate the pieces, and put them on a cookie sheet and then into the oven. She would take the fresh-baked cookies and go sit in the dark. When I used to dress up and go trick-or-treating, my mother would have a spread of candy. Actually, it was a well-ordered regiment. She would arrange the candy in neat, precise rows, and then re-sort and rearrange the rows as she handed out the candy. It was maddening to watch this compulsion, which demonstrated an organization and ardor she failed to exhibit anywhere else. This woman who couldn't file or answer a phone properly could arrange candy in rows on the hall table, alphabetically or by size or according to who knows what exact system, and then dispense the candy in a logic and method known only to her, but in an obviously even way, updating the rows so that they kept their structural integrity. How was that possible?

Once I had stopped dressing up in a costume and bringing home candy, my parents stopped handing it out. It must have had something to do with reciprocity. I could imagine my father running the numbers in his head, seeing the debits, the red numbers piling up with every knock. He always hated kids' coming to the door anyway. "Are there any worse sounds than doorbells?" he grumbled. So now my parents retreated to their usual spots in the house—my father to his den of solitude, and my mother to eat cookies in the dark, so that no one would think they were home.

As we headed down to the Caynes' basement after dinner, a group of trick-or-treaters came to the door. "Where's the witch?" they kept saying.

"No witches," Mrs. Cayne answered calmly. "Only princesses live in this house."

I looked at Anna, but she didn't even acknowledge that anyone had said anything.

the basement

A door off the kitchen led to the basement at the Caynes'. There wasn't much down there, but it was away from the rest of the house, and you could hear anyone coming. No one could sneak up on you or surprise you.

The stairs led to a large room, maybe forty feet by forty feet, almost perfectly square, with a small utility room right by the stairs, that housed the furnace and hot-water heater and all that junk. Behind the stairs was an old bumper pool table, and a beat-up brown sofa against one wall. At the other end of the basement was another sofa, positioned near a wood-burning stove that heated the place. While most of the basement was underground, there was a door that led outside. You only had to walk up a few steps and you were underneath a wooden deck at the back of the house that overlooked the yard sloping toward the street.

Mr. Cayne led us past a stack of boxes left over from

their move and past an ancient TV set. It was the only TV in the house. "Is that color?" I joked.

"It is color, isn't it, Dad?" Anna said. Mr. Cayne laughed, but his soft-boiled features turned menacing, and I could almost see the man who was capable of crushing somebody's wrist and pulling an arm out of its socket. Anna didn't say another word until he left us alone.

"We have six TVs," I said. "Two for each of us. I don't think there's ever a time when one isn't on somewhere in the house."

Mr. Cayne continued toward the end of the room, "This is my workbench." He pointed to a countertop, maybe eight feet long, with four cabinet doors and a row of four drawers underneath. Another pair of doors were above the counter, and a series of cubbyholes in various sizes beside those. A large pegboard covered the wall to the right of the workbench, where his tools hung in haphazard fashion. The top of the bench was covered with more tools, fishing tackle, and empty shotgun shells, as well as old radios and radio parts. There was also a machine to make shotgun shells, and a shortwave radio, a gray box with a bunch of dials set up on a corner of the workbench. "I'm not allowed to have this upstairs," he explained, then turned it on and patiently navigated the static until he found a broadcast.

"This is above the medium-wave band you're familiar with," he told me. "It's a huge space, over twenty times larger than the medium-wave band. There's everything here, news and music, amateur radio operators, Coast Guard ships, commercial airlines, military communications. You can listen to broadcasts from all over the world."

He kept a notebook where he logged the frequency of the stations he liked and what time he listened to them. He consulted his log and tuned to a broadcast from Kuwait and then one from Algeria. I couldn't understand any of it, but he was clearly enjoying it. He seemed like Anna then, his words spilling out and his enthusiasm infectious. He wasn't trying to force it on me; he just thought I would like it as much as he did. I didn't see the attraction at first, but then he tuned to some stations that sounded like the disc Anna had—maybe they were the same ones. It was like voices from outer space, trying to tell us something. Some were happy voices, some sounded like machines, and some appeared to be pleading for someone to understand them.

"There's all this stuff floating around out there," Mr. Cayne said, "and nobody knows what it means."

"Do you ever send messages back?" I asked.

"It's one-way only. I've got a buddy who can broadcast messages, though. I like to listen."

"Can we listen to your friend's broadcast?"

Mr. Cayne ignored me and went back to searching for stations. Anna had left us at some point in his demonstration and was sitting on the couch. After listening a few more minutes he turned to me. "You should think about getting one of these."

"Maybe I will." I don't know if I really meant it when I said it. I was trying to be polite. He nodded and went to the stairs, leaving the door open when he reached the top. I joined Anna on the couch. "How much time does he spend down here?"

"Not as much as he'd like you to believe," she said. "That's what's nice about it. It's a good place to get away from him, actually."

Anna and I spent a lot of time in the basement over the following months. She would turn off the lights and we would lie on the couch and listen to the world woozily making its way across the airwaves to us. It was almost pitch-black in the basement, with only the cool light from the dials of the shortwave and the red glow from the door of the stove. The radio messages would float, hypnotically, rhythmically, monotonously, into the room. I remember especially one broadcast: a woman's voice slowly, calmly repeating, *"Seis, siete, tres, siete, cero . . ."*

Anna moved toward me in the darkness. I could feel her trying to find me, but I didn't want to help. I waited for her to find me on her own. She brushed her hand against my chest and then slowly pushed it up my neck and chin. She pressed herself against me and held my chin in her hand until her mouth found mine. The woman on the radio was still repeating, *"Seis, siete, tres, siete, cero,"* again and again.

"Don't you want to find out what they mean, or where they come from, why we're hearing them?"

"It's almost more fun not knowing," she said. "If you knew what it all meant, then it might not be as interesting or compelling. That's probably half the fun, not knowing.

Sometimes there's more fun in the mystery of things than anything else." We listened for a while longer, and then she whispered in my ear, "Let's make a code."

milk shake

If we weren't in the basement, we were in Anna's room. We almost never went to my house. My mother was always there, either needing help with some small problem or just hovering nearby. A few days after Halloween, I was sitting on the floor in Anna's room, looking at album covers, when she said, "What do you want to do when you leave here?"

"I don't know," I said. "I haven't figured out that far. How about you?"

"I want to write obituaries." She rushed on: "Not for the reasons you're probably thinking."

"It sounds like taxidermy, that's what I was thinking," I said.

"They're not trophies, they're tributes. You have to capture the most important things in a person's life in just a few paragraphs."

She had a couple of notebooks filled with obituaries she had collected, and five more full of obituaries she had written herself. "I have an obituary for nearly everyone in school," she said. "All the students, the teachers, the administration, the janitors, the kitchen crew. I have most of the school board in here, the PTA. In fact, I have a lot of entire families in here."

"Am I in there?"

"Of course," she said, with a finality that told me it was no use to pursue it.

"Let me read one."

She opened a notebook to a page filled with tiny, spidery, almost indecipherable letters. I read:

Mr. Duncan Carmichael, who collected exotic animals, including tapirs, tarantulas, and a Tasmanian devil, was particularly proud of his four monitor lizards. He was discovered in the basement of his home, half eaten by the large lizards. . . . Spared in the carnage were a number of Madagascar hissing cockroaches, which were meant to be the lizards' food.

Of course, Mr. Carmichael was still alive, teaching biology to the freshman class. "Does Mr. Carmichael even have any pets?" I asked.

"Do you want to go to his house right now?" Anna said.

"That might be necessary," I said. "What if Mr. Carmichael doesn't die like this? Then what? Or worse, what if he does? What if everyone in your book dies exactly the way you've described it?"

"Then I will have saved a lot of time for everyone," she said. "You might be missing the point."

"Show me another one. Show me my mother's."

She consulted a master list, an alphabetical listing of all of the names, with the corresponding notebook and page number next to each. "The whole thing would be a mess without this list," she said. She picked up a notebook and opened it to a specific page, took a piece of scratch paper and carefully taped it over something near the bottom of the page, and covered the facing page with a book, then handed me the notebook; but she kept one hand on it, ready to grab it from me if I should try to read what was covered. "It's not yours," she said, "but I don't want you to see it. Not yet, anyway."

Mrs. Emily G_____ was killed on April 27, 2009, in an accident at her home. Her husband, Philip G_____, was cutting down a tree in the front yard of their house at 28 Valley View Road when the tree fell and landed on his wife. Mrs. G_____ was standing in the street to warn passing cars of her husband's activity when the tree crushed her.

Emily Marie Brandt was born on August 19, 1947, in Danbury, Connecticut, where her family had resided for generations. Emily was the first Brandt to leave Danbury and never return, when she left at age 18 to attend Brown University, where she earned a bachelor's degree in 1969. While attending Brown, she met Philip G_____, and the two were married by a justice of the peace on June 21, 1969.

Mrs. Emily G_____ was a housewife for nearly the entirety of her adult life, except for two years when she worked in a number of clerical and secretarial positions in various businesses in the community. She spent a lifetime narrowly avoiding accidents and other mishaps, at least until the last.

She is survived by her husband. Her four children, Denise, Paul (see Volume II, page 68), Joan (see Volume IV, page 107), and [this is where she had taped the scratch paper] preceded her in death.

The odd thing about the obituary is that, except for the deaths, all of the facts were accurate.

"How do you know all of this?" I asked.

"It's mostly public information," she said. "You can find out a lot about people just by paying attention. You should try it sometime."

"But how did you know other stuff? Like the fact that my mother is accident-prone, or her employment stuff?"

"Neither is a well-kept secret," Anna said. "You just have to pay attention. Be curious. Be quiet. You'd be amazed at what people talk about right next to you in public. They forget that other people are around, I guess, or they don't care."

"And why did you kill me off before my mother?"

She smiled. "It's not a rule, but I usually have a parent— sometimes both—outlive the children. I like it that way, having them deal with the loss."

I told her that I wanted to be a writer, even though I had never written anything outside school assignments.

"Write me a ghost story," she said.

"I will."

"Say it like you mean it."

"I'll write one for you."

"Soon," she said.

"Soon."

"I'll make sure," she said. "I'll supply the ghost."

I wanted to read all the obituaries she had written, but she wouldn't allow it. Instead, she invented a game where I wrote my own. It was a version of Celebrity Death Watch. We would e-mail each other a list of names of celebrities, in the order in which we thought they would die, and then write obituaries for each one. There was no way my obituaries could compare with Anna's, so I tended to uncover obscure facts or events in a celebrity's life and dwell on those. If it was a movie star, I would ignore the popular movies and list the TV commercials or bit parts in sitcoms and soap operas, concentrate on the star's involvement in Scientology or PETA, make mention of stays at a Betty Ford clinic or appearances on the Jerry Lewis Telethon. I would inflate the importance of a minor writer or TV star. Politicians were always good because you could find odd voting habits or expenses. I tried to make the obituaries funny and outlandish, and Anna loved them.

You could revise your list every two weeks. Anna was of course uncanny in her picks. She had been playing in some online games for a while, she said, but she didn't really like their versions. "There should be a Celebrity Death Watch site death watch," she said. "Most of them are deadly boring, and have no activity, no action."

. . .

Anna and I had been seeing each other for about a month, meeting before school in the morning and leaving together in the afternoon. Her Goth friends were starting to complain, so I started hanging out with them, standing with them before school in their private spot on the third floor. I am convinced that I looked like a bigger idiot than usual, sticking out in a group that already stuck out. I thought that their conversations would be incredibly interesting, that I would have the inside track on all the mysteries and intrigue of that dark group. I imagined that their talk would be filled with arcane knowledge and insight, a secret world revealed only to me, but instead their morning conversations were like most of the other crap that went on in the other crowds gathered in the school. They were dull, actually.

I also thought that Anna would be the dominant voice among the group, but she was strangely silent every morning. Bryce Druitt did most of the talking. He stood in the hallway with the cast on his leg, his crutches in front of him and his arms crossed casually over the top, going on and on about what he had watched on television or what music he was listening to or what comic books he was reading. Or death. They talked about death a lot. Sometimes they would ask Anna, "Who have you killed lately?" and she would tell them about her most recent obituary. Sometimes they would suggest a gruesome demise—"Why don't you put a busload of them into the river, or crash them into a semi or a culvert or something," Bryce would suggest—

and Anna would nod in agreement, and then ignore the advice.

Bryce liked to talk about *Yith*, a comic-book series he was reading about a time-traveler who could take any shape he wanted and enter people's minds and control them. The name was taken from H. P. Lovecraft, whom I had not read but the rest of them seemed to have. "There are more important things to read," Anna had told me. She had a list for me, and a timetable, it appeared. Or maybe she was trying to steer me away from anything connected to Bryce. He made the comic sound interesting enough, so I went and a bought a few issues. The new one had just come out, and the next day Bryce was talking about it.

"He's in complete control," he said. "Dominating everybody, and they're all going to end up dead and in hell or somewhere in time with Yith, working for him."

"What I liked about it," I said, "was that at the end you think Yith is going to disappear, or at least can disappear. He's got everything so well planned that he knows what everyone's going to do. He can just leave them alone and they'll still do his bidding. That way, they'll all think they've escaped him, but they haven't."

I thought Bryce was going to hit me. "They're not all milk shakes like you," he said.

He had called me that a couple of times before, maybe trying to hang a nickname on me. Nobody followed his lead, but it still annoyed me. There wasn't much I could do about it; make no mistake, Bryce Druitt could kick my ass in his sleep. I kept my mouth shut most mornings after that.

Maybe because I was seething every morning, standing on the fringes, yet there always seemed to be a tension in the group, a feeling that the whole thing could explode or break apart. Bryce's mouth would move and move, and everyone's attention would drift off down the hall. Claire Maenza, one of the other Goths, and Anna would shoot glances at each other, carrying on a secret conversation with their eyes, and Bryce would still go on, unaware that everything had changed. I wanted to go off with Anna, stand alone somewhere with her, but that didn't seem to be an option.

I won't go into detail about each one of them, describing what they were like and what they did. It's not that important. Besides, if they were telling their own story, they wouldn't mention me either.

"I don't really hang out with any of them outside of school," Anna said, "except for when we go to dances or games or whatever." She didn't hang out at all, actually. She had too many books to read and too much music to listen to, and too many notebooks to fill. In the beginning, I wondered why she wanted to hang out with me. She was close to Claire Maenza. I came to like her too, and she became an important link in all that happened.

Claire was a junior. She was tall and thin and had dyed black hair that fell straight down below her ears before breaking into waves that reached to her shoulder blades. She had a small silver hoop stuck through her left eyebrow, and she usually wore black lipstick. Sometimes she put on white lipstick, which was even creepier. I wonder why that is. She was nice, once you got to know her. She was quieter than Anna, soft-spoken. Anna said that Claire got all A's in school. Everyone said she did drugs, and that she got them from her parents.

She lived on Madder Lane, which was kind of an art community. A lot of people in town still called it Hippie Road (my father was particularly fond of "Deadbeat Drive"), since it had been taken over in the sixties. It was the last officially marked street in town, just off Town Street before it turned into Route 63. There were houses past Madder Lane, but the roads were mostly private, gravel-covered drives that led to houses and were referred to by the names of the families who lived there, or more accurately, by the names of families who had lived there years before. Claire's father had moved here from Rochester, New York, when he was a teenager, but her mom's family, the Comptons, had been here for generations. The Compton name was on the church; they had helped build it in 1750, and on the library, which was built in 1861, and all over the cemetery. Claire's mother was an architect, and her father was a sculptor. He made odd-looking contraptions out of stone and metal. None of his art was realistic, but many of his pieces had animal names. One, a group of large stones connected with rusted pipes, was called *Cattle*. "'Bullshit' is more like it," my father said. His work sold for a lot of money, and there were large installations by him in some people's yards. Not too many in town, but you'd see them if you drove into some of the nicer neighborhoods in Hilliker or Joplin. You would often spot Mr. Maenza wandering in the woods on the side of the roads, or wading along the river, hunting for particular rocks or discarded metal objects. He may have appeared like a homeless guy searching for cans, but my father said he was loaded. His grandfather had invented a safety device for slaughterhouses, and that set up the Maenza family for generations. "He can afford to be a bum," my father said. He was a client of my father's partner.

Claire's family had moved into town about six years before. She was normal then, with wavy brown hair. She rollerbladed all over the place, and chewed gum constantly. She played the flute and sang in the church children's choir. She had a beautiful voice. I told her that once and she started laughing. I avoided her for a long time after that. Her parents didn't go to church, so Claire would rollerblade back and forth or, if the weather was bad, her mother would drop her off and pick her up. She was almost always alone in older company as well. You'd see her standing in front of the white church, blowing bubbles with her gum and politely declining rides. Adults seemed to like her— Claire was polite and quiet and respectful. She always made her mother chauffeur her, thinking that she might one day accompany her inside the church.

Claire seemed destined to be a bandoid, one of those people you never have anything to do with unless you're in the band. They all stayed down in the school basement, way at one end, playing their music with the doors closed so they wouldn't disturb anyone else. When you did hear them, it was at an assembly or a game, and they all sat together. When they were in regular class they always sat next to one another, or next to somebody from the choir.

And what could you say to them, anyway? If you told them you liked the way they sang or played, they'd probably just laugh at you as Claire had done. That's what I thought of her, if I thought of her, but Claire Maenza entered the ninth grade as a completely different person. We were in separate schools then, she was beginning high school and I was finishing junior high, but I saw her around. She was taller, thinner, and darker. She had dyed and straightened her hair, and now wore heavy black eyeliner and only black clothes. She had entered the uniformed ranks of the Goths. I didn't even know it was Claire the first time I saw her; I thought somebody new had moved into town. Carl had to tell me who it was. It was a startling transformation, which changed everything. She stopped singing in the choir and stopped going to church altogether. She stopped playing the flute and stopped talking to adults. Before I met Anna, I tried to avoid Claire even more than usual. I never would have believed that we would have anything to do with each other.

I walked home with Anna every day after school. Our usual way was south along the river, sometimes as far as the bridge at the edge of town. We would climb down the bank and sit on the concrete slope underneath the bridge, out of the wind and snow. It was always quiet there, except for the occasional rumble of a car passing directly overhead. It was cold, and Anna wasn't dressed for the weather; she wore the same black jacket I had seen her wear the day she moved in.

"Aren't you cold?" I asked one day.

"No," she said. "I'm training myself not to feel it."

I imagined her in front of an open refrigerator or an air conditioner, or standing in the snow in a bathing suit, waiting to swim with one of those polar bear groups. I didn't think any of it would work. Wouldn't your body just get out of shape again in the summer?

"I started with lukewarm baths," she said. "I would submerge myself in them and stay there as long as I could, then I moved to cold baths, making them colder and colder. I put loads of ice in them now."

"How long can you stay in?"

"I can hold my breath underwater for more than four minutes," she said.

"What are you training for, exactly?"

"I might want to swim around the South Pole." She gave me a mischievous look. "You never know. Or it could be that I hate the winter, and it was either convince my parents to move someplace where it never gets cold or learn to live with it."

She seemed quite comfortable in her lightweight jacket. I was the one who was cold. I had on a heavy coat and a scarf and one glove. Because of my splint, I couldn't wear a glove on my left hand, and I couldn't fit it into my coat pocket, so I wore a thick brown boot sock over it.

"That's the weirdest thing I've ever seen," Anna said. "It's like you have a stump."

"It does the trick."

"You could at least get a color that matches your other glove, or your coat."

"It's only for a couple more weeks."

"I think you should keep it. Maybe wear a sock on the other one too. Have two stumps."

I pulled my right hand up into the sleeve of my coat and reached out toward her with my two stumps. She let out a quick shriek that echoed and amplified against the concrete of the bank and the bridge. A car stopped above and somebody yelled down to us. "What's going on down there?" It was one of the Gurney twins, Derek or Erick. Anna seemed to think it was Derek, but I wasn't so sure. People said you could tell the difference between the twins by the scar Derek had on the right side of his forehead, coming out from his hairline. The only problem was that you hardly ever saw either twin without his greasy green baseball cap. The caps had the word "Gurney's" stitched on the front in yellow. Some people had taken to examining the grease stains on the caps in hopes of finding some dif-ferentiating detail, but that was pointless too, as the caps changed as more grease and grime were added, and be-sides, the brothers might have shared the caps. It was all a guessing game.

We crawled out from under the bridge, and there was Derek or Erick, leaning over the bridge, trying to see for himself. His pickup was barely on the bridge, the door open. He must have gotten out of it in a hurry.

"Everything's all right," I said. He had a smug expres-sion of disbelief on his face. "It's all right," I repeated. What was I going to tell him? That I'd just been attacking my girlfriend with two pretend stumps? Anna didn't say anything, but stayed in the background, watching.

He looked at us for a few more long moments, and then back at his truck. You could tell that he was thinking it wasn't in such a good spot: a car could come along and hit it. The look on his face suggested we would be to blame for that.

"You shouldn't be down there," he said. "You might fall in the river."

"We're just going on home," I said.

"See that you do." He got back in his truck and drove off.

"'See that you do,'" Anna said. "Who's he?"

"We just got scolded by a guy who pumps gas, and we don't even know which Gurney it was."

"I'm pretty sure that was Derek."

"I don't know about that."

get drunk

From the beginning of our relationship, Anna had put things in my locker, or sent things through the mail. On Columbus Day she sent me a postcard with a portrait of the explorer and wrote, "Most people think he went insane, or was insane all along. He had to be dragged back to Spain in chains. He was convinced that his life had been prophesied in the Bible. He thought the earth was shaped like a breast. He argued all his life that he had landed in China and not some new world. He advocated the enslavement and slaugh-ter of the native people. He was a lucky man." Many of the postcards I received were the same ones she had on her bedroom walls. She always wrote "Where?" on the cards she sent me, and I would have to put the cards on my walls in the same spots she had placed hers. I would tape each card up and take a picture and e-mail it to her. "Not even close," she would reply. "You'd better come over and pay attention."

She also sent small boxes filled with objects, an empty prescription bottle, a single glove, a shoelace, discarded letters and notes. These items might be arranged in a collage or tagged with annotations ("Found near the south bridge, November 1"). Other items contained instructions ("Please send to Claire Maenza immediately"; "Send to someone you don't know. Don't delay"). Some messages were anagrams, acrostics, cryptograms, some were in foreign languages, Esperanto. I always had to cheat and go search on the Web to find out what the hell I was getting. "That's not cheating," she said, if she said anything at all. If I didn't mention the mail, she wouldn't either.

Once she sent me an envelope with a single sentence written over and over on it, except for the small block where my name and address appeared in large red letters and numbers. When I opened the envelope, I found the same sentence written over the entire inside—she must have taken the envelope apart, written on it, then folded it back together—except with all the letters backward. The sentence was: "There are realms of life where the concepts of sense and nonsense do not apply."

One of my favorites was a charcoal-and-ink drawing of

her silhouette, with dotted lines around the edges, like out-
lines of pieces of a jigsaw puzzle, with instructions on each
of the sections. "Mail this to Claire Maenza," was written
on one. "Put this between pages 104 and 105 of the book
Literature of the Supernatural, edited by Robert E. Beck, in
the school library," was on another. If you cut the sections
along the dotted lines, her silhouette was transformed into
another silhouette, mine. I didn't follow any of the instructions. I had the drawing hanging on my wall, but took it
down whenever Anna came over. I didn't want her to know
that I hadn't done what she asked.

She made her own stamps. She would take pictures, or
find them, and manipulate them into templates she'd gotten online or created herself, and would then print her own
stamps. Almost everything she sent me had her handmade
stamps: presidents and movie stars, writers and artists,
faces of people in town, her father, a few of herself. You can
imagine my surprise when I saw one with my own picture.
I don't even know where or how she got the picture. Maybe
she took it herself, in her room or at school. I didn't remember it at all, but there I was, at middle distance, looking straight ahead, a little droopy-eyed, my hair slightly in
my eyes. Nothing unusual, except I didn't remember that
picture's being taken.

"They never notice," she said about the post office. "I
don't think I've ever had a letter returned. It must be the
computers—they can't tell the difference between a real
stamp and one of mine. Besides, Archie doesn't care."
Archie Wilkes was the mailman in town. He lived down

the street from us. He didn't have that many stops, he drove his own car, and you never saw him wear a uniform. He delivered the mail whenever he had time, it seemed. He would show up in the evening, or on Sunday morning. It was all very casual. The real work was done in Hilliker, at the central mail facility, where the computers sorted everything out. Once it cleared there, Anna's stamps were as good as the real thing.

It was a game to her. Everything was a game, or a piece in a game only she knew the rules to. Every day there was something new, something surprising.

I now wonder how much of it she planned and how much of it just happened.

I thought that Anna should meet Mr. Devon, take a class from him, or we could go visit him after school one day. She was against it.

"I heard he's a creep."

"I don't think so. Everybody seems to like him."

"He's not for me, then," she said. That was the end of the conversation.

Anna didn't like talking about Mr. Devon. She didn't like him, although she never said why. I always thought they would get along. Mr. Devon was the second most interesting person I knew. You don't have too many football coaches who also teach drawing, sculpture, and photography. He was always friendly, maybe because he was young. He was the only male teacher who still had all his hair, and one of the few who didn't have any gray yet. Instead, he had an overabundance, an unruly black mop that looked like he cut it himself. It was often crooked and asymmetrical, as rumpled as the rest of him. He wore faded blue jeans or paint-splattered khakis, and work shirts, mostly denim. When you saw him in the hallway he always had a tie, but he never wore one in class. We always tried to figure out where he had it hidden in his classroom, and then one day when there was a fire drill and we were lining up to leave the classroom and the building, Mr. Devon calmly opened his desk drawer and pulled out his old, wrinkled tie, and slipped the large loop over his head and tightened it under his denim collar. "It probably wouldn't burn anyway," he joked. "Besides, you have to look respectable for the firemen." The only time he dressed up, without any holes in his shirts or pants, and no stains, was for football games.

All the girls (except Anna) liked Mr. Devon, because he was handsome, in his rumpled, rugged way, and because he was an artist. A lot of girls asked him to paint their portraits, and he just laughed. "Would you settle for a photograph?" he'd say. The guys liked Mr. Devon because he was a jock, and he seemed like one of the guys. Senior players would go to his place after home football games and drink beer. I always thought that if I could be any adult in town, it would be Mr. Devon. He appeared to really like what he did, he always had a good word to say, and he was popular and respected. There didn't seem much wrong with the world of Mr. Devon.

"I hear he's got false teeth," Anna said.

It's hard to look at someone the same way after you hear that. You're constantly looking at the person's mouth.

"What does that matter?" I said.

"It wouldn't matter with anyone else, but he's as fake as his teeth."

"How would you know? You've never talked to him."

"Let's keep it that way, all right?"

Anna and I were walking together after school one day when Mr. Devon pulled up and asked if we wanted a ride home. "Sure," I said, and went toward the car. Anna didn't move. I looked back to her and tried to get a sense of what she was thinking. Finally she followed me to the car and got in the backseat. She wasn't happy.

Mr. Devon drove to my house, even though it would have made more sense for him to drop Anna off first. I could see him glancing in the rearview mirror at her. He was probably wondering why she was in such a foul, quiet mood. When he pulled up in front of my house, Anna got out of the car with me.

"I can take you home too," Mr. Devon said.

"That's all right," she said.

He nodded and drove away.

"You like him, don't you?" she asked me.

"He's nice to me. Why don't you like him?"

"It's not important," she said.

"I want you to like him. It's important to me."

"It only seems important. I'm not telling you to stop liking him. That's why I'm not telling you why I don't. I see him one way and you see him another way, that's all." She moved on to another subject.

I'd first met Mr. Devon in junior high school. He was new in our school when I was in the eighth grade, and there was some tension and nervousness about what he was trying to teach us and how. He had probably learned somewhere, either as a student in his own required teaching classes, or as an on-the-job teacher somewhere else, that there was no use trying to teach a group of seventh- and eighth-graders much technique or form in drawing, painting, sculpting, or whatever. So our class had more activities than art lessons.

There were things to do, which is a radical notion in school. Usually you just sit there and listen to the teacher tell you things, instead of actually getting a chance to do them yourself. Mr. Devon, however, erased that step and had us immediately drawing and painting, and even trying a little sculpture and pottery. Surprisingly, a lot of the kids hated doing stuff. Maybe they wanted to sit around and have Mr. Devon lecture us on the proper way to hold a brush or draw. I liked his class. You didn't have homework and you didn't have to take notes or read a textbook. Best of all, very little attention was paid to a right way or wrong way to do anything, and most of the activities were fun. For instance, Mr. Devon would put a large block of drawing paper on an easel and have one of us go up and draw something on a section of one sheet—a third or fourth or fifth of it, depending on how he had folded it—without letting the rest of us see it. Then another person would go up and, still without knowing what the previous person had drawn, continue the drawing, and then another person would do likewise, and so on until the sheet of paper was filled. The image was always strange, funny, startling, unexpected. After we had done a number of these drawings Mr. Devon explained that the technique had been made popular by the Surrealists. He then showed us some examples of theirs.

Mr. Devon started teaching in high school my sophomore year, and one morning before school he came up to me. "Maybe you can help me out," he said.

"Sure," I answered.

"I have this sculpture in my truck that I need help bringing in. It's a little too heavy just for me. Do you think you could give me a hand for a minute?"

I looked up and down the hall, hoping to find a football player who could help Mr. Devon instead, but there was no one.

"I guess I can help you."

He had an old beat-up Chevy that looked as if it had driven through the woods in a straight line, hitting every tree in the way. It was caked with mud, and the passenger side of the front windshield was cracked from top to bottom.

"Don't worry," Mr. Devon said. "My car's in better shape. I use this for hauling stuff."

In the bed of the pickup was a wooden crate about the size of a thirty-two-inch TV. It was a lot heavier than that, though. I was sure I was going to drop it any minute, but I was afraid to stop.

"You need a rest?" Mr. Devon could tell that I was about ready to drop the crate, and whatever was inside was going to smash to bits on the sidewalk. I kept hoping someone would come along and help, but nobody did.

"I'm fine," I said, and tried to move faster.

Somehow we made it to the back door of the school. From there it was about thirty or forty feet to Mr. Devon's classroom. We had to put the crate down in order to open the door, and then we dragged it through the doorway.

Mr. Teller, one of the custodians, was coming down the hall. "Hold it right there," he shouted.

"I think we're in trouble," Mr. Devon said.

"What do you mean 'we'?" I said. He laughed.

"Don't kill yourself," Mr. Teller said. "Let me get a handtruck and haul that thing out for you.

"Actually, we're coming in," Mr. Devon told him. "This goes in my room."

"All right. Same thing. Just go on about your business and I'll bring this into your room. There's no reason to break your back when I've got a handtruck right around the corner."

"Why didn't you think of that?" Mr. Devon looked at me. "Come on, let's go inside and wait for Mr. Teller."

"I'd better get to class," I said. "I'm already late."

"Let me write you a pass," he said.

I followed him into his classroom. He fished around in a cluttered desk drawer and found a blank pass. "Are you sure you don't want to stick around and see what's in the crate? It will only be a couple of minutes. Besides, I could use your help in getting the sculpture out."

"Yeah, I can do that," I said.

He went into the hall and helped Mr. Teller put the crate on the dolly. They wheeled it into a corner and lifted the crate onto the floor. "Thanks, Mr. Teller," Mr. Devon said. "Thanks for having the brains in this operation."

Mr. Teller left and Mr. Devon started opening the crate. "So what do you think about football?" he asked me.

"I like it," I said.

"You ever thought about coming out for the team?"

"It's a little late for that, isn't it?"

"A little, but we don't have our first game until next week. There's plenty of season left. You should give it a try. We could use you."

"Where?" I said. I doubted that they could use me.

"I was thinking in the secondary. Cornerback, maybe."

"I don't know," I said.

"Well think about it. Or better yet, come to a practice. Just watch. See if you like what you see, and then decide. I bet you'd be good at it."

I actually believed him. Despite my better knowledge of my capabilities and talents, I believed him. I showed up for practice and got my gear—helmet; pads; jersey with number 45 on it, in home and away colors—got my locker, and was out on the field, running drills. I had to borrow a pair of cleats for the first practice, and had my mom go out and buy them the next day. She drove up during practice and handed them to me on the sidelines of the field. But that was later.

Mr. Devon got the lid off the crate. He lifted out a bunch of packing material, under which the sculpture was wrapped in a gray blanket. We reached in and lifted it carefully out onto the floor. Mr. Devon unwrapped it and then stepped back to look. He stood where he could see the sculpture and me at the same time.

It was abstract, a suggestion of something. It was a big bulb of a grotesque blob on a stem, the shape of a head without any of the features of a face, or rather the features torn off in bits and then put back in all the wrong places. That's what emerged out of the gray stone, almost like concrete: a torn face, grimacing, like someone being tortured or in the dentist's chair. Or the way I imagined I was going to look during my first game of football. There were too many misshapen surfaces, globs of stone obscuring detail and anything recognizable, until it was just a creepy blob, but you could feel the tension in it, the struggle or violence. It was vague and powerful, and disturbing. I didn't think anyone would like it sitting there in Mr. Devon's classroom.

"What's it called?" I asked.

"Host."

"Is that your 'Do not disturb' sign?"

"You think it's frightening enough?"

"It's a little creepy," I admitted. "Unsettling."

"What if I told you that some people see it as happy, as exciting or joyful?"

The minute he said it, the object looked different. He

suggested it, sure, but the thing did look different now, not menacing or violent, but like something contorted from a laugh, maybe. I could see it.

"Okay," I said. "Which is it?"

He shrugged. "I just made it. I don't know what it is. Here's your pass." He handed me the yellow slip of paper and I headed off to class.

"Thanks for your help," he called after me. "And I'll see you tomorrow."

"Have you ever been drunk?" Anna asked me. We were sitting on the couch in the basement, listening to the short-wave. Her parents had gone out to dinner, which meant that they would be gone a few hours. It was at least a fifteen-minute drive to the nearest restaurant.

"I've never had the chance," I said.

"You're in for a treat, then." She went to the wall of stacked boxes and dug efficiently until she pulled out a bottle of vodka. "Straight up or in something?"

"I'd better have it mixed with something."

She went upstairs and came back with a jug of cranberry juice and two tall glasses with ice. She filled the glasses about a third with vodka and then topped it off with cranberry juice. "Try this," she said.

It was like drinking something too cold that makes your brain freeze for a second or two. The force of it tapped the inside of my forehead and made me alert, opening my senses. I drank some more, and that initial sensation disappeared. Now it was just cranberry-juice taste.

"What do you think?" she asked me.

"It's good," I said.

"Can you feel it? Can you taste it? Can you tell that it's going to change everything?"

"Not really. Let me try some straight."

She held the bottle in front of her, waving it at me, teasing. She came and sat on my legs, facing me. She leaned into me and kissed me until my lips and tongue were tingling and numb. "You have to know," she said, "that the world is never more perfect than when you're drunk. It's perfect." It was perfect. The way she smelled and tasted and felt. The way her hair fell into my face as she leaned over me, dimming the lights behind her, the way the shortwave crackled quietly in the background, repeating its code like a chorus of some song somebody must know somewhere. It was all perfect. She tilted my head back slightly and held the bottle to my lips. It tasted bad, overpowering, but I didn't mind. She kissed me again and then took a drink of her own.

"So what was it that attracted you to me?" I asked her. I would never have been able to ask her that sober.

"You just seemed so plain and normal that I thought you needed a little weirdness in your life," she said.

I left before her parents came home, and as I made my way through the dark streets, I realized that I was unsteady, drunk. I shivered and felt damp, my teeth chattered and I started running, or at least tried. The snow on the lawns was deep, and I struggled with one lunge after another, happily laboring along. After a few yards, I felt warm again and the world seemed amazing. The lights of the houses reminded me of the illuminated windows in the Advent calendar my mother placed in the front hallway every Christmas. As I walked, the stars trembled brightly above me. The world seemed to spin faster, lurching anxiously into the night, yet I didn't feel any closer to home. It was fine to be stuck in time when I was with Anna, but my nose and face, feet and hands were cold and I wanted to get to my bed, crawl in and go to sleep. I ran down the streets and cut through lightless yards, gaining some time; the pace made my head lighter and my legs weaker. The snow suddenly rose in front of me and I realized I had fallen. Snow had gone into my mouth and nose, and I sat up and laughed. I called Anna. "You should be out here with me. I'm rolling around in the snow like an idiot all by myself. You got me this way, you should be here taking care of me. It's no fun out here alone."

She laughed at me. "We can't be together all the time," she said.

"Why not?"

"It's just not possible. I have things I have to do on my own. So do you."

"No I don't."

"You got along fine without me before," she said.

"You don't know how untrue that is."

"Well, you never know, you might have to again."

"Don't even say that as a joke," I told her.

"I'll see you tomorrow," she said, and hung up. I picked myself up and ran into the darkness.

· · ·

I was sitting on the floor of my room when my mom came in. She wasn't happy. "I shouldn't have to tell you to take your shoes off when you come in the door," she said. I had forgotten. It had never entered my mind. She stood there glaring at me as I tried to take off my boots. They were dripping melted snow onto the floor. They didn't have much of a tread. How much of a mess could they have made? My hand kept slipping off the heel as I tried to pull my right boot away from my foot. I couldn't figure out why it wasn't coming off, until I saw that I hadn't untied it. I pulled slowly on the lace, and the brown string stopped in a knot. I had a hard time picking the knot loose. My mother was still watching me. She didn't say anything. At first I was glad, and then I became angry. I wanted to yell at her. "You know I'm drunk, and you're not saying anything!" I tried to say, "I'm sorry," meaning about the boots, but my tongue had gone to sleep; it felt as if it had been shot full of novocaine. Finally I got both boots off and put them on a T-shirt on the floor. My mother glared at me for a last time, then left the room. I immediately wanted to tell Anna about it, so I went to my computer. I saw that she had sent me an e-mail:

Here's a poem by Charles Baudelaire. It's good advice for you. Get Drunk:

Il faut être toujours ivre. Tout est là: c'est l'unique question. Pour ne pas sentir l'horrible fardeau du

Temps qui brise vos épaules et vous penche vers la
terre, il faut vous enivrer sans trêve.

Mais de quoi? De vin, de poésie ou de vertu, à
votre guise. Mais enivrez-vous.

Et si quelquefois, sur les marches d'un palais, sur
l'herbe verte d'un fossé, dans la solitude morne de
votre chambre, vous vous réveillez, l'ivresse déjà
diminuée ou disparue, demandez au vent, à la
vague, à l'oiseau, à l'horloge, à tout ce qui fuit, à
tout ce qui gémit, à tout ce qui roule, à tout ce qui
chante, à tout ce qui parle, demandez quelle heure
il est; et le vent, la vague, l'étoile, l'oiseau, l'horloge,
vous répondront: "Il est l'heure de s'enivrer! Pour
n'être pas les esclaves martyrisés du Temps,
enivrez-vous; enivrez-vous sans cesse! De vin, de
poésie ou de vertu, à votre guise."

She knew that I couldn't understand French (and she
couldn't either, as far as I knew), but she left it to me to
translate.

carl is dead

"Why don't you write Carl's obituary?" she said. I didn't
want to. "Come on," she said. "I need it for my notebook.
You know him better than I do. You can do a better job than
I can."

In the end, I wrote it. I wrote it twice. In the first one, I had him dying old and rich, after a happy life with plenty of money and no worries. He was married and lived in a big mansion, and was friends with everyone. Anna didn't like it.

"It's not very interesting," she said. "There's not a lot of detail either. I mean, it could be anybody's. Tell me about Carl. Make it interesting. Make him interesting. And have him die young. Like now. Write an obituary as if Carl died now."

thanksgiving

Christmas has the Grinch and Scrooge. Thanksgiving has my father. He hates it. It doesn't make sense, I know; I mean, what is there to hate? There's food and football, and both in abundant quantities, but he hates it anyway. Usually it wasn't so bad, because there would be enough people around that his bah-humbug behavior didn't stand out so much, and if he wasn't complaining, he was holed away in his den and we wouldn't give him another thought. My brother would cook the turkey. It's something he started in college. He and his friends would come and cook a big traditional Thanksgiving dinner at our house. Paul continued even after he married, but he and his family were not coming this year. They were staying down in Baton Rouge.

We went to the club. My father was a member of the country club in Hilliker, and that's where we wound up for the holiday. It had a large ballroom, with enough tables to hold a few hundred people. All the tables had white cloths draped over them and an arrangement of dried flowers in the center. Almost every table had eight people, or ten, or more, large families laughing and eating and enjoying themselves. It was just the three of us at our table, sitting silently by ourselves.

The ballroom looked out across the golf course, covered now in a few feet of snow. My father stood at one of the floor-to-ceiling windows and stared out into the snow, then finally sat down with his back to the window. I'm surprised he didn't go out with a shovel and clear the course, just so he wouldn't have to eat with us.

The waiters and waitresses, in starched white shirts, wheeled a turkey right to your table and carved it with a showy flourish; they also brought huge platters of mashed potatoes, sweet potatoes, stuffing, cranberry sauce, and green beans. There was a buffet where you could fill up on appe- tizers, soup and salad, bread, cheese, and dessert. It was a ton of food, and it was all good. My mother and I made trips to the buffet, but my father never left his seat. He sat and drank his scotch and had a look on his face like he had a big ball of mashed potatoes stuck in his throat. Men came and said hello to him, guys he golfed with or did business with, and he responded with a few words, but he never in- troduced my mother or me, and he kept the conversation as brief as possible. I didn't know anyone there until I saw Billy Godley enter with his family, a big group of parents and brothers and sisters and aunts and uncles and cousins and grandparents. His father was a cop, a detective, and that wasn't the best for Billy. Kids made fun of him at school. He hung out with the geeks on the second floor. He was small and skinny too, which didn't help. Billy was nice enough, but I wasn't about to go talk to him. The two Velveetas weren't going to have Thanksgiving dinner together.

"It's good turkey," I said to my mother. "Don't you think?"

"It is good. Not as good as your brother's, but it's good."

"Maybe we can get him to cook one at Christmas." Paul had promised to come for Christmas. I didn't think I could survive if he didn't come.

My father was ready to go while we were still eating. "Have some coffee," my mother told him. He got up from the table and wandered off. My mother and I went and got dessert. I think I had three pieces of pie. Still, it took only a little more than an hour to have Thanksgiving dinner.

Before we left I went to the bathroom. Someone had thrown up in one of the stalls, missing the toilet, and the chunks were all over the floor. There was the smell of vinegar and fresh-baked bread, the kind of smell that immediately stops you from breathing. I wondered if it had been my father.

He was sitting in the car. Just sitting. He didn't have the radio on, he didn't even have the heat on.

When we got home he made a beeline to his den, and my mother made a pot of coffee for herself. I tried calling Anna, but she must not have had her phone on. I sent her a text message and waited to hear from her. She and her parents had gone out of town for the day, to visit relatives or something; I don't think she ever really said.

My brother called later that night. He talked to my mother for a while and then asked to talk to me.

"So how horrible was it?"

"It was all right," I said. "Not as good as when you cook."

"I'm sorry to do that to you this year."

"That's all right. You've got the baby and everything."

"We'll come up for Christmas."

"That'll be good," I said. It was all done with anyway. I didn't think the day had been so horrible, and at that minute I didn't really care whether they came up for Christmas or not. If you'd asked me a couple of hours before, like when I was standing in the puke-covered bathroom, I would have cared. But right then I was more interested in looking at my phone and seeing if Anna was going to contact me that night. She didn't.

The next day, Anna and I went sledding. She showed up at my house wearing black jeans and boots and her long black coat. I made her change into a pair of raspberry-colored coveralls of my mother's. She hadn't worn them in years. "Everything's going to get wet otherwise," I said. It was going to be a warm day, maybe even above freezing. I had on a pair of ski pants, and Anna asked me if I skied. "I know how," I said. "Maybe we can go sometime."

"Don't push your luck," she said. "I'll be lucky if I survive sledding." She came out of the bathroom and looked at the coveralls and said, "Can we go somewhere where there aren't any other people?"

There was a great sledding hill about five minutes from my house, just north on Lincoln Road, but everybody went there. So we walked east, down Valley View Road and then up Brook Road, with me dragging the two-person toboggan along the sidewalk. My brother and sister had used the same toboggan when they were little. It was still in good shape, although the padding had seen better days. It hissed as it skidded across the snow-covered lawns. The sky was cloudy and the air thick and moist. Sidewalks and streets were clearing as the snow melted, but the curbs were still piled with snow that had been pushed into dirty mounds by plows and browned by sand. I almost wished it would snow again to cover it all up and make it clean. Every once in a while we could hear sheets of snow slide down someone's roof and hit the ground with a muffled thump. The daytime warmth wouldn't last, though; everything would freeze again in the night.

We walked from Brook Road into the woods, and had to take a breather at the top of the steep hill. There was no one around, not even traffic on the road. A couple of hills here had been cleared in the past, for electric wires or something else that never came about, and they made for good sledding. It wasn't as good as the Ashton hill, but it was good enough, and it wasn't crowded like Ashton. My brother was the only other person I knew who had come up here. It's where he brought me sledding when I was little.

A white slide stretched down before Anna and me, a wide trough of snow, bordered by thick trees. The trick was to stay in the middle of the slide, and not go into the woods.

Anna turned around and said, "This isn't going to wind up like *Ethan Frome,* is it?"

I didn't know what she was talking about. It was one of those references of hers that was lost on me.

"Forget it," she said.

"I'm not smart enough for you," I said.

"You're fine."

"I'm a simpleton. I'm simple, like snow."

It was a joke. I meant it to be clever, but she was off again on one of her explanations and investigations, ignoring my point. "Snow isn't simple at all," she said. "It only looks that way. It's actually very complicated." She looked at me and laughed. "I can't help myself." She came over and kissed me with her cold mouth. It was like electricity. "I say stupid things sometimes."

"I've never heard you say anything stupid."

"I'm a freak," she said. "I should just keep quiet. Be more like you."

"I should be more like you."

She wanted to take a run by herself. I watched her slide slowly off the hill and then quickly gain speed as she made the descent. She was fine at first, staying in the middle of the hill, following in the flattened path we had made together, but then, just before the dip of the hill, where it

started to level off, she swerved toward the woods, disappearing from my view. She might have hit a bump or
leaned the wrong way and lost control of the sled, but it almost looked like she wanted to go into the trees. I waited a
few minutes for her to come back out into sight. She didn't
come. I waited a little more and began to think that maybe
she had hit a tree. I ran down the hill, stumbling and
falling into the snow. I followed the path of the sled and
raced into the woods, expecting the worst.

I was sweating and covered in snow and out of breath by
the time I reached the trees. The cold air stung my lungs, and
my breath shot out in cloudy bursts. Anna was lying on the
ground on her back, her raspberry arms stretched straight
above her head, her legs also stuck straight out. She had been
making an angel in the snow. I started laughing at her.

"I could be dead," she said, "smashed against one of
these trees. What would you do then?"

"Leave you here and go on home and act as if it never
happened."

"You would do that?"

"I suppose I could bury you first, but no one would find
you for a long time."

"You would just leave me?" She sat up and made room
for me to sit beside her on the toboggan. Her eyes flickered,
and I thought she might be enjoying herself.

"People might think it was my fault."

"It would have been your fault."

"I wasn't on the sled."

"You brought me here and then killed me and left me in

the woods. That's how they would see it. Just think how sad my parents would be, and you just left me here. It serves you right. You better not bury me in the woods. I'll come back and torment you."

"Just come back," I said.

"Do you think I could?"

"If anybody can, it's you."

"But what if I couldn't come back, what if I could only reach you through somebody else, like a psychic or a medium?"

"I wouldn't recognize you."

"That's why we need a code, or something only the two of us know, something you can recognize," she said.

"Why do you think it's you that's going to be gone first?"

"*You* didn't almost hit a tree."

"And what would our code be?"

"Something simple," she said. "Something as simple as snow. That phrase: 'Something as simple as snow.'"

"You're making fun of me."

"It's easy to remember," she said.

"It's not really a code."

"It's a secret message. It's a signal. It means the message is coming from one of us. That's a code."

"So we start the message with that phrase?"

"That's what Houdini and his wife did."

"What was their phrase?"

"It had a name in it, and then words that corresponded to letters in the alphabet. It spelled out the word 'believe.' The phrase was something like, 'Rosabelle, answer tell pray-answer look tell answer-answer tell.'"

"Was Rosabelle his wife?"

"No, it was from a song."

"Why don't we use that, then?"

"Because it was theirs—it doesn't mean anything to us. Besides, you don't want to use Houdini's code—what if he's still using it?"

"What does our code mean to us?"

She didn't miss a beat. "It means that we know something no one else does. It means that everyone else thinks the world is simple, but it's not. It's like snow—most people think that it's just white, but if you look at it, really observe it, you'll see that there are different shades, from a sort of grayish white to a brilliant white. This book I read, *The Worst Journey in the World*—about Scott's last expedition to the South Pole—described the snow as cobalt blue, rose, mauve, and lilac, with gradations of all of those colors. And then there's texture. Some snow is dry and granular, almost like sugar, while other snow is wet and clumpy. And that's just the superficial stuff—once you start looking at each flake it gets really complicated."

"Maybe you're making it more complicated than it really is," I said. "Maybe it's a myth about the uniqueness of snowflakes. Everybody thinks that no two snowflakes are alike, because they've never really been compared." I scooped up a handful of snow and shook off some of the excess for effect. "Maybe I'm holding in my hand right now the very same sort of flakes, identical in every way, as some guy in Tibet or Switzerland or Iceland or Iowa is holding at the very same instant. But he thinks his are unique and I think mine are unique because we have no way to catalogue and compare them. And that's just the snow that's on the ground right now, what about last year's snow and the year before that? You have billions and billions of flakes that would need to be compared."

She laughed. She laughed at me. "You just proved my point. Think how complicated it would be to catalogue all the individual snowflakes and then try and compare them. They can't even do that with fingerprints, and there's only a tiny fraction of those compared with all the snowflakes in any given winter, let alone all winters."

A freezing rain clicked through the trees and we headed toward home. Instead of trudging back up the hill and then walking down the road, we cut through the woods. By the time we reached Brook Road, the trees were shiny with a thin layer of ice. I wanted Anna to stay at my house for a while, but she changed her clothes to leave. "I'll take your shortcut," she said.

"Be careful."

"I'll call you when I get home."

A half-hour passed and I hadn't heard from her. I called her house and Mrs. Cayne told me that she wasn't home yet. "When did she leave?" she asked.

"Just a little while ago. I'm sure she'll be there soon." I said good-bye and called Anna's cell phone.

"Worried?" she said, before I could say anything.

"Where are you?"

"I'm down by the river, watching the storm, watching the ice."

"Why?"

"Come down and find out for yourself."

I wasn't going anywhere. "I can't figure you out," I said.

"That's good. I wouldn't want you to have it all figured out. Think how boring that would be. Mysteries are the most interesting, the stuff in the shadows or underneath the surface. Don't you think? I mean, certainty is the worst, worse than death."

I could hear ice-covered limbs cracking in the background, and tires spinning on the slippery bridge. "Go home soon, okay?" I said.

"I will."

An hour or so later, the power went out and the whole town went dark. I sat in my room and listened to trucks rumble up and down the hill, fighting the ice with sand and salt and scraping plows. I heard at least two accidents, drivers foolishly trying to make it down the hill and spinning out of control. My father had built fires in both fireplaces and the whole house smelled of wood and smoke. He brought me a flashlight and a candle, but I preferred to stay in the dark.

Anna called me on my cell. "There's nothing but a sheet of ice between us," she said. "Why don't you act like Hans Brinker and skate over here."

I heard music in the background, fading in and out. "What is that?"

"Anton von Webern, I think. Something classical."

"I mean, where's it coming from?"

"My father keeps walking by with a boom box. My mother wants him to start the generator, but he's procrastinating. He likes the dark."

"Is that where you get it from?"

"Not really. My father and I have a lot of the same tastes, but I really get that stuff from my mother. She just chooses to ignore it in herself. How about you, who do you take after, your mother or your father?"

"Neither, really. I guess if I was like anyone in my family it would be my sister."

"Where is she?"

"I don't know. She left."

"Disappeared?"

"She might as well have. She just left and we haven't heard from her in quite a while."

"So that's what you're like? You're going to leave one day and no one will hear from you again?"

"Sometimes I think that way."

"Well, don't leave yet, Hans. I just got here."

"I'm not going anywhere."

disc one

The next day I received a package, a shoe box wrapped in plain brown paper. Anna's stamps were in one corner. The box was filled with turkey feathers, and buried in the feathers was a CD. The cover was a photograph of dead goldfinches, each body tagged and numbered, all laid out in a white drawer. "A drawer full of birds" was written on the spine of the jewel case. She had printed out a list of the songs on the back:

1. The Replacements—i will dare
2. Dinosaur Jr.—freak scene
3. Teenage Fanclub—everything flows
4. Sonic Youth—shadow of a doubt
5. Chet Baker—let's get lost
6. Yo La Tengo—cast a shadow
7. The Bobby Fuller Four—never to be forgotten
8. T. Rex—ride a white swan
9. George Harrison—beware of darkness
10. Pretenders—talk of the town
11. Big Star—daisy glaze
12. Sam Cooke & the Soul Stirrers—mean old world
13. Bonnie "Prince" Billy—death to everyone
14. Nina Simone—i put a spell on you
15. This Mortal Coil—song to the siren
16. Robyn Hitchcock & the Egyptians—airscape
17. The Cure—a forest
18. Calla—awake and under
19. Tom McRae—ghost of a shark
20. Bauhaus—bela lugosi's dead

She had also included a card, a black card with writing in silver ink.

Read Rimbaud. "A Season in Hell":

> I will tear the veils from every mystery—mysteries of religion or of nature, death, birth, the future, the past, cosmogony, and nothingness. I am a master of phantasmagoria.

Listen!

Every talent is mine!—There is no one here, and there is someone: I wouldn't want to waste my treasure.—Shall I give you African chants, belly dancers? . . .

Read the rest. Read it all.

c h r i s t m a s

My brother and his family came up for Christmas. They drove all the way from Louisiana—packed everything and everyone into their big Suburban—which meant that they would spend most of his vacation days on the road and couldn't stay long. "It's a long way to drive for such a short time," my father said, minutes after they had pulled into the driveway. It was about the only thing he said.

I was struck by the fact that my brother looked like a younger version of my father. I had never seen the resemblance before, but sometime since I'd last seen him he had lost the genetic battle and my father had emerged. My brother had put on weight, and his hairline was creeping back across his forehead. He had even started to slouch, ever so slightly. A few years from thirty, and already he looked like an old guy. But then, he had three young kids, twin two-year-old boys and a daughter who was not yet a year old.

The twins were maniacs. They became obsessed with the drawers in the kitchen, and ran to them and pulled them out completely, spilling knives and forks and spoons onto the floor. They wanted the knives, it seemed. They would fight each other over a single knife, even though there were seven more just like it right there. You had to watch them constantly; at any opportunity they would race toward the drawers, and if you didn't beat them there, everything would be dumped on the floor in a split second. "Just let them get at the knives," my father said, "they'll learn to stay clear of them." Finally my brother came from the garage with some yardsticks and bungee cords. He put the yardsticks through the handles of the drawers that were stacked one atop another, and bungeed the single drawers to nearby cabinets. It looked terrible, but it stopped the twins. The problem was, it also stopped my mother. She was frustrated and confused, unable to navigate around the kitchen with everything lashed down. "Can't we just leave the drawers alone, and tie the twins," she said. No one was sure whether she was joking. We might have fasted through the holiday if it hadn't been for my sister-in-law.

At least the house was filled with noise for a change. There was commotion and conversation and life. My parents were miserable. No wonder my brother rarely visited. I imagined when I would be out of the house, off to college and after, when we could get together without our parents, not even invite them. They could stay home in their grumpy silence and the rest of us could have a good time.

.   .   .

My parents put an extra bed in my brother's old room, and the twins stayed there. They put a crib in my sister's old room, which was next door to my room, and the baby slept there. My brother and his wife took over my room, and I had to sleep downstairs on the couch in the living room. This meant that I couldn't e-mail Anna at night, as I usually did. She wasn't supposed to make any calls after ten, so we sent text messages on our cells. I was lying on the couch, waiting for a response from her, when my brother came down and sat in the living room.

"Sorry about booting you out of your room."

"That's all right. It's only for a couple of days."

"We'll try not to mess things up."

"Don't worry about it."

"So how are things around here?"

"Good."

"Mom and Dad still phoning it in?"

"It's like a ghost town. They vanish after dinner."

"That has to suck."

"It's all right," I said. "Who wants to be around them, anyway? They're weird when they don't talk to you, but weirder when they do."

"So what do you do?"

"I've got a lot going on. I've got a girlfriend, she keeps me busy."

"Are we going to meet her?"

"I'll try to bring her over. I've got to warn you, though, she's a bit different."

"What do you mean?"

"She likes to wear a lot of black, you know."

"And you like that?"

"I like her. You'll like her too."

"Well, bring her around, then."

"She'll want your kids, though. For sacrifices or some-thing."

"She can have them. Call her now and tell her to come get them."

d i s c   t w o

There was something cold in the middle of my back. Really cold. I reached behind and felt a freezing wet hard some-thing. I jumped off the couch and saw my brother standing next to the couch, laughing. "Merry Christmas," he said. "That was on the front stoop. I think it's for you."

It was a block of ice about the size of a loaf of bread. Frozen in the middle was a CD case. It had a black-and-white picture inside that looked like fractals or odd geo-metric shapes—they were actually magnified snowflakes—and a title in green letters with red drop shadows—"baby, it's cold outside." A gift tag was also frozen in the ice. You could read it right through the block. "Merry Xmas, love Anastasia."

"'Love,' it says," my brother teased.

I went to the kitchen and put the ice in the sink to let my gift thaw. Anna later told me that she had frozen the two halves of the block most of the way separately, then put the CD and tag on the bottom half, then capped it with the top half and frozen the blocks together the rest of the way. "I had to add a little extra water to hide the seams," she said. "I didn't know if the CD would come out all right, so I made a duplicate, just in case."

"If I'd known that, I wouldn't have thawed the ice. I would have kept it in the freezer."

"Where's the fun in that?"

The back cover was the negative of the front; the song titles were printed on the reverse of the front cover:

1. Dean Martin—a marshmallow world
2. Buffalo Tom—frozen lake
3. The Jesus and Mary Chain—you trip me up
4. The Cocteau Twins—iceblink luck
5. Galaxie 500—snowstorm
6. Damien Jurado—ghost in the snow
7. Kate Bush—under ice
8. Hank Williams—the first fall of snow
9. James P. Johnson—snowy morning blues
10. The Gentle Waves—dirty snow for the broken ground
11. Superchunk—silver leaf and snowy tears
12. Yoko Ono—walking on thin ice
13. Billie Holiday—i've got my love to keep me warm
14. The Handsome Family—cold, cold, cold
15. The Durutti Column—snowflakes
16. Bill Monroe & His Blue Grass Boys—footprints in the snow
17. Tindersticks—snowy in f# minor

18. Nico—winter song
19. The Mountain Goats—snow crush killing song
20. Belle and Sebastian—the fox in the snow
21. Elliott Smith—angel in the snow
22. Nick Drake—winter is gone

Besides the CD, she gave me a portable shortwave. "It's one of my father's old ones," she said. "He had to put some new parts in it, but it works. It's kind of from the both of us. My father says that he'll come over and help put up the antenna." I gave her a copy of *The Devil's Dictionary* by Ambrose Bierce. It was old, and the jacket was stained with coffee or something ("Maybe it's blood," Anna said), and inside were two strange drawings by a child or some crazy person. The first was on the back of the title page. It was a crude ink drawing of two people fighting or wrestling under a bridge or a tree limb. There was little detail, and lines started and ended randomly, or ran together, so it was hard to tell exactly what was going on. The two people (it could have been a man and a woman or a man and a child) looked terrified or crazy. The second drawing was on the inside of the back cover. It was slightly more accomplished, at least in some aspects. It was of a young girl, standing on the railing of a bridge, maybe, or the top of a tall building. She had on a nightgown or a long dress. She was looking up at the moon, and seemed to have tears running down her face. She had three pairs of arms; two arms were folded across her chest, two stretched in front of her, and the last two reached straight overhead, toward the moon.

I didn't know about the drawings when I bought the

book, but Anna thought they were the best part. I also gave
her a portrait of Edgar Allan Poe. It was a page torn from
Harper's New Monthly Magazine. Poe was looking straight
off the page, with his dark jacket buttoned to the top, and
a tie or scarf wrapped around the collar of his shirt, which
was turned up and curled under his chin. He appeared to
have a slight smirk under his dark moustache, as if he were
keeping a secret. I'd found both gifts on eBay and outbid
everybody. "I noticed you didn't have Poe up on your wall,"
I said.

My brother took us bowling. His wife, Kate, stayed home
with the kids. "You think we'd trust your mom and dad with
them?" she said. Anna brought Claire with her. "You can't
bowl with three people," she said. "Besides, I didn't want to
be the only freak there." It was the only time I heard her refer to herself like that. I think she was nervous about meeting my brother, but Paul was all right. More than all right.

We drove into Hilliker and went to SkyMor Lanes. "That
might be the dumbest name I've ever heard for a business
that has nothing to do with flying," Anna said. "But I like it."

"It's a great place," my brother said. "Cheesy as hell."

SkyMor had twenty-seven lanes. If you know anything
about bowling, you know that it's impossible to have an odd
number of lanes. The last lane was an actual lane, but it
was only for show. There was only half a ball return there,
sticking out of the wall, and only half a scoring table—it
looked as if the wall had split the lane in two. It was meant

to be something everyone would talk about, make the place famous. Maybe so, back when the place first opened, but I'd never heard about it. About three-quarters of the lanes were being used, and my brother requested the lane at the far end from the famous half-lane. There was no one down there. I thought he might be embarrassed by his two Goth guests, but he was trying to get us away from everyone else for another reason.

We got our shoes at the counter. The old guy there was comatose; he didn't even notice Anna and Claire; he barely raised his head as he sprayed a cloud of disinfectant into the green-and-red shoes ("For Christmas," Anna said) and swapped them with ours. Bowling shoes are always stupid, but they looked even more ridiculous on Anna and Claire. "I should be a clown in the Goth circus," Claire said. The three of us then went to pick balls while my brother wandered off.

Anna chose a bright pink ball. "It's like a big piece of bubble gum." She wanted me to pick the same color.

"I think I'll stick with basic black for once," I said.

She tried out the bubble gum and threw a strike first thing. "Let's count that," she said.

"It's just practice," I told her. "We've got to wait until my brother gets back."

Anna knew what she was doing, even though she said she had never bowled before. I commented that Claire bowled as if she had taken lessons, flute lessons. It was the first time I made Claire laugh.

Paul came back with four bottles of beer. They were in the shape of bowling pins, which Anna thought was cute.

"Do you guys drink beer?" We all nodded. "All right," he said, "just be careful. We don't want to get kicked out, and I don't want to get arrested." We hid our beers behind the pile of our coats on the row of orange and blue plastic chairs.

Claire and Paul were on one team, and Anna and I were on the other. We killed them. Claire started with three gutter balls in a row. My brother tried to give her some pointers, but they didn't lead to much improvement. Claire didn't seem to mind—nobody did. We had beer, what did we care? Paul's game got worse the more he drank, while Claire's got better. I had the high score in the first game, so I teamed up with Claire, who had the lowest, for the second. We still won. The third and last game had Paul and me against Anna and Claire. We won, but barely. Paul had the lowest score of everyone. "I'm not used to drinking so much anymore," he said. In the end he was the one who got drunk.

He didn't think that he should drive, so he gave the keys to Claire. Claire had her permit, and would get her license at the end of February. He slumped in the front passenger seat, and Anna and I sat in the back. "What's the first thing you're going to do?" my brother asked Claire. "Where are you going to drive?"

"Let's go to the city and see that TV psychic, Preen," Anna said.

"Maybe we'll come back to SkyMor," Claire said. She'd been flirting with my brother all night, teasing him and getting him to blush and laugh. He liked it.

"Let's make a list of all the people we want to run over," I said.

"That's something Bryce would say," Claire said.

"I'll say something else, then."

"Too late," Anna said. "Mr. Devon is on the top of my list."

"Why Mr. Devon?"

"He deserves to have a few things broken."

"Hey, is Mr. Kissler still there?" my brother said. We told him that he was. "We should go run him over. Claire, drive on over to his house. You can hit him with my car." Claire ignored him and drove to Anna's. She dropped her off and then drove to her own house.

"Thanks for a good time," she said, "and thanks for letting me drive. I hope I didn't scare you too much."

"You look fine," Paul said.

Claire laughed. "That's not what I meant."

"I know what you meant." He sat in the passenger seat and watched her walk to the front door. She didn't turn around but went straight inside. The light over the front door went dark, and Paul turned around and looked at me.

"You drive," he told me. I'd never driven before. "C'mon," he said. "It's easy. Besides, no one's going to be out on the roads. Just take it easy."

It was a huge vehicle, and I was sure that I would wreck. I eased down Madder Lane and successfully made the turn onto Kennedy. I was heading home when Paul said, "Take me down by the school."

"We should get home," I said. "Let's not press our luck."

"Take me by the school. We shouldn't get home right now, anyway. I need to sober up a little, or else I'll be in trouble. You want me to be in trouble?"

I turned down Sidgwick. A car was coming toward us. I didn't know where to look; the lights were bright, and I couldn't see the road very well. The driver honked as the car passed, so I thought I might have swerved toward it. "Your brights are on," Paul said. He was resting his head against the glass of the passenger window. It probably felt nice and cool against his forehead. It should have been cool against my head; I should have been the one waiting around to sober up in the car. I didn't like driving that much.

"How do I turn them off?" He told me. "When do I turn them off?" He told me. "Why can't you drive again?"

"You're doing fine," he said.

I pulled into the school parking lot. The building was dark. It looked menacing, a huge beast waiting to pounce. Paul sat up and stared at it too. I was sure he was thinking the same thing I was thinking, and would want to get away from it.

"I can't believe how tiny it looks," he said.

"Did you have people like Anna and Claire in school when you were there?" I asked.

"You mean cute girls?"

"You know what I mean."

"We had them all—the jocks and the Goths, the punks and the geeks, the bandoids and the bussers and the stoners. Did I leave anyone out?"

"Which one were you?"

"I was a geek. I probably wouldn't have admitted it at the time, but that's what I was."

"Does that bother you?"

"Not now," he said. "It's all those guys who did well, both in college and after. And the jocks, the guys the whole town fawned over, almost all of them ended up going nowhere. They peaked in high school. Erick and Derek Gurney were big football stars, that's all you need to know about that. And the biggest geek in school was Bob Fesnor. He made fifteen million dollars before he was thirty."

"Where is he now?"

"He didn't come back here, did he?" Paul kept looking at the dark windows of the school. "I may not come back anymore."

"Home?"

"This place has nothing," he said. "Mom and Dad are a joke. They don't seem to care if we come up or not. They certainly don't seem to want to have anything to do with their own grandkids, and they don't appreciate the effort it takes for us to come up here. So the hell with it. They can come down and see us for once."

"They won't."

He shrugged.

"So you're going to be like Joan, and I won't see you anymore?" I couldn't think of the last time I had said my sister's name out loud. I didn't want my brother to disappear that way.

He looked at me, realizing what he was saying, or realizing how I was hearing it. "You don't need Mom and Dad to come see us. You can come down anytime you want. You're getting old enough to make your own decisions. Come down anytime. I'll pay for it. This has nothing to do with you. I just can't come back up here. You know Mom and Dad."

"They're idiots."

"I don't really want the kids to be around them. I'm truly afraid they'll have an influence on them."

"I'm afraid I'll wind up like them," I said.

Paul sighed. "There's only so much you can do. You can't escape your genes."

"That's comforting."

My brother laughed. "You'll be all right. Just don't stay around. Get out of this shitty town as soon as you can."

I looked over at Paul. He didn't look drunk. He hadn't sounded drunk. I began to suspect that he had been sober enough to drive the whole time. I pulled out of the lot and drove us home. I actually got the hang of it and enjoyed it, felt confident and happy, perfectly content. I would tell Anna how great my brother was and how he had faked being drunk so Claire and I could drive, how he trusted me not to say anything to our parents, anything about him being drunk or me driving. It was our secret.

Paul and his family left the next day, and I thought that would be the last time I would see my brother for a long time. He meant what he had said; he wasn't coming back.

new year's eve

The Tooles had two parties each year, one on the Fourth of July and the other on New Year's Eve. Mr. Toole had worked as a lawyer in the city, and they had used their large house at the end of Garfield Road as a weekend retreat until he retired and they moved up here full-time. It was said that they were originally from Louisiana and had moved north after their son died. So it was just Mr. and Mrs. Toole in a sprawling gray house, with about seven acres of land they kept cleared and manicured so it looked like a park. They'd been having their legendary parties for almost twenty-five years. The Fourth of July party was open to the entire town; lines of cars would stretch for miles, down Garfield Road and then out onto Town Street and beyond. Mr. Toole roasted a few whole pigs on a huge outdoor grill; there were also shrimp boils and piles of corn on the cob. They supplied beer and wine and soda, and all the guests had to do was bring a side dish, salad, or dessert. Hundreds of people roamed around the Tooles' acreage and ate and drank. A band played, starting around ten o'clock, usually after the younger kids had been taken home, and people would still be drinking and dancing the next morning.

The New Year's Eve party, however, was black-tie and by invitation only. A select group of fifty people were invited. My father used to play golf with Mr. Toole (they still might, but I never hear him mentioned), and my parents had been going to the party for the past fifteen years. My father still complained about having to wear his tux. "It's the worst money I've ever spent on clothes," he said. "I only wear it a couple of hours once a year." He didn't want to go, but if you turned down an invitation to the Tooles', you weren't invited back, and my mother loved going. It was her favorite night of the year. She always had a new dress for the occasion and shined brightly and happily on the glum dark arm of my father.

The Caynes were attending for the first time, which was something of a sensation, since they'd been in town only a few months. They had become quite active and popular, the polar opposite of my parents. The event also meant that Anna's parents and mine would be in the same place for hours together. "Your parents are going to hate mine," I told her.

"No they're not. My parents get along with everybody."

"Mine don't get along with anyone."

"So what you mean is that your parents are going to hate mine."

"Probably," I said. "But only because mine are idiots. I wish they weren't going."

I was glad that they were. It meant that our parents would be occupied for the night. My parents would probably leave the Tooles' right after midnight, but even then, it would give Anna and me almost six straight hours together.

A different person answered the door when I went to her house that night, an Anna I had never seen before. She was the person I had imagined she was before she moved to town, before she dressed like a Goth. She wore no makeup, and without the black eyeliner and lipstick her features were soft, powdery, as if she had been dusted with confectioner's sugar. She had just washed her hair and hadn't put in any of the usual stuff, and it too looked soft. She reminded me of a movie star, filmed through a soft-focus lens. We were an odder match than ever.

She wore a dark green dress, not a formal prom type, but

something fancier than the clothes I was wearing: brown corduroys, a blue button-down shirt (with the collar unbut-
toned), and a black sweater. My boots and pants were covered
with snow from the walk over. Her dress looked black at first,
maybe because I'd seen her wear only black, and it wasn't until she moved into the light of the room that I could see that
it wasn't her usual color. It was a slim, simple dress, with short
sleeves and a black ribbon around the waist. She wasn't wearing any shoes. Maybe she didn't own anything other than her
Doc Martens, or maybe she just wanted to show off the fact
that the polish on her toenails matched her dress exactly.

"I didn't know everyone was going to dress up tonight,"
I said.

"You look fine," she replied. "I thought that a little green
in the dead of winter might be nice. Besides, I wanted to
give you first look. I'm thinking about this image for the
new year. Not the dress, necessarily, but the rest of it."

"Don't change on my account."

"You don't think it would make things easier?"

"Not for me, and definitely not for you. Just be yourself.
Isn't that advice you'd give?"

"How do you know that this isn't myself?"

I didn't say anything.

"How do you know that I don't have a lot of different
selves?"

"A lot of people do," I said. She wasn't being confronta-
tional, or argumentative, but I felt things could go that way
very quickly.

"Well, we'll try it for one night anyway. You like it,
though, right?"

"I think you look great either way." It was the dumbest thing to say, sure, but it was true.

She poured two tall glasses of vodka, with a little cranberry juice to give it color, and took me into her parents' bedroom. "I want to show you something," she said. We walked over to a bay window with a built-in bench. Anna removed the cushion from the bench to reveal a mirror covering the seat of the bench. Directly above, on the ceiling of the bay window, was another mirror, of the same shape and size. "Look into it," she said. I leaned over the bench mirror, and immediately my reflection multiplied, over and over, smaller and smaller.

"Isn't that the greatest thing?" she said.

It was hypnotic. The number of reflections depended on the angle at which you approached the mirror: by moving back and forth you could collapse the image to a flat surface, or expand it to a deep, limitless canyon. That was the most fascinating view: looking nearly straight down, past the larger reflections near the surface and at some point deep within the reflections, which gave you the sensation of standing at the top of the world looking down at yourself looking up from the bottom of the world. "It's like the bottom fell out of the mirror," I said, "like it's a crystal-clear ocean and you can see all the way to the bottom."

"Except you'll never get to the bottom of it. That's how deep it is. I also like looking at it this way." She spun around to look up into the ceiling mirror.

"That kind of makes me dizzy," I said. "Is that why you keep it covered up?"

"Yeah, my father doesn't like it. He says he doesn't want any weird illusions in his house, especially the bedroom. My mother says it's because he's afraid of heights, and if he looks down into the mirror he feels like jumping."

"I don't think he'd really hurt himself from this height," I said. An image formed in my head of Mr. Cayne's hairless head repeating over and over in smaller and smaller copies of itself. It made me laugh out loud.

"It wasn't that funny."

"No. I was just thinking of something that struck me as funny. What if the whole room were like that. It'd be your own hall of mirrors."

She put the cushion back on the mirror and sat down. I went over and turned out the light, and we sat and looked out into the darkness. There was a fat-man moon out, wobbly in the sky, nearly full, with part of his head sliced off. "Lobotomized," she said. It was so bright that you could almost go sledding.

"Not in this dress," she said. "Not on New Year's Eve. It's New Year's Eve every night on the moon."

"How's that?"

"A year on the moon is twenty-four hours."

"My father would love that. He can barely tolerate New Year's coming once every three hundred sixty-five days. He'd probably kill the Tooles on the moon."

. . .

She stepped out of the dress in one quick move. "There's a lot to be said for a dress," she said. Personally, I wish they were worn a lot more.

Her body was white, and shimmered with reflected light. My hand shivered, and she reached out and glided her milky hand along my arm. "I'm nervous," I said. It was my first time. It wasn't hers.

"Here," she said, and handed me a ravioli-sized package. It was a condom.

I left her house at midnight, afraid that my parents would be leaving the Tooles' at the same time. If that was the case, it would be a close call to beat them home. I got out of the street and cut across the Bordens' yard, went behind the Morrisons', and then out on Talus Road. The snow was deep enough that I was soon out of breath, and I stopped to rest. I thought that the whole town would be celebrating, that the streets would be filled with cars and people, cheering and kissing and hugging and yelling. Instead, it was dead: there were no cars on the street, most of the houses were dark, and those that had lights on were quiet. Maybe the Tooles had a corner on the partying, because there was nothing going on here. Then my phone rang. For a second I was afraid it was my parents. It was Anna.

"Where are you?"

"Talus Road."

"That's not very far."

"I know. I've got to pick up the pace."

"You took something with you," she said. It was almost a question.

"I'll take care of it."

"Thank you. You sound out of breath."

"The snow's a little deep."

"Maybe you should stay out on the street."

"Maybe. I'll be able to see my house in a few minutes, and then I'll know if I'm screwed or not."

"Don't hang up until then," she said.

I took the phone away from my ear and started running. My feet felt like lead and my legs were tired, a little wobbly. I should have left earlier. I shouldn't have had so much to drink. I wasn't going to fall or anything, but it slowed me down and I was sure that my parents were going to be home. They might not have even stayed for midnight. That would be typical of them—go to a New Year's Eve party and leave before the celebration. I came out onto Burr Road and could see the side and back of our house. It was dark. "I don't think they're home," I told Anna.

"Good," she said.

"What did that sound like?"

"It sounded kind of painful. I could hear you breathing and the snow crunching."

"That's pretty much all of it. I'm going to cut in back of Mrs. Owens's and then I'll be a block from home."

"Don't hang up," she said.

I ran through Mrs. Owens's backyard and noticed her trashcans behind the garage. I dropped the wadded-up tissue into one of the cans. When I got out to the street, I thought I heard a car. I ran down the street and dashed into the dark house. "I think I just beat them," I told Anna. I was almost out of breath. I struggled with my boots, leaning against the wall by the back door and holding the phone to my ear with my shoulder.

"What was that noise back there?"

"I got rid of that stuff I took from your house."

"Where?"

"Mrs. Owens's."

"You don't think she'll come out and find it?"

"There was a bag. I put it in the bag. Besides, what if she did? She won't know where it came from."

"It might give her a scare, though." She laughed.

I had my boots off and made it up to my room in the dark. If my parents came home right now they would see the fresh snow on my boots. I thought about going down and wiping them off, but I was too tired. "I have to go to sleep now," I said.

"It's going to be a great year," Anna said.

"Yeah."

"Listen to me. It's going to be a great year. Things are going to happen that we never expected, never imagined."

"It's great already," I said. I had just crawled under the covers when I heard a car in the driveway. "They're back," I told Anna. "They must have slugged the champagne and gotten the hell out of there. I've got to go."

"Go, then," she said.

I was worried about the boots, but either my parents didn't notice or they didn't want to say anything about it, the next day or any other. I felt as if I had fooled the world. I felt as if we had conquered everything. Anna was right, it was going to be a great year. Everything was going to be all right for once.

j a n u a r y

The Saturday after New Year's, Mr. Cayne and Anna came over to help put up the shortwave antenna. "Maybe we should wait until it's warmer," I said.

"My dad really wants to get this set for you," Anna said. So there they were, all bundled up and ready to go. Mr. Cayne was wearing a bright red stocking cap and chocolate-brown coveralls. He looked like a lit cigar.

My father was sequestered in his den, so I didn't even bother to ask him about where to put the antenna, or even if we could borrow his ladder and tools. I simply went to the garage with Anna and Mr. Cayne and let him take over. He outlined the procedure and assigned us our specific duties.

Mr. Cayne and I carried the ladder to the side of the house and extended it to reach the roof, and he made the ascent as far as my bedroom window. I went to my room while he was climbing the ladder, then handed him the antenna and wire through the open window. "You can close the window right over the wire," he said, and made his way to the roof. I left the window open and looked down to

Anna, who was stationed at the bottom of the ladder to keep it steady. She didn't look up at me. She was stamping her feet in the snow and trying to wind her long black scarf higher around her ears and nose.

Mr. Cayne shouted to me to turn on the receiver. As I turned to go to my desk I heard a thump and a skid. I rushed to the window and saw Mr. Cayne getting up from the edge of the roof. "Where the hell were you?" he yelled at Anna. "I could have fallen off this fucking roof thanks to you." He kicked the ladder violently, knocking it over onto the lawn. I ran downstairs and outside and helped Anna pick it up.

Her eyes were red, ready to cry. "Don't worry about it," I said. "It's all right."

As we steadied the ladder against the house, my father emerged, shuffling his slippers in the snow. He looked half asleep, and tried to rub the afternoon nap out of his face. He stood and watched us for a few seconds and then retreated into the house without a word. Mr. Cayne was still furious as he stood at the edge of the roof. He ordered me away from the ladder. "Let her," he said. "It's all she had to do. One thing. Let's see if she can do it and not get one of us killed." He came down the ladder and glared at her. "Nicely done."

We returned the ladder and the tools to the garage. "It's not the best antenna," he said, "but at least you'll get a taste for the shortwave. If you like it, we can always upgrade to something better." I thanked him for his gift and his help, and he started for his car. "Let's go," he told Anna.

"I think I'm going to stay here for a while," she said. "Is that okay?" Mr. Cayne didn't look as if he approved, but he dismissed her with a shrug and then left.

"He's got a short fuse today," I said.

"Let's go inside."

We went up to my room and she closed the door. It was cold from the open window, and Anna quickly crawled under the covers. My father was probably back into his nap. I got into bed.

She was clutching my hand with hers, and when I turned to face her she was already asleep. She was flat on her back, peaceful and still, and I watched her sleep, listening to the measured rhythm of her breathing. I wanted to turn off the shortwave, but she had a tight hold on my hand. The woman on the radio was calmly saying, *"Seis, siete, tres, siete, cero . . ."*

The next Monday we got our report cards. I made the honor roll; Anna kept her consistent D's for every class. Her parents told her that she couldn't see me until her grades improved. "It doesn't make any sense," she e-mailed me. "I was getting horrible grades long before I met you."

"Maybe it's about the ladder," I replied.

"It doesn't matter," she wrote. It didn't matter; we kept on seeing each other.

She would leave a text message on my cell phone, or IM me at home. "Come to the basement door in a half-hour. It will be unlocked." I would sneak in through the basement door and we could spend some time together. "My parents usually aren't this stubborn or stupid," she told me. "I don't know why they're suddenly being dramatic." I noticed in the dim light of the basement that she had bruises on both arms, just below the shoulders. When she saw me looking at them she sat up and put her long-sleeved shirt and sweater back on.

"You can't be cold," I said.

"A little."

This was one of those times when she wasn't supposed to be in the basement either. She had sneaked down after her parents had gone to bed, and we couldn't risk lighting the stove. It was freezing on the couch, but this was better than some of the alternative meeting places. "Meet me at the river," she would say on the phone, and I would run down to her spot at the river and we would kiss and shiver in the cold until we couldn't stand it anymore, until our toes were numb and our ears and noses were frozen, and we would have to leave each other again.

She aced her next test, and the ban was lifted. "It was just an excuse anyway," she said. "My parents have never cared about grades before. Something else is going on with them."

"They don't like me."

"It's not that simple," she said. "It never is with them. Besides, they do like you."

journal entry

We had all moved into a barn in the country. It was a huge old barn, bigger than most of our houses. It had to be about a hundred feet long and maybe fifty feet wide, but the most impressive thing was the roof. It had to be more than eighty feet high. There was a second story, with three cutouts in the floor and wooden ladders hanging down to the dirt floor. The whole thing was made of wood and smelled of fire. There was a thin cover of straw in some of the old horse stalls. It seemed perfect.

We had built our own little rooms in the barn. The Goths took the top floor—they were like bats in the rafters, lurking in their black clothes—except for Anna, who was on the first floor, next to me. Carl had been the first to finish his room, and as we hammered together partitions, moved in bed frames and mattresses and personal belongings, he stayed on his bed reading *Why We Buy*.

There were a lot of us in there, maybe twenty or twenty-five; we had all moved out of our houses, away from our parents. No one knew whose barn it was. We had electricity for lights, but that was as modern as it got. Mice ran around all the time, and birds flitted from ladder to ladder and swooped from high in the ceiling. There was at least one owl. These were problems, sure, but I thought we could take care of them.

Then one day I came back to the barn and Anna wasn't there. She didn't return for a couple of days, and no one could tell me what had happened to her. While I was worried, no one else seemed to be concerned. She wasn't at her parents', she wasn't at school, she wasn't anywhere. I thought that maybe she had found some other place, someplace better, and was there by herself. She didn't want anyone to be with her. She didn't want me.

Finally she returned to the barn, to get her things. I pleaded with her to stay. "I can't," she said. "I have to go somewhere else." I told her that things would be better. I told her that we were all new at this, that we were learning things every day. It wouldn't stay like this. I was practically crying. "Just stick it out," I said. "Things will get better."

"I can't stay," she said.

She had persuaded me to keep a dream journal. This was the dream I had three nights in one week, 30 January, and 2 and 5 February.

m u m l e r

"How's the ghost story coming?" she asked me.

"I'm not doing so well," I said. I had been trying, but I began to think that I wasn't really cut out for this type of stuff. I had gotten myself into a situation where I didn't have anything good enough to show her, but the longer I waited, the greater her expectations were. I would think about it at night, sitting by my window and look out into the night, the snow shining in the moonlight, and I would try to think about what kind of ghost story she would like, one that I would like to write, one that I could write. I couldn't think of anything. So then I would read some of the books she'd given me, old ghost stories, but that only made things worse because then I couldn't think of anything that hadn't been done before. I wanted to write something that would surprise her.

"Maybe you need some inspiration," she said.

She told me that there was a legend about a place across the river called Mumler. You wouldn't find it on a map anymore, and there was no town there now, only a few acres of woods. I had never heard of Mumler before Anna told me about it. She said that the town was founded more than two hundred fifty years before, that it grew and prospered and then, through a series of strange events, died off. The only things left were some ruins and the legends. What had happened to Mumler was a mystery, and the woods where it used to be were said to be haunted.

She showed me a bunch of websites with the story. A lot of the details were different, but the general story was the same. Something horrible had happened across the river, and the people who had survived finally abandoned the place and moved into our town or far away. Most of the websites agreed that the town had been founded by George Tomias in 1737, but was overrun by the Mumler family a few years later. One site indicated that the three Mumler brothers had escaped England after a failed plot to over-

throw the king, and that a curse had been put on them. Not
long after they moved into the small settlement, strange
things began to happen. The youngest of the brothers, Abel,
went insane, and shortly after that, another resident, Gri-
sham Pyn, fell to his death during a barn raising. According to one site, he was murdered, and Hiram Tanner, who
owned the barn, was under suspicion. Tanner eventually
went crazy from a curse put on him by his own sister. Some
families left Mumler, but trouble seemed to follow many of
them. In 1760, the Carter family abandoned their house,
which was formerly Abel Mumler's, and moved to Bing-
hampton, where they were slaughtered by Indians. Around
1800, General Gideon Swann's wife was killed by light-
ning, and soon afterward he went mad. The last events mentioned involved the Proby family in the late 1800s. William
Proby's wife died of an illness, and then his children disappeared in the woods or the river, depending on which version you consulted, and then Proby burned his house down
and tried to set the whole town on fire, before disappearing
himself. In a few years the town was gone, its residents either dead or moved on to a safer spot.

One website had a photograph of a washed-out road that
had once run through Mumler and was now overgrown
with plants and grass. To the left of the ruined road were a
number of trees, with a white cloud suspended between
two of the trees. The site identified the cloud as some sort
of spirit, caught on film. "This is the kind of physical evidence skeptics hate," the caption read. "There is obviously
no way anyone could have created the spirit cloud, but
there it is, plainly captured by the photographer."

"Have you ever been there?" I asked Anna.

"It's private property," she said.

"Who owns it?"

"Some association. There's no one there to stop us, if that's what you're worried about."

"I don't need to go there."

"Come on," she said. "You can't write about the place unless you see it, soak up the atmosphere."

"Who said I'm writing about it? It looks like enough's been written about the place already."

"Well, write about something else, then," she said. "But this is the only place that I know of that's supposed to have ghosts. You're going to write a ghost story, right? So let's go get some ghosts."

Anna took me to Mumler. She brought along a picnic basket with sandwiches and fruit and a thermos of hot chocolate and a little bottle of brandy. It was cold and snow was everywhere. "Maybe we should wait until spring," I said. We walked across the southern bridge, and then north about a mile and a half. It was a Saturday afternoon and there was only about an hour of daylight left. That's the way she had planned it. She wanted to get there during daylight, but stay until it got dark. "I've got a flashlight if we need it," she said.

It wasn't anything more than a big, thick clump of woods. I had seen it a million times and had never thought anything about it. No one had mentioned it before Anna, and she was a newcomer to town. An old hiking trail led into the woods, but across it hung a chain with a "No Trespassing" sign.

"Do they think that's going to stop anybody?" I said.

"Shouldn't it say 'Enter at Your Own Risk'?"

"Well, it doesn't look like anyone's been here lately." I didn't see any footprints in the snow. There weren't any animal tracks either.

We trudged through the woods until we came on an old chimney sticking out of the snow. It was crumbling at the top, but otherwise was in good shape. Anna scooped away the snow from the base of the chimney and found the stone hearth. She brushed it off and pulled a blanket out of her picnic basket, spread it out on the hearth, and sat down. "This is a good-enough spot," she said.

"Isn't it cold?"

"Sure, but what are you going to do?"

"I could start a fire," I said.

"Somebody would see the smoke and think the whole forest was on fire," she said. "Besides, this will warm you up." She took a drink of brandy and handed me the bottle.

I sat down beside her, and we took sips of the brandy and ate the food she had brought. She peeled an orange and handed me one of the segments. It was a brilliant curve of color against the white of the snow. Everything was sharp, the smell of the brandy, the crisp air. I could have stayed there forever.

It started to get dark. The sky was a deep blue, and stars were visible. There was going to be a full moon. "Let's wait for the ghosts," she said, and moved against me. We sat huddled in the freezing darkness and waited.

"Do you believe in ghosts?" I asked her.

"I would like to believe," she said. "I would like to think that there's something beyond this life, something that connects us. It would make the world more interesting."

"So you think this place is haunted and all that stuff we read about Mumler is true?"

"I doubt it," she said. "That's the problem, too many people have junked it up with legends and hoaxes and schemes."

She told me about Houdini.

"One of the tricks he designed, and even patented, but never performed was to be frozen in a block of ice, or at least a theatrical representation of one, and escape, walk out of it, without disturbing it at all.

"The Water Cell Torture was like a phone booth filled with two hundred fifty gallons of water. Houdini was locked inside, upside down, and then a curtain was placed between him and the audience. His attendants would be visible, at least one holding an axe, to break the glass booth just in case. Houdini would ask the audience to hold their breath with him. The audience waited and waited. You could hear people gasping as they couldn't hold it any longer. Still, nothing happened. They say that some people in the audience would become frantic, start screaming for the attendants to free Houdini, save him from drowning, and then, just when the audience couldn't take any more, when no one could possibly be holding their breath, Houdini would emerge from behind the curtain."

"That's some trick," I said.

"It was a trick," she said. "Houdini could get out of the Cell whenever he wanted. Some people claim that he would sit behind the curtain reading a paper, waiting for the right moment to come out. What's most amazing is that it's a performance where nothing happens—the audience is just looking at a curtain and a couple of guys standing around. It's what they *think* is happening that gets them agitated and excited, anxious and nervous, and finally relieved and amazed. The trick wasn't so much in getting out of the Cell—he had figured that part out long before he ever took it onstage—but in manipulating the crowd. He knew how to play the crowd so well that he knew fake mediums and spiritualists were doing the same thing.

"His friend Sir Arthur Conan Doyle was the biggest sucker, he fell for the cheapest tricks. Doyle had lost a son in World War One and wanted desperately to believe in séances and mediums," Anna went on. "Houdini thought that this type of desperation was dangerous and allowed people to exploit Doyle's grief and desire. So Houdini tried to convince Doyle that the mediums were really nothing more than skillful magicians. He wrote Doyle letter after letter denouncing mediums Doyle believed, and he described exactly how they had managed their tricks. Doyle refused to believe and told Houdini that the problem was that Houdini didn't approach the mediums with an open mind. The friendship turned into a feud, and Houdini changed his act to include the exposure of the tricks used by mediums.

"The funny thing," Anna said, "is that both men wanted

to believe. Doyle wanted to believe so much that he was willing to accept any medium as genuine in order to hear from his son, and Houdini wanted to communicate with his dead mother so badly that he refused to accept the frauds and the fakes."

"That's why he used the code?"

"Exactly. He had tried to contact his mother through a medium, and one told him that she had made contact. Houdini wanted to know what his mother's message was. 'I'm through. At last, I'm through,' the medium told him. Houdini's mother couldn't speak English, so he knew it wasn't true, and that's why he created a code for himself and his wife."

We sat in silence for a few minutes, giving the woods an opportunity to live up to their reputation. Nothing happened. It only got darker. There was no moon, and I couldn't see farther than ten feet. The closest trees were like enormous columns, and everything behind them was a solid black wall.

"Do you want to wait for the moon?" Anna asked.

"Not really." I was colder than I wanted to be. She handed me the flashlight. "Do you think we need it?" I said, and took a few steps away from her. She almost disappeared in the darkness, only her blond hair visible, dimly shining. She came over and took my hand. "Listen," she whispered, and gripped my hand. We stood for a few seconds in the cold silence. "What?" I finally whispered back.

"You can almost hear that Cure song I put on that first CD for you, can't you?" she said out loud, and started singing the first verse, before breaking into laughter. I turned on the flashlight and we slowly made our way out of Mumler.

"Now we're cursed," she said when we left the trees and the darkness and the Cure behind us.

"I'm ready for it," I said. "I feel like I've already been cursed."

"That's not a nice thing to say." She came up to me quickly and kissed me, then ran down the road. I chased after, keeping the beam of the flashlight on her back, the light bending around her black clothes. She ran off the road and through the snow, down to the river. "Let's walk across," she said.

"I don't think we should. I mean so soon after we've been cursed."

"You think we should wait a half-hour?"

"Like swimming after you eat?" I groaned.

"You're the one who wants to wait." She took a step out onto the frozen river.

"Let's at least do this during the day," I said.

"Everybody does that." She took a few more steps. I took a step onto the ice and shined the flashlight across the surface. There was a layer of brittle snow. I couldn't see any water or fishing holes or other breaks, but that didn't mean they weren't there, waiting under a thin patch of ice. Anna was about twenty feet out. She turned back into the beam of light and looked at me, her black-mittened hand in front of her face, shielding her eyes. "Come on," she said, seeing I was still at the shore. "Come on."

I took the picnic basket and swung it back behind me and then tossed it forward onto the ice. I thought that I could slide it to her and test the ice between us, even though the basket weighed a fraction of what I did. Instead, the basket skidded to a stop a few feet away from me, slowed by the snow.

"You're definitely cursed," she said. She waited for me, but I told her to go ahead, we didn't need to double the weight on a small space of ice. I knew this river; I had skated on it and walked across it hundreds of times in my life, but always in daylight. Anna acted as if she owned it, walking confidently across the surface, as if she did this every night, while I treaded more cautiously, examining every inch of ice between us and the other shore. My heart was thumping in my chest as I imagined us both breaking through the ice into the swift current just beneath our feet.

Finally we reached the opposite bank and I scrambled off the ice and collapsed. Even though I had been moving slowly and carefully, I felt as if I had just run the hundred-yard dash. I was out of breath and sweating. I turned the flashlight toward Anna, kneeling beside me; she was beaming, her face reflecting the light with the stars thrown out across the dark sky behind her. "How fun was that?" She was right; even though I'd been half scared to death, it was the most fun I'd had in a long time.

7 february

"I've finished my obituaries," she said.

"The whole town?"

"Everybody. Do you want to see the last one?" She grabbed her notebooks and flipped through the pages, then handed me one. "I know you like him and everything, that's what took me so long with his."

It was Mr. Devon's obituary:

William Devon, former art teacher and high school athletic coach, was found dead in his home after a fire that started sometime around 4:00 a.m. Mr. Devon's girlfriend, and former student, Jana Chapman, escaped the blaze through a second-story bedroom window, but firefighters could not rescue Mr. Devon, who was asleep on a couch downstairs, where the fire started. It is still unclear how it began, and Hilliker police are actively investigating the scene at 32 Eddowes Street. "There are some inconsistencies with an accidental fire," George Godley, Hilliker detective, said, "and we will continue to work with the fire department and investigate the scene until we can come to a determination for the cause."

William Devon was born on June 3, 1969, in Tacoma, Washington. His father was an itinerant carpenter, and the family moved frequently, living in New Mexico, Arizona, Texas, Arkansas, and Florida before William was in high school. He lettered in football, track, and base-ball at Fort Kelly High School, excelling particularly in football, where he was named to the all-state team his junior and senior years at running back. His 1,283 yards rushing set school records in season rushing yardage and total offense in 1983. He scored 130 points that season, and had 307 yards rushing in a single game against Stride. In the first quarter of that game, Devon lost four teeth on a play in which he also lost his helmet at the yard of scrimmage but continued to run for nearly fif-teen yards before being tackled, and was struck in the mouth by a Stride helmet. Despite the injury, Devon played the rest of the game.

After graduating from the Rhode Island School of Design in 1992, he spent two years traveling and study-ing in Europe, before returning to the United States, where he began his teaching career in 1996.

Mr. Devon was forced to leave the teaching profession after a series of scandals in his classroom and the athletic department became too troublesome for the school board. He had spent a few months traveling before returning to town and beginning his residence with Ms. Chapman on Eddowes Street.

"That's a little mean-spirited, isn't it?"

"Not all of it," she said, and took it away from me. "I'm not changing it. They're all finished."

I didn't know what to say. I looked at the stack of note-books. "How many are there now?"

"One thousand five hundred and sixteen," she said. "That's everybody in town, including everybody in school, even the bus riders, and everybody who works in town but doesn't live here."

"So what now?"

"I don't know. I got it all finished a lot faster than I thought I would. It took me a long time last time, but there were more people, and I didn't have anybody like you to help."

"You did this before? What happened the last time you did this?"

"Everybody started dying, exactly the way I had described."

Her eyes were black and still. I couldn't tell if she was joking or not. I didn't know whether she wanted me to laugh or not, so I just sat there with her notebook in my lap. I handed it back to her and she started laughing.

"I didn't make them die," she said. "People die, that's what happens. And when they do, you need an obituary."

I left through the basement door before midnight. She kissed me and said, "With this kiss, I pass the key."

"What does that mean?"

"It's how some magicians, maybe even Houdini, got the key or pick for the locks in their tricks. Their assistants passed them the key with a last-minute kiss, sliding it over."

"I didn't get anything," I said.

"Maybe next time."

. . .

It had started to snow again. The fine, dry powder blew along the streets and sidewalks like sand, forming small dunes against the wheels of cars. I took my usual route home, cutting through backyards to shorten my time in the biting air, leaving a fresh trail of footprints. If it snowed all night they might fill up. I disposed of the tissue with the condom and its wrapper in Mrs. Owens's trash. This had become something of a ritual.

I was awakened in the night. I thought my phone was ringing, but when I checked it there was nothing. No one had called. I went downstairs to the kitchen for a glass of water. It was a few minutes past four and I was wide awake. I went back to my room and read until I was tired, and went back to sleep.

My father came in and told me to wake up. I lifted my head off the pillow and looked at the clock. "It isn't time," I said. "I've got another hour."

"Mr. and Mrs. Cayne are here," he said. "They're worried about Anna."

I wiped some of the sleep out of my face and saw the three of them standing in my room, my father in front and Mr. and Mrs. Cayne behind him. "What's going on?" I said.

"Anna wasn't home this morning," Mr. Cayne said. "We were wondering if you could tell us what you two did last night."

Mrs. Cayne pulled my desk chair up by the bed, and my

father moved my clothes off the other chair and brought it over beside her. Mr. Cayne sat down and they both looked at me. I know it's wrong to think about things like this in serious moments, and I probably shouldn't tell this, as it doesn't reflect so well on me, but while the two of them sat there in front of me, Mrs. Cayne's wild hair practically screaming off her head, Mr. Cayne with his completely bald face, I couldn't help myself: I tried to imagine what Mr. Cayne would look like with his wife's hair on his head. I had to turn away to keep from laughing. I'm sure they thought I was hiding something, smirking with some secret knowledge about their daughter. I didn't know what they were talking about.

"I don't know what you mean," I said. "We were over at your house last night. I left her at your house."

"What time was that?" Mr. Cayne said.

"Around ten or so, I guess."

"She didn't leave with you, walk you outside or part of the way with you?"

"No," I said. "I left through the basement and she stayed inside."

"She didn't say anything to you about going anywhere?" Mrs. Cayne asked.

"Nothing."

"You don't know any reason why she wouldn't be in her room this morning?"

"No."

"What did you do last night?"

"Nothing. We just hung out in the basement. Listened to the shortwave, played some pool, drank some soda."

"You didn't have a fight, anything to upset her?"

"No," I said. "We never fight."

"Something else happened," Mrs. Cayne said. "What was it?"

"Nothing." I could feel the redness rising from my stomach, and I tried to take an unnoticeable deep breath to keep the shame of the lie from appearing on my face.

"Did you have sex with Anna?" Mrs. Cayne continued.

"No," I said. I thought I was going to pass out, fall off the bed and drop to the floor, unconscious. I almost wish that had happened. It might have been better.

I could see that Mrs. Cayne was angry. She had been calm, all things considered—she was nervous and frantic that her daughter was missing, but she wasn't yelling or babbling or anything like that. But now she was mad.

"What's this, then?" she said, as Mr. Cayne pulled a torn and empty condom wrapper out of his pocket.

"We found this by the couch in the basement. This morning," he said.

My brain froze. It hung, like an overloaded computer, the screen frozen. My face must have been a red, frozen screen. I could see that my father and the Caynes could see that I was blushing, but my mind was whipping around in uncontrollable circles. How could they have found a condom wrapper? I had taken it and thrown it away. I made sure. I saw it go into the trash. Part of me wanted to run out of the room and out of the house and go straight back to Mrs. Owens's and dig in the trashcan and confirm what I knew to be true. But what did that mean? Had they followed me? Had Anna had someone else over after I left?

Had she planted the wrapper for her parents to find? Were they just bluffing? Nothing was making sense.

Mr. and Mrs. Cayne sat staring straight at me. My father stood looking down at me. They weren't happy. I wasn't happy.

"Well, son?" My father's voice said, We all know what happened, so now be a man and admit it.

"We were careful," I said, looking at Mrs. Cayne. She slapped me in the mouth and then started bawling. I knew it was the wrong thing to say, but I didn't expect to get hit for it. I couldn't think of any other time I'd been hit. I'm sure my parents spanked me, but not that I remember. I'd never been in a fight in school, and I'd never done anything that provoked somebody to haul off and hit me, especially not a grown woman. And here Mrs. Cayne had slapped me full force in the face and no one was doing anything about it. I sat on the bed and put my cold, sweating hand up to my burning face. My father didn't say anything. Mr. Cayne didn't say anything. They looked at me as I sat in my bed, the left side of my face red and shamed.

Finally Mr. Cayne spoke. "Is there anything else you can tell us? Anything else you might know about where Anna might have gone?"

"I don't know anything," I said. "I wish I did, but I'm at a loss. She didn't say anything to me at all."

"Has she left like this before?" my father asked.

"Never," Mrs. Cayne replied.

"Her coat's gone, but it doesn't seem like anything else. Probably her phone, but she's not answering it," Mr. Cayne said.

"Or can't," Mrs. Cayne added. "Maybe we should call the police."

"They'll probably want you to wait awhile," my father said. "At least today. To see if she'll come back."

"I'd like to call just the same," Mrs. Cayne told him.

My father took them out of the room, to the phone.

He came back alone. "You don't know where she is?"

"I told you, I don't," I said. "I wish I did."

"I heard you last night," he said. "Around four. What were you doing?"

"I got up for a drink of water."

"Downstairs?"

"I couldn't sleep."

"She wasn't over here? You'd better tell me what you know right now. This isn't a joke or a game—this is serious. The police are involved. If you're covering for her or hiding something, you'd better stop right now."

"I'm telling you the truth, Dad. I don't know anything about it."

He stood in the doorway, glaring at me, trying to figure out if I was telling the truth. "All right, then, get up and get ready for school." He turned and went downstairs.

I reached for my cell and called her. There was no answer. I checked my log to see if I had missed a call from her. There was nothing.

I had to go to school and sit through every class. Nobody was really paying attention; we were all waiting for the principal to announce something, or for somebody to rush in and say that she'd been found. Part of me thought that she would walk into class any moment and surprise everybody. There was a lot of talk, a lot of speculation, but no one spoke to me, except Carl. He didn't know anything, but he said that most people thought she had run away from home. Others thought she had been kidnapped. Some said she had been abducted by aliens. Carl said they weren't joking. There were some people who thought that I was involved and that I shouldn't be in school. I should be down at the police station, locked up. That hadn't even occurred to me until Carl mentioned it. "Who's saying that crap," I asked, "Melissa?" It wasn't Melissa. She wasn't saying anything.

The school day ended and people started going home. There was still no news. I walked to Mr. Devon's room. He was loading a bunch of cameras with film. I sat and watched him for a while. He didn't say anything, and neither did I. That's what I liked about Mr. Devon.

Finally I spoke. "What can I do?"

He knew what I meant. He shook his head. "Wait. That's the hardest thing anyone can do right now."

"What are the teachers saying?"

"We're all hoping that everything turns out all right."

I looked at him, hoping he would give me something more than the official, politically correct crap, but he didn't.

"It's all your fault," I said.

"How is that?"

"I met her in the library."

We both laughed a little. Then I left. "If you hear anything, would you let me know," I said when I was at the door. "I feel like I'll be the last person to know anything."

"I'll call you as soon as I hear something," Mr. Devon said.

It was almost dark outside as I started to walk home. I was a couple of blocks away from school when a car slammed on its brakes and the driver rolled down the window. It was Kevin Hermanson, a senior. "They found your girlfriend down at the river," he said. "Dead." He was excited, practically yelling at me from the street. He pulled his head back into the car and drove off. I just stood there, staring at the spot where Kevin Hermanson's head had been.

I ran back to school. The door I had come out of a few minutes before was locked, so I ran around to the side of the building where Mr. Devon's classroom was. His light was still on, and I pounded on the window. He came to the window, then motioned toward the front of the building. I ran there and waited for him.

"Kevin Hermanson just told me that they found her dead in the river," I said.

Mr. Devon grabbed me and hugged me. It was one of those hugs where I didn't know if he was hugging me or needed the hug himself.

"Let me take you home," he said.

"Take me down there."

"That's not a good idea."

"I'll go by myself."

He didn't want to go, but he didn't want me to go by myself either. He slowly put his coat on, trying to think of a way out of it. "Maybe I should take you home first," he said. I shook my head. "All right," he said, and then drove us to the river.

There wasn't anything when we got there. I guess I expected to see ambulances and police cars and a crowd of people watching as Anna's body was pulled from the water, but there was only the river. It was dark by now, and Mr. Devon drove until he saw a police car parked along the road, just above the water. He parked and told me to stay in his car, then went over and talked to the officer sitting in the squad car. Mr. Devon walked back and said, "Come on." He kept his headlights on and grabbed a flashlight.

We walked down the shallow bank to the river. Yellow police caution tape stretched between some trees, blocking our way to the edge of the frozen river. Mr. Devon swept the flashlight beam across the surface of the ice and we saw a hole about halfway across. There was snow on the ice, and the tracks and markings made it look as if there had been a lot of activity between us and the hole.

After a few minutes I heard somebody walking behind us. The beam of another flashlight reached toward us and then out across the river. It was another police officer.

"Let's take you home," he told me.

. . .

I told the police everything. They told me almost nothing. I told them how we had crossed the river once before in the dark. I told them about Anna and me, and the night we spent together before she disappeared. I told them about the condom and Mr. Cayne's pulling it out of his pocket like some magic trick. We sat in our dining room while my mother made coffee for the police officers. She put dinner aside for later and I told them everything. Almost. I didn't tell them about our code.

My father had wanted to get a lawyer to make it all official, but I didn't see the point. I had nothing to hide. "Once you talk to the police, that's it," my father said. "That's the official story. You can't change it later. You know that part, 'Anything you say can and will be used against you'? That's what they're talking about." There was only one story, the truth. Why would I change it? I wanted to help. I thought it might help.

I told them about her notebooks, about the fact that she was constantly writing obituaries. The officers seemed interested in this. They asked what the notebooks looked like, how many of them there were, all that stuff. They hadn't found them. I wondered if she had taken them with her. Maybe she had destroyed them or hidden them.

I told them about the strange marks I'd seen on Anna's body, the bruises and scratches. I didn't tell them about the cuts on her arms. Maybe they knew about those already, maybe they had seen them on her dead body. They probably thought it meant that she was suicidal. I didn't want to support that. It didn't make sense. Anna was ravenously curious. She read all the time, she listened to music, she watched movies, she was always online reading about more things to read, and more things to listen to, and more things to look at. There didn't seem to be anything she didn't want to know. I can't imagine a person with that much interest in the world wanting to leave it. It didn't fit.

My mother looked at the officers. "What do you think about that?" They didn't respond. "Maybe you should be over at the Caynes' asking them about this?"

"We're talking to everyone," one of the officers said. My mother was about to continue, but my father's hand on her shoulder stopped her.

"What can you tell me about what happened?" I said.

The officer was writing in a small spiral notebook. He had his head down and kept writing. He clicked his pen and pushed it through the spiral and then put the notebook into the pocket of his leather jacket. I realized that I hadn't taken my jacket off either. I wasn't hot; in fact, I was still cold. I wanted some coffee, I guess, even though I'd never had any before and couldn't bring myself to ask. I had to wait for the officer. He put his right hand on the table and leaned on it. He looked at the hand as if studying how it supported the weight of his body. He looked at his partner, and then at my parents.

"This is not official," he said, "but we believe that Anna Cayne drowned in the river. We've started a search for her body."

"What? I thought you found her body."

"No. We haven't recovered the body."

"Then what was out there on the ice?"

They hadn't found her body after all. They'd found only her dress, arranged neatly beside a hole in the ice, like someone lying facedown, looking into the water. "That's bizarre," my mother blurted. The officer didn't say anything, but only shifted his eyes from my mother to me.

"So she killed herself," my father said.

"We're not speculating at this point," the other policeman said. "We need to locate the body and then go from there."

The officers left, and my mother took the coffee cups to the kitchen. My father sat at the table, his hands pressed together in front of him. "You don't know anything more about this?"

"Somebody told me they found her body," I said.

"Did you think they would?"

"I didn't think anything. I don't know anything. I wish I did."

"Is that your story?"

"It's not a story," I said.

"I saw you lie to the Caynes this morning," he said. "I hope I didn't see you lie to the police tonight."

"It was the truth," I said. "Everything I know about it, and what happened."

"Let's hope so."

.   .   .

I had a dream about Anna. Or about a book. Or both. There was a book in the dream, and her name kept appearing in odd places on the page and then disappearing. I turned a page and her name jumped around, like a floater in your eye that moves every time you try to look at it, always remaining just a bit ahead of you, elusive and fleeting. The book didn't make any sense, the chapters and pages were all out of place, but I kept riffling through them, hoping they would provide some meaning, some sense. Carl and Claire were in the dream too, suddenly asking me what I was doing. I tried to tell them about Anna, but they didn't know what I was talking about. "You don't read," Claire said. "You can't read," Carl told me.

"That's not true," I said to Carl. "We read Sherlock Holmes together."

"I remember that. Who do you think is smarter, Sherlock Holmes or Sir Arthur Conan Doyle?"

"You can't imagine someone smarter than yourself, can you?" Claire asked.

"No," I said, and when I looked down, the pages of the book were empty.

When I woke up the next morning, I was surprised. I was shocked that the world could continue, that I could wake up as I did every morning. I didn't wake up and think that the day before was a dream, or any of that crap; I was too acutely aware of what had happened. She left. She was taken. She was gone. She was dead, or she wasn't, but she was still gone. That's what made everything so shocking. There was a disturbing ordinariness about everything. How could such a terrible thing happen and the world just go on? Everything should stop and wait until it had everything figured out before everything started up again. Everyone should be at the river, searching, smashing every last piece of ice and straining through every drop of water until she was found. But it wasn't like that at all. My father was finishing up in the bathroom, as he did every morning, combing his remaining strands of hair in the proper place, adjusting his tie, brushing a spot out of his suit. My mother was in the kitchen, drinking coffee from the pot my father had programmed the night before to start brewing at seven-thirty sharp. Everything seemed programmed. My father showered and shaved and left for work as he usually did, my mother appeared to do or not do the things she usually did or didn't do every morning, and I had to go to school. The world had a hole torn in it yesterday, but today it would go on as normal. Maybe it was too used to these sorts of things. To me, the world wasn't unhappy enough. I was afraid that I wasn't unhappy enough.

Before that day I had always imagined that it took strength to continue after a tragedy, but I now realized that it was really weakness. I didn't want to face directly what had happened, or imagine what might have happened, so I tried to ignore it from one moment to the next. I didn't go up to the third floor before school; I didn't want to hear what Bryce had to say. Instead, I searched the first floor for Billy Godley. He was on his way to homeroom, and I stopped him and asked him what he knew. "I don't really know that much," he said. He knew more than anyone else, though. He said people were down working at the river, cops and the volunteer fire department and a couple of rescue teams from nearby towns, all looking for her. He said his father had mentioned that it was strange that all they found was a dress. "No coat, no shoes," Billy said. "No body, though that could be good."

grief can really fuck you up

I wasn't even there and I can't get the image out of my head. If this were a movie or a graphic novel, there would be an overhead view of the snow-covered river, with her black dress laid perfectly on the ice, the hem curving in a dramatic arc, the arms stretched straight out on each side. It would look like a black snow angel, with the neck stopping just at the edge of the jagged hole in the ice, exposing the churning water below. It's a great image—and I can say that only after knowing Anna—she would have appreciated it, and I have thought about how well the scene was set, how perfectly the image was composed, and I wonder if maybe she didn't appreciate it too. I was still confused by it, though. Why weren't her coat and shoes there? She wouldn't walk all the way from her house through the snow and then across the frozen river without a coat, and without shoes. "Maybe they went with her," Billy had said. He meant that maybe she had run off, sure, but I couldn't help thinking of her going through that hole, like Alice through the looking glass, slowly drifting through the cold water, her boots weighing her down.

After school I walked along the river. Carl had said that he would come with me, but he had some business to take care of at the last minute, and Bryce was driving Claire and the other Goths. I didn't want to go with Bryce. You could see cars streaming in the same direction, seniors and parents and everyone else who shouldn't have come. They were all coming to gawk, but there was little to see. Her clothes were gone, the ice was gone, and the hole she had gone through was gone. The only thing that was still there was the yellow caution tape. The police had to put up barricades to keep the crowds back. The rescue-and-recovery team had brought in an excavator to claw through the ice and break it up so they could get boats into the river and start searching. The boats were in the water when I got there, men in red jackets dragging poles through the river and peering over the side. Somebody said they had been there all day. Somebody else said they wouldn't be coming back to look tomorrow. Another person said the river would be frozen again by morning. This proved to be wrong, but it was frozen again in the next few days. Just walking by after those few days, you'd never have known that anything had happened: the crowds were gone, the barriers were gone, the yellow tape was gone, the water was gone. There was nothing but ice and snow and cold; everything looked the way it had before, as if the clock had been turned back, before everything changed.

Anna's locker became a memorial. People taped poems and prayers on it, and it was covered with yellow ribbons. There were flowers and unlit candles on the floor in front of it. The pile grew and spread throughout until finally an announcement was made, telling everyone to stop blocking the hallway. A designated area in front of the principal's office was now the official receptacle of the school's anguish. There was a large cardboard box with a handwritten sign above it: "A. Cayne." You had to laugh. Carl told me that he saw the janitor shoveling the pile that was in front of the locker into the box. "He was using the same shovel he uses to clear the sidewalks," Carl said.

"Anna's just going to throw it all away when she comes back anyway," I replied.

People held a vigil down at the river. It was bitterly cold, well below zero, but about a hundred showed up and threw bouquets of flowers onto the ice or piled them on the snowy shore. I don't know who organized the thing or how people knew to show up, but they did. Police tried to keep them away from the river, but Bryce pushed his way through and placed a lit candle on the ice. A number of people followed, until there were a dozen or so candles flickering in the darkness not far from where she had disappeared. Finally one of the police officers spoke. "Please stay back, just stay back, away from the river. We don't want another person falling through the ice." That seemed to get people's attention.

Mr. and Mrs. Cayne were there. They stood off to the side, and then Mrs. Cayne moved down toward the river and stood in front of the blue barricades. The flames from candles in the crowd threw a tenuous light on her face. She spoke tearfully, thanking everyone for coming and for giving strength to her and her husband. "We still have hope that Anastasia is alive," she said. "We still have hope that she will be returned to us, safe and sound."

Bryce moved to her side and put a reassuring arm around her. He was like a dark tower beside her, with his black stocking cap pulled low over his shaved head, and his long black overcoat. He was smart enough to stand on the other side of her thrashing hair. "I just wanted to assure the Caynes that we're doing everything we can to help," he said, but you got the idea that he was talking about himself, not a group. He mentioned his car wreck and how everyone said it was a miracle that he had survived, and he was certain that the same sort of miracle would happen for the Caynes.

I couldn't believe that Bryce would speak like that. I was embarrassed by him, embarrassed for him. It wasn't his place, and then the thought occurred to me that people might expect me to say something. I could feel myself blushing and I moved to the back of the crowd, hoping no one would say anything. No one did, and in fact the crowd slowly dispersed, with some people approaching the Caynes and speaking to them in quiet, somber voices.

I had reached the road and was heading to a shortcut toward home when I heard Mr. Cayne call out, "Do you need a ride?"

I looked up to see who it was he was talking to and realized he was looking at me from inside his car. When I didn't move, he motioned toward me with his gloved hand. I didn't want to go with him—I thought of him and Mrs. Cayne as somehow responsible for what had happened to Anna. Even if they weren't directly responsible, they had failed to take better care of her, watch over her, protect her. Isn't that what they were supposed to do? He motioned to me again, and reluctantly I walked over to his car. Mrs. Cayne was sitting in the passenger seat, looking straight ahead.

"It's too cold to walk," he said. I couldn't think of any reasonable way out of it, so I got into the backseat. Mrs. Cayne didn't move. We drove in silence until Mr. Cayne said, "That was nice."

"It was nice of Bryce to speak," Mrs. Cayne said.

"Have you heard anything more?" I asked. They didn't have any information that I didn't already know, or at least they didn't tell me any. I couldn't help being suspicious, distrusting everything they told me and the way they acted. I was the one who had lied to them, and now I didn't trust them. The difference was that I knew I didn't have anything to do with Anna's disappearance, but they might have. I didn't know. I didn't know anything about them, really.

Mr. Cayne pulled up in front of my house and I got out.

He got out of the driver's side and came around the front of the car, his body cutting through the beam of the head-lights. I waited for him on the sidewalk.

"Mrs. Cayne is still very upset," he said, almost apologizing.

"She has every right to be."

He nodded quickly. "I can't say that I'm not upset. I mean with you. For the other night. It's just that I also wanted you to know that we are thinking about you, that we know this is hard for you too. Just know that."

"Thanks," I said. "Can I ask you a question?"

"Sure."

"Did Anna take anything with her that you know of?"

"Not that we can tell. Even her backpack is hanging on the back of her chair. We don't think she ran away. Is that what you're asking?"

"No." I could tell that I shouldn't have asked in the first place.

"Well, if we hear anything, we'll let you know, and we hope that you'll do the same."

"I will," I said. He reached out and patted me quickly on the shoulder, then hurried back to the car. Mrs. Cayne was still staring straight ahead.

I realized that there was a connection between my parents and the Caynes: they had now each lost a daughter. Maybe it should have drawn them closer—I wondered if it would. My parents might be able to help them find comfort, but that was probably hoping for too much. I don't even know if my parents had found comfort. The Caynes were probably better off not knowing them. I could see them using my parents as role models, the Caynes becoming just like them, withdrawn and inactive, quietly removed from the world.

I went inside and ate dinner, then went to my room. After a while my mother came and told me that Mr. Cayne was on the phone for me. "I just wanted to let you know that I looked all over Anna's room again," he said. "She might have taken her purse and her phone. I checked with the police, and they didn't find them at the river." He said that he had called her cell and there was no answer, but why would there be, I thought. I spent the night dialing and redialing, just to hear her voice say, "I'm sorry we're not talking right now, but leave a message and I will get back to you." It sounded like a promise.

4 e v e r ,

There was the problem of her body. They still hadn't found her, and I wondered how long they would look. If she had gone through the hole in the ice, what would happen to her? Would she be caught in the current and float beneath the ice? How far was the river frozen? I looked at a map and followed the river as it meandered southeast across the state, lazily marking curves across the yellows and greens before widening and spilling into the sea. The river was more than two hundred miles long. Did it all freeze in the

winter, the entire length of it? And if it did, could the current carry her all the way to sea underneath the ice? It was
like a math problem: If a body weighs 100 pounds and the
current of the river moves at 16 miles an hour, how long
would it take the body to travel 200 miles? Somebody had
to be thinking about this, working through these problems,
and once they had been solved, it would be time to work on
getting her back.

I tried not to think about it for too long. It drained me,
and I sat in my room and looked at the walls of things she
had sent me. She had turned one of my walls into a duplicate of one of hers, each postcard and picture in the same
position as on her wall. Our walls were almost identical, a
double dactyl. The thought made me smile.

I looked at a card she had sent me, not on the wall, but
taped to the side of my computer. It was blank, except for
the sentence, written in her own hand, "The way to solve
the problem you see in life is to live in a way that makes the
problem disappear." The words were written in a spiral, in
such a way that they got smaller and smaller, circling
around the period at the end. The word "disappear" was so
small that you needed a magnifying glass to read it.

I had to wrestle with the options, question which ones I
preferred—dead but in love with me, or alive and probably
not in love with me? If she were alive, why did she leave?
Why did she leave me behind? Had I done something to be
left, or to drive her away? But if she left, there was always

the chance that she would come back, that she might change her mind, or that she would at least contact me from wherever she was. We had made a code. Why make one if you weren't ever going to use it?

Sometimes she closed her notes and letters and postcards with "4 ever," then signed someone else's name. She rarely used her own, and she never used mine at first. They were all addressed to me, of course, but she used names that had something to do with what she was writing about. "Dear E.W.," she started one postcard about Houdini, and closed it with "4 ever, B.," referring to Houdini's real name, Ehrich Weiss, and his wife's name, Bess. Sometimes I had to investigate her references. "Dear Seldon," a letter began, and ended, "Your friend, Lily Bart." I often thought that if it hadn't been for Google our relationship wouldn't have lasted longer than a week. A few times even the Web couldn't help. "Dear K.," she addressed me on 4 January, and started to describe a small Greek island and how we should both go there to look at the moon sometime. "Maybe you will meet me there. Perhaps you will come and look for me, searching frantically, afraid that I have fallen down a well on the island. There are no wells, teacher. Don't be afraid. I love you, Sumire." I thought "K." might be a reference to Kafka, or to Kerouac. The postcard was a photograph of the Russian Sputnik satellite soaring through a fake blue sky. Sputnik was launched on 4 October 1957 and fell back to earth on 4 January 1958, but I could never find what "Sumire" meant.

I looked at other cards on the wall, and thought about events that had happened in our months together. The numbers 4 and 14 were recurring details. She had disappeared at 4 in the morning (at least that's what the police report said) on 2/8 ($8 \div 2 = 4$), not far from Route 521 ($5 - 2 + 1 = 4$). Our first date had been on 4 October (October is the tenth month, $10 + 4 = 14$). We'd gone out for a total of 4 months and 4 days. Her proper first name had 4 letters; the name she preferred to be called, "Anastasia Cayne," had 14. The significance of the number 4 might be in her initials ($A = 1, C = 3$). She used "4 ever" 14 times in her writings to me. There were five words in the code she made for us, but only 4 unique ones, and the word "as," when repeated, had 4 letters total. These were just the 4s I noticed then; there were possibly even more. It was either a maddening coincidence or something planned. I felt that I should know, and that if it was planned it had to mean something. She was trying to say something, and I should be the person to best know what it was. I wanted there to be clues and signposts; I wanted to examine the patterns and find a solution.

m a p

Two days after Anna disappeared I received a map. At first I didn't think it was from her, because there was a real stamp, but after looking at it I had no doubt it was from Anna. It's funny, the time she used a real stamp, her mail

took the longest to get to me. There was nothing in the envelope except the map. She had drawn it herself, and it
looked like no other map I'd ever seen; in fact, I didn't know
what it was at first. It was a folded sheet of paper with dots
and letters and numbers. The dots were clustered mainly
in twos, threes, and fours; there were a few groups of five,
and a number of single dots. Near some of the groups
were numbers followed by a letter or letters, like 14 EC, or
19 ABH.

I didn't want to decipher it; I didn't think I could stand
one of her games, but the more I thought about it, the
more important it became. What if it was the last thing she
wanted to say to me? What if this was the puzzle that answered what had happened to her, and why—what if this
answered everything? I couldn't ignore it, so I began the
unavoidable, painful process of deciphering it.

I started with the numbers, since only four of them were
used on the map: 5, 14, 19, and 23. The clustered dots were
arranged in rows, vertically and horizontally, and the numbers were usually at the end of the rows, followed by the
letters. There were a greater number of 5s and 23s. They
zigzagged through the little rows of clustered dots and into
a space marked with an X. Then the idea hit me that it was
a map.

She was giving me directions. The numbers 5, 14, 19,
and 23 corresponded respectively with east, north, south,
and west. If she used numbers for letters, she must be using
letters for numbers, I thought, so EC must mean 53. Did
that mean 53 feet? 53 paces? 53 yards? I didn't know the an-

swer, but I soon solved it by deciding that she had written everything upside down and backward, so you had to read the map opposite to how it appeared. Now I had to figure out where the directions started and ended. That's where the dots came in. They were the houses in town. Actually, they were the number of people in every house. I began with my street and tried to see whether it was on the map. It wasn't. That would have been too easy for Anna. It didn't start at her street either, or Claire's, or that of anyone else who might be obvious to me. It took me a long time to crack that part of it, but I finally determined that the map started at the first row of houses you could see from the high school library, looking south. Then it was easy.

I went out and walked off the directions on the map, and went south through town and then into the woods, not far from where we had seen Carl holding his hand over his eye. It was getting dark and I hurriedly paced off my calculations. I got close enough to see her marker. Near one of the trees in the woods, barely sticking out of the snow, was a short stick with her photograph stapled to it. It was just her head, cut out like a mask, wrinkled and wet from the snow. She had pasted pink hearts over her eyes, and across her forehead had written, "Dig here." I hadn't brought a shovel or anything to help me get through the dirt. I pushed away the snow and tried to dig at the ground with my gloved hands, but it was too hard and frozen. I put her picture in my backpack and cleared the area of snow so I could find it the next morning. When I got home, I put her picture on the wall, to take its place with all the other faces.

I couldn't sleep, thinking about what might be buried underneath that spot. It had to be something important— a key, a solution, an answer to all my questions. Maybe it was the announcement of an elaborate hoax; maybe there was a phone number, and when I called it she would answer and laugh at everyone for believing she was gone, and then she would come back. I fantasized about her return, or even better, that she would invite me to wherever she was and we would be together out of this town. I knew better, but I couldn't stop myself.

The next day I ran out first thing in the morning, before school. This time I had a shovel. I consulted the map once I got to the woods, and found the spot. I dug in the ground until I hit a metal container about a foot deep. It was a rusted tackle box. I yanked it out of the ground and opened the lid. Inside were a sealed envelope and a square package wrapped in red paper. I opened the envelope and found a cheesy Valentine's Day card inside. "What buried box of luck could you not find here? You will find me. You will be mine. Love, Anastasia." She had drawn an anatomically correct heart with a realistic arrow piercing through it. The arrow had my name on it. The map hadn't gotten to me too late; it had arrived too early. Or maybe she thought it would take me that long to figure out. In the red paper was another CD she had made for me. The front cover was a black-and-white photograph of a couple buried up to their necks on some sandy beach, straining to kiss each other. The title of the CD was "you stay dug." The back cover was a photograph of those candy hearts with phrases like

"All mine" and "For keeps." The song titles were printed over that:

1. Björk—violently happy
2. The Get Up Kids—valentine
3. My Bloody Valentine—when you sleep
4. Cab Calloway—hep cat's love song
5. Robert Johnson—from four till late
6. Matt Suggs—western zephyr
7. The Byrds—one hundred years from now
8. Jeff Buckley—i know we could be so happy baby (if we wanted to be)
9. The Cure—the walk
10. Felt—all the people i like are those that are dead
11. Elvis Costello—my funny valentine
12. Hole—softer, softest
13. The Band—whispering pines
14. Bright Eyes—a perfect sonnet
15. Kate Bush—Houdini
16. The Sisters of Mercy—valentine
17. Bob Dylan—blackjack davey
18. The Stanley Brothers—meet me by the moonlight
19. The Smiths—asleep
20. The Flatlanders—keeper of the mountain
21. The Handsome Family—don't be scared
22. The Beach Boys—be still

I almost put everything back in the hole and covered it back up. I felt cheated. It should have been more. The map

and the card and the CD had nothing to do with her leaving; they didn't answer anything. There wasn't anything
except a joke card that wasn't funny anymore. If she was
still alive I would have been happy about the map and the
card and the disc, I would be happy about the mystery and
anticipation, and she would be so happy that I had figured
everything out, but just then I hated her stupid games and
her creepy sense of humor and her music. I didn't want any
of it, or I wanted things the way they used to be, the way
they were meant to be, with her standing in the hall at
school, and I could go show her the gift she had made for
me, and tease her that I had found it a few days earlier than
she had expected. She didn't have everything figured out. I
put the stuff in my backpack and headed off to school.

m o r e   m a i l

Two days after I received the map, her obituary arrived in
the mail. There was nothing unusual about the envelope; it
was a plain white business envelope with my name and address typed across the front. There was no return address,
and the postmark date was smudged. It looked like double
digits, but it was hard to tell. It had come through Hilliker,
but that didn't tell me anything; all the mail in our area
came through Hilliker.

It was an obituary she might have written. It was an in-
furiating, frustrating, fucked-up document. It was typed,

on the kind of notebook paper Anna always wrote on. It
was filled with information I never knew about her, which
meant either that it was all lies or that I didn't know her as
well as I thought. It also had a number of glaring omis-
sions. It never mentioned that she was dead or how she
died; it merely stated that she was "gone," which could
have meant a number of things. It was another puzzle
within a puzzle, and I wondered how long the puzzles
would continue. I pored over it for more patterns and signs:

Anastasia Cayne is gone. She was born in the middle of a
thunderstorm on March 28 in Charlottesville, Virginia.
While he was driving to the hospital, her father's car
failed and he was forced to leave his wife and go for help.
He ran to the nearest house and called for an ambulance,
and when he returned to the car, his wife was holding
their new daughter. "I don't remember the rain, but
I remember the blood," Anastasia would always say
whenever her parents told the story.

She was given the name Anna Cayne, but everyone
who loved her called her Anastasia. She was the youngest
daughter to Nicholas and Alexandra Cayne. Her father
had emigrated from Russia as a teenager, and her mother
had moved from Germany when she graduated from
high school, in order to attend college in the United
States. Anastasia spoke both German and Russian as a
child. She had three older sisters, Olivia, Tatiana, and
Maria, and a younger brother, Alex, who died of a brain
hemorrhage when he was four years old. Shortly after

Alex's death, the Cayne family moved to Oyster Bay, Long Island. Anastasia's two oldest sisters, Olivia and Tatiana, became nurses with the Red Cross. Her sister Maria ran away from home on July 16, 2000, and although the Caynes hired a private investigator, Maria has not been found or heard from since. Anastasia had a small scar on her right shoulder blade where a mole had been removed, a star-shaped scar on the bottom of her left foot, and a scar behind her left ear. She also had a scar at the base of her left middle finger, from when her brother accidentally slammed a car door on her hand.

Her friends indicate that she enjoyed pranks and practical jokes, but could be demanding, stubborn, and suspicious of those around her. G_____ called her Anna.

The last sentence was a knife. Whoever wrote it knew what it would do to me. If Anna wrote it, what did it mean? Was she doubting that I loved her? "Everyone who loved her called her Anastasia. . . . G_____ called her Anna." Why would she even suggest it? But if someone else had written it, it meant nothing. What did anyone else know about us, anyway? Everything in my head was screaming, a constant, torturous metallic collision of everything I thought I knew with everything I didn't know, everything I thought to be true with every lie, everything I expected with every inconceivable exception, everything I wanted with everything I wouldn't wish on my worst enemy, everything I felt with everything I didn't want to feel.

.   .   .

Comparing the Anna Cayne described in the obituary with the one I knew, she seemed nothing more than an apparition, a haunting presence of veiled secrets, an elusive girl who had disappeared in the night fog. She had always been a ghost.

I couldn't sleep, couldn't concentrate. It was like I had suddenly been struck with ADD, how I used to feel right before football games, excited and nervous, full of adrenaline and anticipation and dread, waiting for something to happen. I would lie in bed at night, completely exhausted, trying to sleep, but I would continue to be wide awake. I would get up and pace in my room or go online and jump from site to site, not able to read even a few sentences but not able to lie still either. I called Anna's phone and listened to her voice over and over, but then I got worried that the message might somehow go away, so I recorded a version on my computer and began editing different versions, taking the words and trying to make more sentences, more things she could say to me. In the end I always returned to the original message, or just the last part. "I will get back to you."

After Anna left I was in a numbed daze, living in an aquarium where everything was murky, underwater, in slow motion. Everything inside me seemed tied down with lead weights, or was turning into lead. I had trouble breathing and seeing, and had to go about the easiest of tasks with great effort and deliberation. School was nothing more than a long ringing bell and shapes passing in front of me. I sat in class, but had no idea what anyone was saying. I did all my assignments, but barely remember doing them. I wrote a lot of things down, but little of it had to do with school. I wrote about Anna, and what had happened to her, or what might have happened. Mrs. Wyrick (English) had started a series of free-writing classes every Friday, where we spent the period writing about anything we wanted. I used one of those periods to write about the possibility of Anna's not coming back, the possibility she had been killed. I developed a list of suspects:

1. Mr. and Mrs. Cayne. They should be at the top of anyone's list. According to some research I did on the Web, only fourteen percent of all murders are committed by strangers—though that number increases significantly for victims under age eighteen. Still, the Caynes or some other acquaintance of Anna's is probably responsible, if she was murdered.

2. Bryce Druitt. He's a jerk, so he goes on the list. Actually, it's more than that. While it's true that they were close friends, after his accident I noticed a real tension between Anna and Bryce. They spoke less and less, and he seemed to avoid her. I'm not sure that they even liked each other anymore. Sometimes I thought that if it weren't for the facts that they dressed a certain way and that there were so few of their clique around, they

wouldn't ever have anything to do with each other. There was never any reason for me to think that Bryce would want to hurt Anna, but he certainly had the ability.

3. A stranger. This seems the least plausible. For one thing, there aren't any strangers in town, and what are the odds that one would have been passing by the Caynes' house, and how would the stranger have drawn her out of the house? I suppose the stranger could have come across Anna by the river, but it seems unlikely. It does raise the question of what she was doing after I left her. Did she go to the river by herself, as she often did, or was it something else?

4. Anna Cayne. Suicide. But if she wanted to kill herself, she could have picked a hundred better ways to accomplish it.

5. Nobody. She wasn't murdered at all. Maybe it was an accident. Maybe she was trying to save someone from drowning and she was reaching for the person and choked on the icy water and drowned. Maybe she was reaching for something else; maybe she had thrown her notebooks into the river and then suddenly wanted to retrieve them. Maybe she was trying to see how long she could last in the frigid water, holding her breath and steeling her body, pushing herself like Houdini. Maybe she was testing death and failed the test.

6. Maybe it was a setup. There was no body falling or slipping through a hole in the ice. She staged the scene

and escaped her life. She could be anywhere, someplace better.

This didn't help; it only made me more anxious and hy-
per. I couldn't sit still, I couldn't read, listen to music, watch
TV. I couldn't sleep. I would try to do all of those things,
but would end up doing them for only five minutes. I felt
horrible and looked worse. My eyes were fiery, glassy. My
skin was waxen, worse, sweaty wax. And my face was completely broken out. I couldn't keep my hands away from the
line of zits that had spread across my chin. I scratched and
poked them without thinking. "Am I going to have to tie
your hands behind your back?" my mom asked me at dinner. I wouldn't have minded.

By the third day without sleep I was desperate. I asked
Carl to sell me something. "Never," he said. He wanted to
help, but he told me to go to a doctor. "I don't need a doctor," I said. "I just need some sleep." Finally, on the fifth
day, he gave me a single pill, a capsule in a plastic sandwich
bag. "Take this about half an hour before you go to bed," he
told me. I didn't care if I became a burnout, addicted to
pills and whatever else. I didn't care if I became dependent
on Carl and the drugs he stole or bought and sold. I just
wanted some relief. I didn't even hesitate; I took the pill.

I slept most of the night, but didn't feel any better in the
morning. "I slept, for a while anyway," I told him the next
day. "What was that pill?"

"Sugar," he said. "It's my best seller. The mind just be-
lieves it's a drug, because that's what you want. People buy

the drug they want, but it's not what I sell them. Most people never notice the difference. I'm out of the drug business, for the most part. I'm in the mind management business."

"So why'd you tell me?"

"To prove to you that you don't need it. You're going to get through this. You're going to be all right."

"What do you know about it all? What are people saying about Anna?"

"No one knows anything," he said. "It's all rumors, you know that. There's always been rumors. Just remember that you know Anastasia better than anyone else. Don't forget that. You know her, they don't."

valentine's day

It was about a week since Anna's disappearance; I had dreaded every day since then, and I especially dreaded this day. Both my mother and my father told me to stay home from school, but that might have been worse. I needed the distraction. For somebody used to being ignored, I was not prepared to be ignored in the way it was happening now. I was a car wreck on the side of the road; when people saw me they slowed and quietly surveyed me and then sped up again. They didn't say anything, they looked and moved on. They just wanted to see how bad the damage was. And on Valentine's Day it was even worse. People were obvious in their avoidance of me, averting their stares in jerks of the head as I walked down the hall. When I got to my locker, just a few minutes before class, it was already filled with cards.

I had never liked the holiday much, had never had a reason to like it. I gave out few cards and received even fewer, but this year was different. I collected the white hill of envelopes at the bottom of the locker (people had stuck them through the vents in the top) and stacked them on the shelf to open later. I was almost afraid of what they might say. But when I opened them later in my room, almost all of them were sympathetic, wishing me well and hoping the best for me. I separated them into stacks. There was the "Hang in there" stack and the "Don't give up hope" stack, which were about equal in number. These phrases appeared so often that the words lost all meaning and I mindlessly shut the cards and put them in their respective pile once I read them. Most of the cards started, "I don't know you very well, but . . ." and proceeded to express sincere sympathy and good wishes. Some of them related stories about people who had disappeared for months, had been kidnapped or had run off, and then came back safe and sound. I should have been touched by the fact that so many people had taken time to drop a card in my locker, but I was also reminded that it would end there, all the emotion and concern would stay in the card, no one would approach me in the halls, hardly anyone who had written "I don't know you very well" would make an attempt to change that.

I almost preferred the handful of asshole cards, from

people honest enough to admit that they took pleasure in Anna's absence. Maybe they didn't want her dead, but they were happy that she was out of their lives and happy that I was alone, that we both had suffered. A few cards even said it was my own fault, and one quoted the Bible and said that I would one day join Anna in hell. They were honest enough, but only to a point—they were all unsigned.

There was another unsigned card, handmade—a heart cut out of black construction paper, decorated with tiny white flowers in rows and a white clock face in the middle, without hands but with the numbers in white ink. In the middle of the clock face were the words "Love is just an excuse to get hurt. And to hurt." In the upper right corner of the card was an old three-cent stamp with a bust of Abe Lincoln. You could make out the cancellation across it: "Water is precious, use it wisely." In the narrowing bottom of the heart were the letters NYCS, written in white ink. Somebody had gone to a lot of trouble to make this card, and it seemed like something Anna would have done. Or maybe it was Claire, but there already was a card from her. She had written a biblical passage I had seen before: "And I gave my heart to know wisdom, and to know madness and folly; I perceived that this also is vexation of the spirit." I couldn't place the quotation, even though it should have been familiar, and put these two cards in their own pile.

There was a card from Melissa. "I am truly sorry for everything that has happened," she wrote sympathetically. "I can only imagine what you are going through. If you

need anything, please let me know if I can help. I mean it."
It was nice, but the handwriting reminded me of the writing on another card. One of the asshole cards. I spent a long time comparing the two, looking for any exact matches in the way the letters were formed or slanted across the page. Some things were similar, but I concluded that I was just being paranoid. I desperately wanted to find out who had written the asshole cards, and kill them. I wanted to take the cards to the principal or the police and have those responsible kicked out of school or arrested. I wished I hadn't received any cards. I wanted to leave town. Instead, I went down to the river.

Someone had made a huge, ragged heart in the ice. It must have been twenty feet from the top to the narrow tip. Anna's name and mine had been written in the middle, the letters scraped with feet or a shovel. I didn't know whether it was meant as a memorial or a mocking insult. It didn't matter.

When I got home my dinner was waiting on the stove. I assumed that my father was in his den and that my mother was watching TV or already asleep. But they both joined me in the kitchen before I even had a chance to get my coat off. My mother prepared me a plate, and I sat down to eat. "When you finish up there, why don't you come see me in the den," my father said.

When I went in, he was sitting in one of the large leather armchairs, reading the paper. He wore a pair of those half-glasses you can buy in drugstores, and when he saw me he pulled them from his face and put them between the cushion and the arm of the chair. He stood and motioned me to sit in the other chair. "You want something to drink?" he asked as he poured himself a scotch. His words passed between us like clouds, changing shape and meaning, and by the time I realized that he was actually offering me alcohol I had already said no. He put the bottle of scotch back on the bar in the corner and said, "I won't ask again. Soda?"

The room itself was a foreign country. On the wall were photographs of people I had never met and did not recognize, some of them standing with my father on this or that golf course, their arms around each other as they smiled for the camera. On the shelves, where most of the books were about golf or accounting, I tried to see if there were any that Anna had in her room, or that she might have liked, but I could barely concentrate. I noticed the door on one wall, a door that led to the front of the house. I had never noticed it before. I was in my own house, where I had spent my entire life, and I didn't know the place. I wanted to leave; I wanted to go someplace that I knew, someplace safe. But I sat quietly, watching my father move around the room.

He went over to a console and opened the front doors to expose a big TV and stereo. He popped a video into the VCR and said, "You might like this."

It was a series of instructional golf films made with Bobby Jones in the early 1930s. I have no idea why my father thought I would be interested in watching them, but he was mesmerized. He blurted out things as we watched. "That's James Cagney." "That's the Riviera." "You couldn't get away with that now." "He's completely inside the ball." I didn't know what to do with most of the information he tossed at me, but I started to get into it.

Bobby Jones was kind of a stiff—you could see him struggling to read the cue cards in some of the scenes—but his golf swing was beautiful to watch. I don't even like golf, not in the least, but I began talking to my father about Bobby Jones.

"Completely self-taught," my father said. "Never turned pro. He was a lawyer, a practicing lawyer, and he could golf like that. Look at him. It's a completely natural swing. No one could play like that. You couldn't teach somebody to play like that, you wouldn't want to, but it worked for him. He was maybe the greatest golfer of all time, and he died a gruesome, painful death. Some rare disease that destroyed his central nervous system."

My father was talking more to himself than to me. He drifted off into silence and we both watched the black-and-white images of Bobby Jones as he demonstrated his technique on how to get out of a sand trap. There was no editing, no second takes, just one long shot of him placing the ball near the pin time after time. There was something calming about watching him controlling the ball so easily in his shirt and tie. I sank back into the chair and felt my body relax for the first time in days. I could have gone to sleep. I looked over at my father, who had turned his head away from me slightly. He was crying. I wanted to say something, but I sat there and in a few minutes I was fast asleep.

On Friday there was a dance at school. I had no interest in going, but Carl talked me into it. "What are you going to do," he said, "sit around at home by yourself and mope? You can do that any night." His mother would drive us, he said.

She sat in the car and honked the horn when they arrived. Carl came and knocked on the door and said hello to my parents. They talked for a few minutes while Carl's mom kept honking the horn.

The gym was decorated with red and white hearts and streamers. At least the place was dark so you couldn't see how horrible everything really looked. There was a dj at one end of the basketball court, a concession stand at the other. In between, everyone was dancing. I had no intention of doing that.

Carl, of course, had his own reasons for going. A dance was always good business. But that night there were more chaperones than usual. Mrs. Crenshaw, who taught algebra, was stationed by one of the exits, where she kept track of who was leaving, or trying to leave. Carl discovered that you had to have a good reason to leave. "I thought she was going to follow me," he said. "Going out to get some air" proved to be an excuse that she wasn't buying. Mr. Davies, the history teacher, was stationed near the boys' bathroom, making it impossible for Carl to conduct his transactions there. And

Mr. Devon and Mrs. Wyrick wandered around the gym, along with Mr. Vorhees, the principal. Suddenly Carl's job was more difficult. "This has to be your fault," he told me.

"Suicide watch?" I said. "Or Columbine?"

"Either. Just don't make any sudden moves." He wandered off among the crowd, talking to almost everyone he passed. He was like a politician, shaking hands and nodding, smiling at everyone. I could almost hear him saying, "I'm counting on your vote."

Mr. Devon came over by me. "It's good to see you."

"Thanks."

"I think Mrs. Crenshaw is going to ask you for a dance," he said. Mrs. Crenshaw was about ninety years old.

"Only slow dances," I said.

"I'll be sure to tell her."

"Don't make me spend the whole night hiding under the bleachers, Mr. Devon." He nodded and we were silent for a while.

"How's your hand?"

"Good," I said. "Like brand-new."

"That's great. I expect to see you ready for baseball this spring, then."

"Sure," I said.

Mr. Devon stood there a few minutes more, then excused himself. "If you need anything," he said, "anything at all, just ask me. All right?"

"Thanks, Mr. Devon." He reached out and patted the back of my head with his hand. I watched him walk toward one of the exit doors and stop and talk to Carl. They walked past Mrs. Crenshaw and went outside. As I waited for them to come back, I saw Claire come through the doorway.

"I called your house and they said you'd come here," she said.

"I hadn't planned on coming, but Carl talked me into it. I'm sorry I didn't call." Actually, it hadn't occurred to me. I thought that she would be with the rest of her friends. I didn't really think that my relationship with her would continue. "Is anyone else coming?"

"I don't know," she said. "We didn't talk about it. I was like you—I hadn't planned on showing up."

Carl came back, and the three of us went and got some soda and stood around and watched people dance. Almost everyone was on the dance floor, and almost all the girls tried to get Carl to join them. He politely declined.

A slow song started and the dance floor emptied except for couples. Claire turned to me and said, "Come on." She led me onto the basketball court and leaned into me, and we swayed in a little circle.

It was the first physical contact I'd had with anyone since the night before Anna's disappearance, and it caused a sudden rush of feelings. I was nervous and embarrassed. I thought people might be staring at us, but I didn't want it to end. It was relief; I knew things were going to get better. We continued to move with our small steps, circling around each other. My mind drifted there in the dark, a pleasant, drunk dream, with the soft lights swirling across the ceiling, the other couples shadows swaying in time with the music. I didn't even look at Claire, I just tried to imagine that it was Anna, that she and I were dancing together. We had never danced together. Then I realized that Claire was crying. She wasn't making any noise, but I could feel her tremble, and feel her tears dropping on the back of my shirt and soaking through to my skin. She lifted her face to mine and I felt the tears on her cheeks. "I'm sorry," she said.

"It's all right." I held her tighter, and before I knew it I had started to cry. We kept swaying to the music, holding each other and weeping. When the song was over, she hurried to the restroom, and I tried to find Carl.

"What were you guys doing out there?" he said.

"What did it look like?"

"It looked intense."

"She just started crying, and that got me started. Did everybody notice?"

"I don't think they thought you were crying," he said.

"That's fucked up."

"It's a hard time for everybody," he said.

Claire came back. "Did I make a spectacle of myself?"

"Carl seems to think that we're the talk of the night."

"I didn't say that."

"What did you say?"

"It's too goddamn dark in here," he said. "Who knows what's going on?"

"You're making less and less sense," I said.

"I'm having a bad night. This was a bad idea. Why did you drag me here, anyway?" He wandered off.

"I'm really sorry," Claire said.

"There's nothing to be sorry about."

"Is everybody really talking?"

"I don't know. It doesn't matter. There's nothing we can do about it. You could do nothing, and people would still talk. This was a bad idea. I'm going home." I went to the coat check and got my coat and started to leave. Mr. Devon caught up with me.

"Mrs. Crenshaw's going to be really disappointed," he said.

"Tell her maybe next year."

"Hey," he said, "I'm going into the city tomorrow for an art exhibition. I was wondering if you wanted to go with me."

"Sure."

"You can bring someone if you like. Maybe Claire would like to come?"

"Yeah, maybe. I'll talk to her about it."

"Great. I'll be by about ten to pick you up."

a step away from them

The next morning Mr. Devon tapped the horn on his pickup and waited for me. It was freezing cold outside, and maybe colder in the truck. I could see my breath forming clouds that drifted away from my mouth and nose. "I think there's some warm air coming out," Mr. Devon said, waving a gloved hand in front of the air vents. It felt like he had the air conditioning on. I wasn't prepared for this. I had on a pair of khakis and a black turtleneck; and not even my warmest coat. I was shivering and tried to scrunch my head down into the warmth of my scarf.

"Is anyone else coming?"

"Just us," I said.

"That's too bad. At least it would be warmer. Instead, you'll have to try this trick. Do a math problem in your head, you won't feel as cold."

"Are you serious?"

"It's true. The area of your brain that registers cold is also responsible for solving mathematical problems. So if you give it a math problem to work on, it'll get distracted from the cold problem."

I tried it. I stopped shivering, but I was still cold. Mr. Devon looked over at me and laughed. "Don't worry," he said. "We'll take the train. My treat."

Mr. Devon sat across from me on the train. He was wearing brown corduroys and a heavy blue denim shirt. His black leather jacket was unzipped and a navy blazer edged from under it. A camera hung around his neck. He reached into his backpack and pulled out a thermos. "Do you drink coffee?"

I nodded and he poured me a cup. I took off my gloves to get the warmth from the plastic cup. "I don't think I'm ever going to be warm again," I said.

"Just wait until the ride home," he said. "We might have to set the dashboard on fire."

I had a book, a biography of Houdini that Anna had given me, and my CD player in my backpack, but Mr. Devon talked most of the trip.

"What did I tell you about the show?" he said.

"Not much."

"Well, did I tell you that some of my work is in it?"

"No," I said.

"Nothing to get excited about, but I've got a few pieces. It's a group of us who have known each other for a while, and we periodically rent a space and exhibit some work and try to sell it. There's some good stuff there, some stuff you will like. Not mine, I mean some of the others'. There's also a theme to this show, which I thought you might get a kick out of. It's called *A Step Away from Them*, and every piece has to be based on or influenced by another work."

"What works did you use?"

"You'll have to figure that out for yourself," he said. "I just hope that you like it. I hope it's not a waste of a Saturday for you."

"I didn't have anything planned."

"I imagine it's been tough."

"It's been tough," I said.

"Have they been good about getting you information?"

"I guess," I said. "I'm not so sure there is any information."

"I haven't heard anything," Mr. Devon said. "Everybody's hoping for the best, though." I nodded. "I'm not going to say that I know exactly what you're going through, but I know a little about it. I lost a girlfriend myself."

"How was that?"

"A fire," he said. "She fell asleep on the couch, with a lit cigarette in her hand. I was asleep upstairs." He lifted his left foot onto the seat and rolled his pants leg to his knee. A pinkish-white scar ran up the front of his leg, from below his sock to above his knee. "It's sort of how I came to teach here. After it happened I just wanted to get away for a while." He pushed his pants leg back down to his boot and put his foot back on the floor.

"I'm sorry about that, Mr. Devon. I didn't know."

"Not too many people do. It's not something I want too many people to know about, if you know what I mean. Anyway, as I said, that was part of the reason that I came here, to try and . . . not forget—that isn't the right word—but move on a little, put some distance between us."

I nodded and we lapsed into silence.

We walked out of the train station and into the bright, cold noon light. We made our way to the exhibition space. I guess I expected the place to be a museum, with clean white walls and guards standing around watching to make sure you didn't touch anything. I expected the quiet and sterility you would find in a hospital. This was nothing like that. As you walked in off the street, there was one large room with a couple of old couches haphazardly placed near the center. A short hallway on the left led to a room that was being used as a theater—a few rows of folding chairs, and even a few armchairs, which looked as if they had been saved from the dump. A staircase in a corner of the main room led down to another, smaller room. We put our coats in an office near the staircase. There were about twenty people in the studio when we arrived; they were sitting on the couches or standing, smoking and drinking coffee or beer.

Mr. Devon introduced me to the five other artists who were exhibiting. They were all younger than he, guys just out of college, and they all looked deliberately unkempt. Their clothes had holes, and one guy had duct tape holding his worn-out army boots together. A few of them had scraggly goatees, and all of them had filthy hands, stained with paint and tobacco and who knows what else. They seemed nice enough, but after meeting them I hoped that I wouldn't have to talk to them again, at least not about their art.

Most of it looked worse than the stuff we did in Mr. Devon's class, and only a few pieces were better than the things Anna had sent to me. A few I liked, though. There was a smashed boat in the middle of the room, between the two couches. Its splintered planks stuck up from the floor like a broken rib cage, and each board was painted with a different scene, like a marauding band of Indians or the starry night sky, or with lines from a poem. The piece was called *Le Bateau Ivre*. "It means 'The Drunken Boat,'" Mr. Devon told me. "That's a poem by Rimbaud. Do you know Rimbaud?"

"I know who he is," I said, "but I don't know that poem."

"Well, there it is," Mr. Devon said, nodding at the wreck on the floor.

The rest of the exhibit wasn't really worth commenting on, except for his stuff, which was the best in the room. He had a series of black-and-white photographs, disturbing pictures of bare, burned backs and shoulders and arms. They were obviously women in the photographs, except one that showed a naked couple embracing, just their shoulders and arms, blistered and scarred. I didn't say anything. Mr. Devon explained that the photographs referred to a movie, *Hiroshima Mon Amour.*

"I haven't seen it," I said.

"You will," he said. "In college, probably."

Next to the photographs was a collage. It included a photograph of him in the middle of pictures of girls from school, stretching and arching their backs during gym. The expressions on their faces made them look as if they were in pain, and the collage was put together so that Mr. Devon, his arms folded across his chest and a stern smile on his face, appeared to be torturing them, or at least responsible for their torment and getting some satisfaction from it.

"Anna would have liked these," I said.

"They cheer up the place, don't they?"

"I really like this, though," I said. The last piece of Mr. Devon's was an aquarium with a wineglass, a pipe, old specimen jars, balls of cork, and other objects suspended in a clear, solid solution. Scraps of newspaper, maps, and postcards floated on the surface. It was called *Lycidas.*

"I may not try to sell that piece after all," he said. "I might be too attached to let it go."

. . .

Mr. Devon said that he needed to hang out in the place for a while, so he suggested that I wander around outside. I had intended to do just that. First, though, I wanted to watch the film that was running in the theater, so I waited until the next showing. It was called *Window Fan Baby Moving*, and was the view of a baby from its swing. The camera moved back and forth in slow motion, showing a fan in a window, and through the blades of the fan the leafy branches of a tree brushing against the window in the breeze. Everything was blurry, patches of colors moving slowly across the screen. I was sitting in one of the armchairs, and a few minutes into the movie I fell asleep.

When I woke up, I was disoriented, not immediately sure of where I was or what time it was. The baby was still swinging, the blades of the fan barely turning, the branches of the tree sweeping across the screen. I didn't know whether it was the same showing of the movie, or whether another one had started. I got up and left the theater. As I entered the main room I saw Mr. Devon near the stairway, leaning against the wall and intently holding a woman's hand near his chest, writing something on her palm. At first I thought it was Claire—she had the same straight dark hair, the same long, black overcoat—but when she turned her face away from Mr. Devon and started to laugh, I could see that it wasn't Claire. She was about the same age, though, maybe a little older.

I tried to change direction and walk away from them, but it was too late. Mr. Devon saw me and immediately started walking toward me. "Back already?" he asked.

"I never left," I said. "I fell asleep watching the movie."

"It does that to everybody." He looked at his watch. "Are you hungry? Let's go get something to eat." He got our coats and backpacks, and we walked a few blocks to a bar.

Mr. Devon didn't seem to give a second thought to taking me in, and I didn't say anything. It was my first time in a bar. It was disappointing. The place was gloomy, with a few groups littering the tables, and a row of men at the long wooden bar, hunched over their drinks and watching basketball on televisions crammed into the corners. We sat at a booth near the back, and Mr. Devon positioned himself so he could look out the front window at the street.

"Do you mind if I order a beer?" I asked.

"If they'll serve it, you can drink it. Just know that I won't take you home drunk and I won't take you home sick."

We each ate a hamburger and an order of fries, and I had two beers. Mr. Devon had five or six vodka and tonics. We barely made the train.

It was dark as the train pulled away from the city. The train car was filled with an antiseptic white light. I wished that I could turn it out and peer into the night outside. The seat had a hospital-bed smell, bleach hiding urine. The whole train was like a rolling hospital, quiet and sterile. Mr. Devon sat across from me again; he seemed nervous, agitated. He folded and unfolded his arms and shuffled his feet, unsuccessfully trying to get comfortable. His bottom lip jutted out in an angry pout, and he looked over at me and noticed me watching him.

"Did you have a good day for yourself?"

"I did," I said. "Thanks again for bringing me."

"What was your favorite thing?"

"I thought your stuff was the best by far. I especially liked the aquarium piece." We'd had this same conversation in the bar.

"It's called *Lycidas*," he said. "What did you think of the photographs?"

"Unsettling," I said. "I'm going to have to check out that movie you told me about."

He nodded quickly. "Let me tell you something I haven't told very many people. I told you about my girlfriend and the fire. But what I didn't tell you was that the official report didn't say the fire was an accident."

"I don't understand."

"I know you don't," Mr. Devon said. "That's why I'm telling you this. There was some evidence that the fire wasn't started by her falling asleep with a cigarette on the couch, but was set deliberately, with a match. Seems like a hard way to go about it, doesn't it, especially with me asleep upstairs?"

"Does that make sense to you, that she would do that?"

"You never know what people are really thinking," he said. "I try to tell myself that it doesn't matter, it doesn't make any difference. I'm not giving you advice, but it's not bad advice either."

"Do you think there's a heaven and all that stuff?"

"I don't think I'm the person to ask about that," he said. "But I'll tell you that I don't think this is the end of the story. I think that people, especially people who are important to you, don't ever leave. And I don't mean that as just memories, I mean those people stay with you in a physical sense. You might think I'm crazy, but there's science behind what I'm saying. There's a physical law that says that energy cannot be created or destroyed. It only changes form. It's is a biological fact, a fact that the human body contains energy. We're little more than walking test tubes of chemicals acting and reacting with each other, firing off energy inside us. And once you're dead, well, the physical body might be gone, but your energy has to go somewhere. It has to. It can't be destroyed, so where does it go?

"Now, this is where we get a step away from the science, but just a step." He was locked in on me; his eyes never left mine as he talked, in a measured, soft voice. It was hypnotic. "Now, follow me," he said. "There are waves. There are frequencies. Light and sound exist along a spectrum, with only a small percentage of the light and sound within ranges we can see and hear. We have to use special instruments to see light or hear sounds out of those ranges. The periodic table is another spectrum, with elements arranged in a certain order, from hydrogen, with a single proton, to lawrencium, with one hundred and three protons. At that end of the spectrum, the one with lots of protons, are elements that could not be seen until recently, and some of those elements can only be observed for a very short time under laboratory conditions. There are also atomic particles we know exist today that they couldn't see twenty years ago, and that they never imagined existed a hundred years ago.

"All of these things are true. There are aspects of our fundamental universe that we can experience for only very brief periods of time, under very special circumstances, or see with special instruments. No one would deny it. So why can't this be true for ourselves? Why can't our energy simply change to a different frequency, a different wave along the spectrum? Why can't we continue to exist in a space in the physical world that can't yet be seen or measured, or that can only be experienced in brief moments and under special circumstances, but is there all the time? If you look at an airplane propeller when the engine is off, you can see the blades of the propeller perfectly fine, but when the engines turn on, the propeller disappears. There are plenty of things that exist in this world that we can't see, that we can't hear. There are entire worlds around us that we never encounter. Why is it so hard to believe that this could be true for ourselves?

"Does any of this make sense to you?"

"A little," I said.

"Well, it barely makes sense to me. Was I ranting?"

"A little."

"I'll stop, then," he said, and folded his arms across his chest and closed his eyes. He leaned back in his seat, and before long his head was rolling back and forth with the motion of the train. I watched his body sag and slack into sleep. I imagined his girlfriend sitting on the couch, falling asleep the same way, with a cigarette in her hand. I couldn't see how you could fall asleep with a burning match in your hand. There wasn't enough time, and it would burn you

awake, I thought. If she had done it on purpose, dropped
the match on the couch with Mr. Devon asleep upstairs, it
seemed like a difficult, painful way to kill yourself.

I used to think about the different ways I could do it: as-
phyxiation, gunshot, overdose, poison, hanging, jumping
from a tall building (I'd probably have to get to Hilliker for
that), cutting my wrists, drowning. There were a lot of easier ways than fire. I thought that people might think differently about me after I had killed myself, that they would
wish they'd been nicer to me. And then I would think that
if I killed myself they would be glad they hadn't been
friends with me; after all, who wants to be friends with
somebody who's going to kill himself? They wouldn't feel
sorry for me at all; they would make fun of me and even
humiliate me after I was gone. I hadn't thought about it for
a long time, since before Anna, except for once in January,
when she brought it up.

"Do you think it's a sin to kill yourself?" she said.

"You're the one with the Bible in your room," I said.
"You tell me."

"I don't think the Bible says anything about it."

"How about 'Thou shalt not kill'?"

"But then look at all the killing in the Bible. And a lot of
it God has something to do with. He's killing people all the
time. He even kills his own son."

I started to say something, but she cut me off.

"And if you want to get technical, while you could claim
that God murdered his son, you could also say that Jesus
committed suicide."

"Explain that to me."

"Well, Jesus knew what was going to happen to him, and he let it happen. He could have stopped Judas, or simply gone away, or done something. This is a guy who performed miracles, right? He walked on water, turned water into wine, fed the multitudes. But he did nothing. He knew he was going to be killed and he let them kill him. It's not that different from a guy who walks into traffic or lies down on the railroad tracks."

"I think you could say that being a martyr is not the same as lying down on the tracks. It's more like being a soldier in combat, on a mission."

"I think they call those 'suicide missions,'" she said. "That's the name. You can call it being a martyr, but it's just a different name for the same thing. He ended his life, instead of allowing life to take its natural course."

"But that was his natural course," I said. "That was his whole reason for being born." I stopped. She was looking at me, her blue eyes shining happily in the warm light of the basement, encouraging me, getting a kick out of what I was saying. "This is why you're never supposed to discuss religion with anyone," I said. "You always end up splitting hairs or getting into issues that can never be resolved, like angels-on-the-heads-of-pins-type stuff. You wouldn't think they would make it so complicated, with so many loopholes and contradictions."

"It's not very clear, is it? The Bible is full of contradictions and ambiguities and mysteries. That's why I like it. That's probably why it's still around and still read at all.

People want to try and figure it out, and there's room for everyone to interpret it the way they see fit. If it was all crystal clear, if it all made sense all the time, nobody would care. It would be boring."

She was ready to move on, but we hadn't even started.

"Okay, then," I said. "For the sake of the discussion, if suicide is not a sin, then what?"

"Then what do you do?" she said.

"What do I do? I don't do anything."

"Why not? You don't think this is a horrible world with horrible events and horrible people?"

"I guess. I don't really know, though. I haven't seen any of the world."

"But you know about it. Don't weasel out of it. You know what goes on in the world. Is it a place you would want to bring a child into?"

"No. Absolutely not."

"Well, you're a child. So what are you doing here?"

"If I had my choice, I guess I wouldn't have been born, but now that I'm here, I might as well see how it all turns out."

"So you wouldn't take the easy way out?"

"Not this second. No. I mean, it's something you can do anytime, so why not wait?"

"Then you'll always be waiting."

"Maybe," I said.

"You're so practical," she said. "It's what I like about you. Really."

"Your turn," I said.

"My turn?"

"Yeah. What would you do?"

"I don't know. I honestly don't. Sometimes I think I could end it all, but it takes a lot of strength, or courage, because you don't know what's going to happen. Frank O'Hara said that he wished he had the strength to kill himself, but if he had that kind of strength he probably wouldn't need to."

"What happened to him?"

"He was run over by a dune buggy on the beach at Fire Island. I wonder, if he had known he was going to die young anyway, whether that would have changed anything."

"Like what?"

"If you knew a car was going to run you over, would you end your life yourself, on your own terms, or wait for the car?"

"I'm not sure it matters."

"I'm not sure either," she said. "I guess that's why you don't know. Unless you have cancer or some other terminal illness, it's a mystery. So you might as well stick around to see how it turns out, instead of jumping to the last page and spoiling it."

That's the part I sift through. Those are the words I roll over and try to examine again and again. Like so much of what Anna said, or what I remember, there are a number of perspectives and aspects. She was rarely definite. Things were never black and white. She was opinionated about everything, but she could also argue both sides of almost any subject with seemingly equal conviction. "Convince me," she would say. I couldn't even convince myself.

She was a mystery. Did she want it spoiled?

. . .

Mr. Devon's head jerked forward and he looked at me, his eyes wide open. "Do you think she'll call me?"

"Who?"

"That girl," he said. He rubbed his palms up and down his face and looked around the train. "I mean about my photographs."

"I don't know," I said. "Did you take any pictures today?"

He reached down and held his camera as if noticing it for the first time. "No," he said. "I wear it to try and re-member to take more pictures, but I never seem to take them." He slipped the strap over his head and handed the camera to me. "Here," he said, "take my picture." I held it to my eye and he suddenly shouted, "No." I still had it to my eye when he rose unsteadily from his seat and grabbed it from me. "I said no."

He sat back down and held the camera to his own eye and took my picture. There was no flash. "That should be all right," he said. "I think it's bright enough in here." He then carefully placed the strap over his head and let the camera again rest in front of him. "I should have had you be the team photographer this year. That was dumb of me. And next year you'll be playing. You will be playing, right?"

"I don't know," I said. "Maybe I could help the team more taking pictures."

"We'll see. A year can make a big difference." He leaned his head back against the seat, and in a few minutes his mouth slackened and dropped open.

Mr. Devon didn't awaken until we were pulling into the station. He was back to his old self. We walked out to his truck. "Let's hope it starts," he said. It started all right, but the heat still didn't work. We both shivered as he drove, laughing at the sound of our teeth chattering and the white clouds of breath filling the cab. "If you have a match, use it," he told me. "Light something on fire, anything—a book, the seat, my coat, anything. Have you ever been this cold?"

"Maybe you should try math," I said. He didn't seem to think that was funny. We drove the rest of the way to my house in silence.

"It probably wasn't worth it, was it?" Mr. Devon said.

"No, it was. I had a good time. Thanks for inviting me and everything."

"I thought there would be some other people from school there. People you'd know. I guess it's a long ways to go."

"It's really not that far," I said.

"The exhibit's going on for another week."

"I'll spread the word," I said.

"Just leave out the part about the bar," he said. "It was a good time, though, right?"

"It was."

That night I couldn't sleep. I turned on the shortwave for the first time since Anna had been gone, and listened to the same strange voices sending the same incomprehensible messages to someone or no one that Anna and I used to listen to. When a broadcast would end or fade, I would move up or down to another frequency, just killing time.

I stumbled across a weak broadcast of a woman's voice reciting a long list of numbers. The voice was almost buried in static, sounding distant and faint, but I recognized it. She might as well have been shouting in my ear. It was Anna's voice. It sounded just like her. I sat up in bed and moved the radio around, holding it to one side, over my head, out in front of me, trying to get better reception, a clearer signal. It improved only slightly. I could make out only some of the numbers. "One, nineteen . . . nineteen, fourteen, fifteen, twenty-three." And then it was done. There was nothing more, only static. It was about twenty minutes after eleven. I frantically got out of bed and turned on the light. I wrote down the time and the frequency and the numbers I could remember. I didn't even know whether I had gotten the order right, but I scribbled everything down as fast as I could, as close as I could remember.

The next day I received an e-mail identifying the frequency I had listened to the night before and "2310 est." It was from a Yahoo! account. I sent a reply, "Who are you? What are you trying to tell me?" but received nothing in return.

I started listening that night at nine, but there was nothing on the radio at that frequency except static. At eleven-ten, I heard the same person, sounding just like Anna, reciting the following message: "Count. Nineteen, fifteen, thirteen, five, twenty, eight, nine, fourteen, seven." Pause. "One, nineteen." Pause. "Nineteen, nine, thirteen, sixteen, twelve, five." Pause. "One, nineteen." Pause. "Nineteen, fourteen, fifteen, twenty-three." The message repeated a few times and then stopped.

An e-mail from the same Yahoo! account was in my mailbox the next day. "What does it mean?"

"That's what I want to know," I replied. "Who is sending this?"

I listened to the same numbers the next two nights, and became even more certain that it was Anna's voice. The broadcasts were exactly the same, as if they were a recording. I received no other e-mails.

I began to think less about the broadcasts and more about the numbers. What did they mean? I wrote them down on a piece of paper and studied them. Nothing. I studied them again. Nothing. Then I wrote them down in five groups, separating the numbers where there were pauses in the broadcast. The first group contained nine numbers, the second two, the third six, the fourth two, and the final group had four numbers. The second and fourth groups were identical, one and nineteen. Nineteen was in every group. What did nineteen mean? What did it represent? I looked at the numbers again, and then at my transcript of the broadcast. It had started with the word "count." I wrote the alphabet on a separate piece of paper and put a numeral 1 under A, 2 under B, and so on. The nineteenth letter was S. The second and fourth groups spelled "as." The rest came easily. The numbers worked out. "Something as simple as snow," was the message. Anna had sent the code.

I had to find out where the broadcast was coming from.

I went online and researched how to track down a short-wave broadcast but there wasn't much information, and what I could find was too technical for me. I needed help—the only person I could think of to ask for help was Mr. Cayne. I didn't want to, but I didn't have another option. I called him and asked if I could come over for help with a problem.

"I've been listening to a strange message on the short-wave," I told him when I went over. "This might seem crazy, but it sounds like Anna."

"What's the message?"

"A string of numbers."

"Anastasia saying a string of numbers?"

"I know it doesn't make sense," I said. "But it sounds like Anna. I mean, I'm almost positive it's her. I want you to help me find out where the broadcast is coming from."

He looked at me straight in the eye. It always frightened me a little when he did this, looked at me dead-on with those bald eyes of his. "What do you think the numbers mean?"

"I don't know. But if we can find out where the message is coming from and who is broadcasting it, we might be able to figure it out."

"I don't think that will help."

"How can you say that?"

He was silent for a long moment, then said, "Because I've been broadcasting that message."

"You?"

"Yes. I was hoping that someone could help me figure it

out. I found it on Anastasia's computer. She had recorded it a few days before she . . . before she left," he said. "I listened to it and thought I could get some help with it."

"So you sent the e-mails too?"

"I sent it to all her friends. Everyone on her contacts list, everyone I could think of, everyone she might have known. I thought people might help more readily if they didn't know that it was me behind it."

"Did anyone help?"

"No. I have to find out what it means."

"I know what it means," I said.

"You said you didn't."

"I know. But I think I do. The message was for me."

"What is it?"

"I can't tell you, Mr. Cayne."

"You have to."

"I can't. It wasn't really a message. It's just the beginning, a signal. It was a phrase we agreed on to start a message, a secret that only the two of us would know. In case we ever got separated. I can't tell anyone what it means."

"What do you mean, in case you ever got separated?"

I told him about how Anna wanted to make the code, the way Houdini had done with his wife. "It was just a contingency," I said, "but then there's this." I handed him Anna's obituary, the one I had received in the mail. He read it and then read it again. "Did you write this?" he said.

"Someone sent it to me."

"Who?"

"I don't know. I thought maybe Anna."

"No," he said, very sharply. "She didn't send this."

"How can you be sure?"

He studied me for a moment, then replied carefully. "There are things in here that Anna wouldn't know."

"What things?" Mr. Cayne didn't answer; he just looked at the paper. "Did you have another daughter who ran away?" I said.

"One has nothing to do with the other," he said.

"I thought she was an only child."

"Is that what she told you?"

"I thought so, but now I'm not so sure. What else is true in there?"

He handed the sheet of paper back to me. "This won't help anyone. You should just forget about it."

"Maybe we should take it to the police."

"You could do that," he said, in a way that suggested that he knew I wouldn't. I folded the paper and put it back in my pocket. He had answered nothing, really; he spoke almost exactly like Anna—saying only what he wanted to say and ignoring everything else. A worried sadness suddenly came over him, and I thought that he might cry. He didn't look at me, but dropped his gaze to some indefinite spot on the floor between us. "She's not coming back," he said.

I couldn't believe that he would say it. Out loud. We had all been thinking it—it was the thought we tried to avoid, had to constantly push aside—but no one had said it out loud. You'd never think that the first person to say it would be one of the parents. I stared at him in disbelief; I didn't know what he wanted from me, agreement or denial. I had come to him for help. I stood there, afraid to say anything. I was afraid that the next thing he might say was that she was dead.

Mr. Cayne's attempt to reach out, to make contact, made me want to do the same. I called a telephone psychic. I was embarrassed and didn't expect anything, but the woman on the phone was friendly and something about the way she spoke made me feel better. She was calm and comforting and positive. She told me that good things were going to happen. For a few minutes out of the day she could almost convince me that I wasn't depressed and desperate, or at least wouldn't be that way forever.

"I see things changing for you real soon," she said. "You're not staying in one place for long. It's bigger and better things. It's someplace sunny and warm, where people love you and will take care of you. It's going to be good. I'm telling you, it's going to be good very soon."

"Where will I be?" I said.

"It's a place marked in red. There are tigers. And it's warm. You're going from a place of water to a place of water. There's a connection there somehow."

"That's vague."

"It's all I know about it," she said. "I can try to get more, but you'll have to stay on the line." I didn't.

"What's your name?" I asked when I called again the next night.

"Cassandra. What's yours?"

"Carl," I said. "What's your real name?"

"It's still Cassandra," she said.

"Good-bye, Cassandra."

I called the next night too. When Cassandra came on the phone I could tell at once that it wasn't the same person. I called back a few times before I recognized the voice from before. She gave me the same story, and I thought that maybe she described the same vague sunny scene to everyone. Then she startled me.

"You called before," she said.

I didn't say anything.

"I don't know what city it is, but it all looks the same," she said. "You don't have to worry, Carl, things are going to be okay."

We talked for a while, not even about psychic stuff. We just talked. For five or six nights I lay on my bed in the dark and listened to her. It was a kind of infatuation, I guess; I was infatuated with the world Cassandra was describing. I liked it when she described all the good things that were coming my way. Actually, they were coming Carl's way. That I could believe.

"I'll call again tomorrow," I said.

"Okay."

"But I want to talk to you. You have to tell me your real name."

"I can't do that," she said.

"I won't call, then," I said.

She was silent for a moment. "I can't give you my name, but how about if we use a code?"

"What kind of code?"

"When you call and ask for Cassandra, also ask for extension thirteen."

"That's not a code," I said.

"I know, but it sounds better that way." She laughed. She thought it was funny. My heart was racing.

I talked to her for a few more days and then finally told her. "My name's not Carl," I said.

"I know."

"I'm trying to find somebody. I'm waiting for a message."

"I can't help you with that," she said.

"I want to find out what happened to a friend of mine," I said.

"I can't help you."

"That's not what you're supposed to say."

"I know. But it's the truth."

I didn't want the truth. I had that the rest of every day. I wasn't calling for the truth. "Tell me what you're supposed to say." She didn't want to. "I'm paying for the call," I told her. (My father was, but she didn't need to know everything.)

She started to tell me some vague things, but it was no use. Her voice had changed. Everything had changed. I stopped her.

"She had something to say to me," I said. "Something specific."

She didn't say anything.

"You have to tell me what it is."

"I don't know what it is."

"Come on, tell me."

"I don't know anything about it."

"Tell me."

"She says that everything's going to be all right. She says don't worry. Not to worry."

"I thought you could help me," I said.

"I thought I was," she said. "It doesn't change what I said before. Things are going to be better."

"You shouldn't lie to people," I replied. I wasn't angry. I was sad. I wanted to keep calling her. I wanted to have a few minutes in the day when I could feel better. It was just like it had been with Melissa—all of a sudden there was nothing. I didn't know what the attraction was.

"I wasn't lying," she said. "I'm trying to help you."

"You're not helping," I said, and hung up.

I was awakened in the middle of the night by a beep on my cell phone. I opened my eyes and saw the brief green flash inches from my head. I must have fallen asleep with the phone still on the bed, although I didn't remember doing so, but there it was. I had a new text message. I opened the message and saw the letters "SaSaS." That was all. It didn't mean anything to me.

I tossed the phone onto the floor and put my head back down into the pillow to go to sleep. Suddenly I sat up. "Something as simple as snow." It couldn't be. I grabbed the phone and looked at the message again. "SaSaS." There was no one listed as the sender. There was nothing except for the tiny document icon on the left. I had received the message at four a.m.

I couldn't go back to sleep. My mind was racing in circles, chasing some imaginary tail, or was it real? Was the message a disturbing coincidence, a hoax, or the real thing? It couldn't be a hoax. The code was our secret. Anna would never tell anyone. Besides, why would a hoax use only the initial letters and not the actual code? It wasn't the code we had agreed on. But it was close, close enough to keep me awake the rest of the night. I looked at the message again and again, and even replied. "Hello. ????" The more I thought about it, the less sense it made. If it was Anna, why wouldn't she stick to the original code that we'd agreed on? And if she could send a message, why would she send it to my phone and why would that be the only one? But then what did I know about it? Maybe that's all she could send. Maybe it was all she could ever send. On the one hand, I was getting all freaked out about some strange coincidence, overreacting to an odd but insignificant occurrence. On the other hand, I had to keep trying to make contact. After Houdini died, his wife tried to contact him for ten years, patiently waiting for him to utter the code.

the channel

Carl's mom drove us to the train station. I don't remember what we had told her, maybe that my mother was already in the city, and Carl and I were meeting her for the day and she was going to take us around. Whatever it was, Carl's mom agreed to let him go. She was safe, because I knew she would never talk to my mother.

Once we got to the city, we walked to the studio where the television show *The Channel* was taped. The host, Gerald Preen, is a medium who gives audience members messages from lost loved ones. A lot of people cry. It's really popular. I had filled out an application on the show's website to see if I could get on; I wanted to know whether Anna could be contacted through the medium. I knew enough to be skeptical, cautious, but at the same time I was willing to try every available option. They wanted a lot of information, but I tried to keep my answers as brief and general as possible. I played up our ages and the mysteriousness of Anna's disappearance. "I am afraid that something terrible has happened to my friend," I wrote. "My friend might have committed suicide or been murdered or worse. My friend had a strong faith in the afterlife and believed in the ability to communicate through *The Channel*. I am sure that my friend is trying to send me a message. Our entire town is waiting to hear."

I received a response the next day, which invited me to the taping. "We receive so many requests," the e-mail stated, "that we cannot guarantee that you will receive a reading, or even that you will be selected to be in the studio audience. But if you are at the studio at the specified date and time, your participation will be considered."

I had printed out maps from MapQuest, and Carl and I had studied them on the train so we would know where to go once we got to the station and wouldn't stick out like dumb tourists. The city was like a hive or an ant farm, with people scurrying along their paths, looking sure of where they were going. There was something inviting about it all. When we got to the studio, Carl tried to leave me to wait by myself on line. He wanted to go wander around. "You don't need me," he said. I thought that maybe he'd go talk to the real businessmen, the guys standing in the park, whispering their wares as people passed by, dealing in cash and secrets. Or maybe he would be one of those guys himself, make a few deals and head home with some easy extra money.

"Come on," I said. "I need the moral support."

So he stayed, and we both stood there in hopes of being selected for the taping. The longer I stood, the more I knew it was crap. Anna had told me that Houdini spent the last part of his life trying to tell people just like me that it was all a lie, but I was almost ready to believe a lie. The cold of the concrete seeped through my shoes and into my bones as we waited. Somebody from the show handed me a questionnaire and told me to fill it out, even if I'd already answered the same questions before. Once again I kept my answers as short and vague as possible; I didn't want to give any hints, do the staff's job for them. Finally someone came and led us inside.

About twenty of us had been selected to be in the studio audience. We were brought into a small waiting room that had only one couch and a few chairs. Those of us who didn't sit there sat on the floor or stood. Carl and I were the youngest people in the room by far. An assistant asked me where my "parent or guardian" was. "I'm eighteen," I told him. He looked at Carl and me for a long second, then handed us more paperwork. "Read and sign these," he said.

Assistants walked in and out of the room like waiters, and put food and drinks out for us. They casually asked if we needed anything, and began talking to us. Though we had been instructed to be quiet, people started speaking about the relatives they wanted to hear from and how they had died, and mentioning other things that the assistants could easily hear.

After an hour or so, we were escorted into the studio and shown to our seats. There were still a lot of empty seats, and I wondered why they had turned away so many people who had been waiting on line. After a few more minutes, another group, about fifteen people, arrived and sat with us. We were told that they were audience members, exactly like us, but afterward someone in my group said that they had arrived together in a van. This group was very talkative and asked a lot of questions. I knew I had to provide some information or else the host wouldn't talk to me, but I was careful about what I said. "I can't believe we're wait-ing around this long," Carl said. "I could be getting things done."

Finally Gerald Preen arrived. He was smaller in person than I thought he would be. "They all are," Carl told me later. Preen was young-looking, like my brother, but he had to be older than that. He had dark hair, very short, and combed to the front to conceal a receding hairline. He wore a black turtleneck sweater and gray wool pants, and spoke in a calm, quiet, voice. It was supposed to be soothing, but he spoke so rapidly that you had difficulty keeping up with him. The rhythm of his speech reminded me of the first time Anna had spoken to me, in the library; the words flowed out in a steady, seductive stream. There was a big difference, though; he had nothing interesting to say. He explained what was going to happen during the show, and surveyed the audience. "No one here has met me before?" he asked. "No one has seen me in person or even talked to me before now?" No one had, or no one admitted to it, and the show started.

He started with easy stuff, low-hanging fruit, and with obvious methods I had read about in books Anna had given me, and things I had read about online. "I'm getting a J over here. I don't know what this means. It's a male name. John, Jonathan, Jack . . . He could be someone who has gone across, he could be someone here, he could be some-one that you know." A number of hands went up. After all, who didn't know someone named John? Some of the tech-niques I had read about indicated that many psychics rely heavily on probability and statistics (like the fact that many male names begin with J and many female names with M). They relied on different styles of reading, both "cold" and "hot." Cold readings start with very general information and move to specifics, gathering and building on informa-tion and feedback from the subject. Hot readings rely on information gathered about the unsuspecting subject that is then told to the subject, to that person's amazement. I had read about psychics who had enlisted aides to go to subjects' homes and pretend to be salespeople or people in trouble who needed to use the phone, in order to notice things about the subjects and their homes. During the reading the psychics could then provide specific details about the people while honestly stating, "We've never met before today, and I've never been to your home." Preen seemed to be using a combination of techniques.

He continued to ask questions or make vague statements and then move to specifics, until he had narrowed his comments to one person in the audience. Now he concentrated on very specific things about John. Nothing seemed impressive, but this was exactly the type of thing I had read about. It was fascinating to see in action, like watching a magic trick when you already know the trick, but Preen's performance was so convincing that you almost forgot it was a trick. The way he operated was magnetic, and like a magnet, the closer he got to you, the more he pulled you in. The most compelling aspect of his routine was how he reacted when the subject denied a bold statement he had made. Instead of moving to another area, Preen would insist that what he was saying was accurate and that the subject was mistaken. "You may not have been aware of this," he would offer. "Or maybe this didn't happen, but the deceased had wished for it to happen." If these assertions didn't stick he usually proceeded to another subject.

After talking to six subjects, Preen looked at me.

"You're trying to find someone," he said. "You're trying to tell this person something, something important. The name starts with C."

"Which name?" I said, fighting myself from nodding and offering him a tip.

He hesitated. "The last name." When I nodded, you could hear a gasp from the audience, as if he had just solved some incredible problem, instead of guessing correctly on something he had a fifty-fifty chance of nailing.

"The first name is more difficult," he said. "This person doesn't like to be called by her real name. I'm getting a long name, quite a few syllables."

This part was taking forever. I wanted him to get right to the real stuff. He worked the crowd, however, building suspense. "I'm receiving an A."

He rattled off a lot of general, but true, information. "It's a woman's name. She was someone close to you, a mother, sister, girlfriend. She was a girlfriend. She left suddenly, recently. Very quickly."

He then went down a road of wrong information, and returned to her name—which he never gave in full, only the initials—and I was afraid that he was going to abandon me. He was trying to manipulate and lead me, and I was trying to do the same to him. I wasn't going to help him; I was convinced that he was a fraud, nothing more than a good practitioner of the art that Houdini and Dr. James Ryan, a "psychic hunter," and others had described. Dr. Ryan had even offered a public challenge to Preen, inviting him to exhibit his skills in a controlled environment, supervised by Dr. Ryan. He would give Preen a million dollars if he successfully demonstrated "evidence of any paranormal, supernatural, or occult power." According to Dr. Ryan's website, Preen had never responded to his challenge.

But I wanted him to continue talking to me; there was a small degree of hope that he had something to offer. He asked to see a photograph of the person, or anything of hers. I had read that this was a familiar ploy of fake psychics, so I had made sure not to carry anything with me. Though he was agitated that I didn't have any personal effects, he continued. "You want to say something to this person," he said. "She wants to say something to you. You have talked about this." He stopped abruptly, and changed direction as another thought struck him. "There is an agreement," he said. I tried to become a stone, a blank piece of paper, but I must have given something away, a hint in my eyes or mouth that he picked up on. "There is a code," he announced. This was dangerous. If he couldn't tell me anything more and I confirmed this much, then everyone would soon know about the code between Anna and me. Anyone who watched the show would know, and then it would be a guessing game. I waited and said nothing, and Preen looked at me, his eyes almost burning into me, searching for something, for anything, and then almost pleading with me. Finally I gave him a short shake of my head, a tiny no, and he moved on to other wrong information and quietly abandoned the reading altogether.

This was typical. He hit only about fifteen to twenty percent of correct information throughout the taping. He stopped some readings more abruptly than mine and simply started over with another person. After a complete miss he would usually move on to someone from the group that had arrived after us at the studio, and this seemed to support the theory that they were ringers. I wondered how it would all play when the show aired, and when I saw it a few weeks later, most of the misses had been edited out, while some of the more accurate readings had been edited to appear more dramatic. I wasn't in the show at all.

After the taping, as we were filing out of the studio, an assistant approached me and asked me to follow him. Carl said that he'd wait outside; without asking any questions, I went along with the assistant. I was led to Preen's dressing room, where he was sitting on a leather couch, sipping a cup of hot tea. At first he didn't look at me. "Why did you lie to me?" he said, as he shot his gaze toward me.

"I don't know. . . ."

"There is a code," he said. "You shook your head when I said it. Who are you working with? Are you working with Dr. Ryan?"

"No."

"But you've talked to him? He's helped you, instructed you?"

"No," I said. "He wouldn't talk to me." It was true. I had e-mailed him, told him some of my story and the fact that I was going to try to be on *The Channel*, but I'd never heard from him.

"What do you want?"

"I think I'm being contacted," I said. "Things have happened that make me think that an attempt at contact is being made, but nothing more than that. I want to make contact. Real contact. I want to know what happened and what's happening."

He put his cup on an end table and got up from the couch and approached me. He put his hand on my shoulder. "I can help you."

"How?"

"Do you know what happened to this person?"

"No," I said. I was a little annoyed—I had just told him that I didn't know.

He looked at his cup for a long time and then swung his dark head back to me. "She's passed. That's how I'm able to know what I'm going to say to you."

"You're sure?"

"I'm sorry," he said. "She's dead, but she is still trying to tell you something."

How could he know that she was really dead? It took some balls to say it, and I was angry that he had. I didn't know where this was going. I didn't know why he was telling me all this, maybe to save face, maybe to get me back on the show. I didn't know. Once again I tried to keep calm, but I wanted to hear what he had to say. I wanted to hear what Anna had to tell me. "What is she trying to say?"

"She says that you're not trying hard enough. That you're not trying. That's what I'm getting."

"Who is saying this?" I said.

"A.C."

"What's her name?"

He paused. He closed his eyes. "Is it Anne, or Abby, or Alice?"

"You have to tell me," I said. I wasn't going to supply any answers.

He looked at me with his hard gaze again. "It's Anna."

"What does she want to tell me?"

"That you're not trying enough."

"What else?"

He closed his eyes again, and his face contorted slightly in what was meant to be intense concentration. When he opened his eyes, he seemed to have come to a sudden realization. He looked surprised.

"It's something simple," he said. "That's what she wants to tell you. Something simple." He paused and concentrated again. "That's the code. Something simple. Something simple."

He looked at me for confirmation. I wanted him to continue. I wanted him to get everything. I wanted him to tell me everything. But that was it. He was finished.

"What else?" I was practically pleading with him to get it.

"The code is simple. Isn't it?"

"You have to tell me," I said. "What is she saying?"

"Would you be willing to come back?"

"You can't tell me what I need to know," I said.

"I think I can. This isn't the right time or place. With a little more preparation, and a little more receptiveness on your part, I think we can help each other, and help Anna deliver her message."

I was in a corner. I wanted him to go on; I thought for a moment he was going to get the code, get the start of her message. He was close. How could he get that close and not get closer? I wanted him to continue, but he was finished. He almost had me convinced, and I would have agreed to come back; but then I thought that he was stalling for more time, so he could talk to people I knew, read up on what had happened to Anna, and then use that information. I could imagine Preen's people snooping around town, sticking their noses in all of our lives, digging up just enough stuff to convince a TV audience.

"I can't," I said. "It was hard enough to come this one time. I can't."

Preen looked sadly toward his cup. "I'm sorry," he said. He walked me toward the door. "Let me leave you with one thought. The greatest gift you can give Anna is to acknowledge that she is with you always." It was one of those things that sounds profound the moment you hear it, but if you think about it, it's really meaningless. A lifetime with my father had prepared me for sayings like that. Preen hadn't provided any answers, only platitudes and playacting.

Carl was waiting near the door when I left the building. "How'd that go?" he said.

"Strange." I told him most of what had happened. "What do you think about this Preen guy?"

"He's done some amazing stuff, I think."

"You think so? You think he can really communicate with the dead?"

"I don't know," Carl replied. "But I think it's possible to communicate with the dead, so why not Preen?"

"How do you think it's possible?"

"Some people are blessed with better senses, or are in tune with things we don't notice, like dogs that can hear sounds we can't. The crazy thing about the mind is that it's more capable of things than the mind itself can imagine. What do you think?"

"I don't know," I said. "This might have been a big waste of time."

"That's not true. You tried. That's not wasting time."

The lights went out as the train inched its way through the tunnel and out of the station. Long rows of bare bulbs hung from the tunnel ceiling and cast a harsh glow that barely reached the ground but made the tracks glisten in the darkness. Water dripped from the ceiling in a number of spots, and I wondered where it came from. Was it from just overhead, or was it rain or snowmelt that had worked itself from the sky down to the street and then patiently squirmed through minute cracks and fissures until it found release all this way underground, where it fell for a brief moment and was trapped on the floor of the tunnel? Or did it continue, wriggling down into great free-flowing rivers below us, or even greater confinement, moving from one spot to another—freeing itself from one trap only to land in another, over and over until it evaporated and returned to the air to start the process again?

On the ride home I tried to sort out what had happened. Had Mr. Preen gotten lucky, or had he actually received something? He didn't seem to know what he had. He used the phrase "something simple" four times but didn't seem to know what it meant.

After they found Anna's dress, I had stopped going to the third floor at school every morning. I would go there a few times a week, to see Claire, but I couldn't stand to be around Bryce and listen to him talk about what he thought or felt. When I got back from the *Channel* taping, I stopped going to the third floor entirely. Instead, I hung out on the eastern end of the second floor, talking with Billy Godley. He knew that I was talking to him only in case he had any information from his father, but he was nice enough to tell me if he did. Sometimes Claire would join us; this usually made the other kids scatter like birds, flitting off to safety elsewhere.

No one was looking for Anna, Billy told me. He said that she was considered just another missing person and that the police suspected she was a runaway.

"I don't believe that," Claire said. "Why would she go through all the elaborate setup, with the dress and the hole and all that?"

Billy shrugged. We'd had the same conversation over and over. Sometimes I thought that we might be the only people who talked about her still. It had to bore Billy, since he had never known Anna. He barely knew Claire or me. He patiently listened to us until the bell rang and we headed off for class. Sometimes it even bored me; I would

rather have spent my days thinking and talking about any-
thing else, but if I had stopped thinking or talking about
Anna she might have been gone forever, and whatever hope
I had of making contact might have slipped away, lost.

A couple of weeks after the taping, a man from Gerald
Preen's office called the house. "We were wondering if you
could come in and meet with Mr. Preen," he said.

"I don't think so," I replied. I didn't see the point.

"We have an item we think you might be interested in
taking a look at."

"What is it?"

"It's a photograph of you and your friend."

Anna and I had never had our picture taken together.

"Are you sure?"

"That's why we want you to come in. We think you'll
agree it's a very interesting photograph."

The man had a menacing tone, as if threatening me. Did
he think he could do something worse to me than had already been done? Good luck, I thought. I told him I'd call
back, but I never did. The same guy called the next day, and
the day after that. Then a woman called. She had a different tone. It turns out that they wanted my help. Why
couldn't the man who called before have told me that, instead of going through all the drama and mystery? The
woman said that the people at the show wanted my help
with a photograph they thought was of me. I agreed to go
and we made an appointment.

This time my father went with me. I didn't know what

Preen's people might try to pull, and I figured my father could help me. I told him about the taping and how I had met with Preen afterward.

"So what do they want with you now?"

"I don't know," I said. "I don't know what to think."

We went on a Saturday, and they made us wait in the lobby of the building for twenty minutes. My father was almost ready to leave after ten. "They can't keep an appointment?" he said. "This isn't the doctor's office, for Christ's sake." It was a good thing he hadn't been with me for the taping. He paced back and forth in the lobby. Finally we were led to Mr. Preen's office. Three of his assistants, dressed identically in black pants and black turtlenecks, were there, but no Preen. They motioned for us to sit on the couch.

"How old is your son?" one of them asked my father.

"He's sixteen."

"He has lost someone recently, someone close to him."

"Yes," my father said. "Get to the point. What's this about?"

"Mr. Preen made a strong connection with this individual, a connection that seems to have manifested itself in a very real way. As we explained, Mr. Preen has come into the possession of a particular photograph. One that we would like you to identify."

The assistant showed us the photograph. It was the one Mr. Devon had taken on the train. I was staring straight at the camera, and in the background, looking through the window of the train, was a ghost. It was blurry image of Anna's face, looking at me.

"Where did you get this?" my father wanted to know.

"Mr. Preen is an avid collector of spirit photographs," the assistant said.

"Where did you get this?" my father repeated.

"We just want you to verify that this is the friend, behind you in the photograph."

My father shook his head. "If you're not going to answer my question, we're leaving." The assistants said nothing, and we left.

By the time we reached the street, my father's face was red with rage. "What the fuck is going on?" he asked.

On the ride home, we went over my trip to the city with Carl and the earlier trip with Mr. Devon. I told my father most of what had happened, but I didn't tell him everything. I didn't tell him the specifics of Preen's conversation with me after the show, and I didn't tell him about Mr. Devon's taking me to a bar or his getting drunk.

"Let's have a talk with Mr. Devon," my father said when we got home. I called him on my cell, and we drove to his house.

"I need an explanation," my father said as soon as Mr. Devon opened the door. "I need to know how a photograph you took of my son winds up on a TV show."

"What photo? What TV show?"

I told him about the photo and that Preen had it, but not on his show.

"I don't know how that could have happened," Mr. Devon

said. "I took the picture of your son, but that's the end of what I know about it and the end of my involvement."

"How did the Cayne girl's picture get in it?"

"Someone probably put it there."

"How?" my father asked.

"You used to need two negatives to create the effect, or you had to double-expose a single negative. But now, with a computer, it's easy to create what I think you're describing. I'd have to see the picture, and even then I might not be able to tell how it was done. If it was done well."

"And how would they have gotten the picture in the first place?"

"I don't know about the picture of Anastasia, but I have photographs and negatives all over the classroom, my office, and the darkroom at school. Any one of a hundred kids could have come across it and taken it."

"Why?" my father asked.

"You'd have to ask them," Mr. Devon said.

"So someone just stole something out of your classroom and you shrug it off."

"Dad, you don't understand," I said.

"I understand that this guy doesn't have any control over his students."

"It's not like that," I said.

"What is it like?"

"We make a lot of different kind of artwork in class," Mr. Devon said, "using all sorts of materials, pictures from magazines, old photographs people bring from home, pictures that I've taken or that the students themselves have taken. It's not that I don't have control over my students, it's that someone happened upon this particular photograph and decided to use it for this particular purpose. Maybe they meant it as a prank or a hoax, or maybe they were just trying to get attention. Other than that, I'm not sure what harm's been done."

"None, really," I said. "We were just trying to get to the bottom of something. Come on, Dad." We left.

Driving home, my father turned to me and said, "I might have overreacted, but I'm just trying to help. Don't you want to know who's responsible?"

"Not really. It's probably just some asshole at school, trying to be funny." Even then I was fairly certain who was responsible, and I wasn't in any hurry to find out for sure.

cemetery

Claire had started driving me home whenever she could use her mother's car. Sometimes she would drive it to school in the morning and we'd leave from there in the afternoon, and other times we would walk to her house after school and then she would drive. It was almost the same distance from the school to my house as it was to Claire's, but I didn't mind. I didn't even mind when we would get to her house and the car wouldn't be there. I'd just warm up a bit and then head out.

She invited me into her room once. Everything was black. She had painted the ceiling and walls a deep black. On the floor was a futon, which was covered with a black sheet and a black comforter. The only other things in the room were a black dresser and a TV set on the floor near the futon. There was a Bible on top of the TV. When she closed the door behind us, the room was completely dark.

"How do you see anything?"

She turned on a light. "There's nothing to see," she said. "But look how good the TV looks." She turned the TV on and switched off the light. We both sat on the futon. It was like being in bed in a movie theater.

"You don't have a computer?"

"There's one in my father's office," she said. "He lets me use it, but I don't like it that much."

"How about a stereo?"

"No," she said. She made it sound like I was crazy even to think it. She had that in common with Anna: she seemed to be able to move the conversation where she wanted, shutting down subjects she didn't want to discuss and making you feel stupid to continue talking about them.

"I'm hardly ever in this room anyway," she said. "I use it for sleeping, and that's about it."

"You're taking the word 'bedroom' a little literally, aren't you?"

She laughed. "That's exactly what Anna said the first time she was here."

I asked Claire if she would drive me somewhere nearby, and she agreed.

As you come into town from the south, on Route 521, the cemetery is the first thing you see. It's just on the left, surrounded by an old stone wall. The cemetery covers about five acres, and I always wondered how people knew so long ago how big the cemetery would need to be. I guess they figured that people would be dying forever, so they marked off a big enough area to keep people satisfied for a long time. There were graves that went back to the late 1700s, the first families of the town, their stones almost smooth, their names and dates and inscriptions faded away until you couldn't tell who was buried there at all. A lot of the stones were broken, or tipping over.

Claire parked the car and I got out. "I think I'll stay here," she said. I was approaching the gate when I heard her car door close. I waited for her to catch up. The gate was locked, so we climbed over the stone wall. I walked through the straight rows of graves to a place near the back. There was snow on the front of my coat from the stones, and Claire came over and brushed it off. "You should at least look nice," she joked.

Claire and I stood over Denise's grave. There wasn't a headstone, but a plaque at ground level with her name and the dates of her birth and death. "That's my sister," I said. What else was there to say, what else did I know about her? There weren't photographs or stories. There was no time for that. I wondered what it meant for my mother and father, who had held her and brought her home from the hospital, only to return her to the hospital a week later, and then return her to nothingness.

"I didn't know," Claire said.

"We never come here." There were empty spaces on either side of the plaque, plots for the rest of us, so we could all be in the ground together. It seemed like a bad joke; it seemed like a waste. I turned and looked at the length of the cemetery, the headstones sticking up stiffly in their rigid rows. I wondered how long the Caynes would wait until they decided to mark Anna's life with a stone.

I imagined a big funeral for her, with the whole town there, everyone dressed in black. I had only one suit, which my parents had bought, for times like this ("weddings and other appropriate occasions," I think, were their exact words), but I'd never worn it. I could see everyone standing in deep snow, solemnly listening to the preacher as he said some trivial words over her grave and her black coffin, smelling of wax and rosewood, was lowered into the open grave. I had imagined a similar funeral for myself hundreds of times, the whole town wailing and weeping, almost unable to go on without me. I imagined it because I knew it would never happen, but this was nearly real, this was sadness. I could see Mr. and Mrs. Cayne standing in the cemetery snow, quietly crying beside the casket. They probably had buried her hundreds of times in their minds already, trying to prepare themselves for the day when they really would bury her. Or bury something. What would they do if they never found her? Bury an empty box, or just put up a marker? These weren't questions you could ask out loud.

"Where do you think they'll put her?"

"What?"

"I'm sorry," I said. "I was just thinking about if she doesn't come back, wondering where they might put her grave."

Claire looked at me like I was crazy. "Would it matter?"

"I'm sure it matters to Mr. and Mrs. Cayne. And it matters to me. I mean, let's say they never find her. What do they do, just put a marker here somewhere? I don't want that, but the Caynes may want one spot where they can go and be reminded of her."

"Like your sister?"

"That's the idea, but we never come to see her. Never. It might be different for the Caynes, though."

We walked slowly through the headstones. "What do you know about them, anyway?" I asked Claire.

"The Caynes? Less than you do, I'm sure."

"I don't know anything. We never talked about it. Anna never said anything about where they came from. I don't think I heard her talk about one thing that happened before they got here."

"She never talked about it with me either. They're from down south, I think. That's about all I know."

"They seem to know everybody in town, but nobody seems to know them," I said.

"My mother thinks something happened to them that they're trying to forget. That's why they don't say anything."

"Why does she think that?"

"I don't know, people talking, I guess. Wondering what their story is, just like us."

"What could have happened worse than this?"

Claire pulled up in front of my house, as she had a number of times, and I suddenly remembered something. "I completely forgot your birthday," I said. "I can't believe that you've been driving me around and it didn't hit me until right now."

"That's all right," she said. "It's not that important."

"Thanks for taking me down there. I hope it wasn't too morbid."

"We're the ones who are supposed to be morbid," she said.

"You're not, though."

"Keep it a secret—I've got a reputation."

"Thanks again," I said, and leaned over and kissed her. It wasn't a conscious thing. I hadn't thought of kissing her before I did so; I don't recall ever thinking about it beforehand. But there we were.

"That was nice," she said. "But I don't think it was meant for me."

She had me at a disadvantage. I didn't know what I was doing, and I was embarrassed. "I don't know," I told her.

"You don't have to say anything." She leaned over and kissed me and then returned to her place behind the wheel. I sat and waited for what would happen next, but nothing did, so I got out of the car and went inside.

s a l a m a n d e r s

Winter broke off, finally, a long ash crumbling at the end of a cigarette, burned out, weak and emptied. In late March the thermometer jumped almost thirty degrees, launching itself above sixty during the day. I started walking to school along the river. It was out of my way; I had to walk over from our house, then wind north along the banks, then cut along Town Street about half a mile to school. It took me almost an hour, forty minutes if I walked fast and didn't stop, but I didn't mind. I liked the walk.

The river sighed and snapped, the ice finally melting. I watched the water splash up from beneath the cracked surface, pushing its way around, trying to wrench itself from its deep sleep. Or maybe the ice was just tired, tired of hanging on all winter long, tired of gripping the same stone, the same spot in the bank, and was just giving up. Across the river I could see large chunks breaking free and disappearing under a shelf of ice, dragged into the water and taken off somewhere before disappearing. If it stayed warm, all the ice would be gone by the end of the week, and the river would move again, the fish could return to the surface, and fishermen would follow and try their best to outsmart them. It would all happen as it always had, as though nothing had changed, or had changed so naturally that you barely noticed.

The grass was almost free of snow, and looked brown and spent and ugly. The snow retreated to its final holdouts, piles on the edges of parking lots, the shadow of the woods. The days were bright and warm, but I found myself following the snow into the woods after school. It was calm and cool and quiet. Once spring came, the place would be filled with people smoking and making out and who knows what else. I wandered through the woods by the school and then walked along the river and into the woods where I had last seen Anna's face, stuck on a stick in the snow. I wanted to find the spot again, but without useing the map, so I ended up wandering through the thick evergreens, wasting time until I had to head home for dinner. One afternoon, just before April, I heard two voices arguing.

"Do you want me to call her?"

"It's none of your business."

It was Carl and his father. Carl was not happy. I didn't move. I stood there in the snow, afraid they might hear my clumsy boots if I moved. I couldn't see them, but from their voices I assumed they were behind me. I was afraid they might see me and recognize me. If they said something to me, I'd run, but if they couldn't see me, I would wait until they left, and they would never know that I'd been there. Their voices were raised loud enough to hear clearly.

"You get your nose in enough of my business," Carl was saying.

"Well, stay out of this."

"If you do the right thing, I won't have to get involved."

Mr. Hathorne didn't answer.

"Where are you going now?" Carl asked.

"I'm not going over there, don't worry about it."

"Just go home."

"I've got things to do."

"What?"

Again there was no answer.

"Do you have any money?" Carl said.

"No."

"Good, then you can't buy anything to drink."

I could hear someone coming closer, and before I could do anything, he was behind me. Carl didn't look surprised to see me. "Did you hear?"

"A little. Just the end. I'm sorry. I didn't know what to do, so I didn't do anything."

"That's all right. He was wandering around in the woods. I don't know what he was doing."

"My mother's name didn't come up, did it?"

"No," Carl said. "We were talking about something else. Do you want me to ask about that?"

"No," I said. "I'd rather not know."

"Me too." He flashed a smile. "What are you doing now?"

"Nothing."

"Come on, then."

We walked over to his house. Mrs. Hathorne had the kitchen smelling good; a huge pot of stew simmered on the stove, and biscuits were baking in the oven.

"That's a winter meal, Mom. Winter's over."

"I wouldn't bet on it. You may need this stew after all. The both of you. Do you want to stay for dinner?"

"Sure," I said.

We went to Carl's room. I sat at his computer while he unlocked his file cabinet and updated his books. He had just finished locking the cabinet when the doorbell rang. His mother called for him and he left the room. When he came back, Claire was with him. I thought she might have been looking for me. Her black hair was pulled up through a white scrunchie, so it fanned up in the back. From the front, the rising tuft looked ceremonial, like a tribal headdress. She might have been a beautiful Indian woman, a princess from some dark and secret land. I didn't want to stop looking at her.

"Did you drive over?" I asked.

"I had to walk—my mom's got the car. I'm thinking about getting my own."

"Get a BMW," Carl said.

"If you pay for it."

"Who's the first person you'd hit with it?" I said. Claire didn't say anything. "Put me at the top of the list, would you?"

Carl's mom drove us home. We were going down McKinley Road, near Glass Pond (Anna always called it "See More Pond," I guess because there wasn't much of one, it was more like a swamp or a marsh, except when there was a lot of rain or snowmelt, like now), when we saw some rubbery things glistening on the road in the headlights. They were four or five inches long and their bodies looked wet and silvery, like curious little snakes with their heads raised into the air.

"It's the salamanders," Carl yelled. "Be careful, Mom." Mrs. Hathorne slowed the car to a near-stop and tried to avoid the animals as they worked their way across the warm pavement. Every year, near the end of winter, the salamanders migrated from their winter home in the woods to the swamps and ponds and pools where they could breed. There were hundreds of them on the road, and Mrs. Hathorne was swerving wildly to avoid them. Finally she sped up. "Someone else is going to run over them, anyway," she said.

"Stop," Carl shouted. She stopped. He jumped out of the car, and we could see him bent over, pushing the gray salamanders toward the side of the road. He moved forward a few feet, continuing his rescue effort. Claire and I got out and helped him. The salamanders froze when we approached them, so we had to pick them up and carry them, placing them gently on the dirt in hopes they would continue toward the pond, not venture back onto the pavement.

It was a good night for salamanders. The air was thick, with a flavor of damp earth that filled our noses and mouths. When we finished moving the damp salamanders, Claire playfully wiped their slickness off on the front of Carl's blue jeans. He pushed his palms toward her face, but stopped just short of touching her. I thought about going over and wiping my hands on her dress, but didn't. I watched them laughing in the headlights of the car, while Mrs. Hathorne waited impatiently inside.

I had almost forgotten Carl's affection for animals. When we were little we had made a pact to become forest rangers, or Greenpeace activists: we would live and work in Alaska or Africa or at the Bay of Fundy, helping preserve the wilderness and protecting the animals living there. Carl had it all figured out. He had become a vegan and had read a lot of relevant books. He knew what needed to be done. But as he researched more and we got older, he determined he could do more good by making money and supporting

organizations than by working for one of those organizations. Then it seemed that he forgot about what he was going to use the money for; the point, it seemed, was to make
money. But seeing him there in the dark, pushing and
prodding and carrying the salamanders to safety on the
side of the road, I thought that he might still be operating
according to his plan. Maybe he still had it figured out, but
he just didn't talk about it anymore. It also made me think
that I was no longer part of his plan. Carl had left me behind.

hay in a stack
of needles

My father took me to the first Saturday home baseball
game. He hadn't even told me that he had bought tickets,
or maybe they'd been given to him. Either way, he told me
at dinner Friday night. We had never been to a game together, and I couldn't remember him ever going. But there
we were, driving to the game. I had wanted to take the
train, but he insisted on driving.

My father refused to get an SUV. My mother was always
telling him that we needed one, that she needed one for all
her errands—which she never ran. We might have been
the only family in town who didn't have a huge vehicle, an
SUV or a truck; my parents both drove Volvos, my father a
little brown two-door coupe and my mother a brown four-
door. They looked like cardboard boxes on wheels. But

really safe cardboard boxes. My father wanted the smallest, safest car built, and I'm sure he would have driven a single-passenger model if they had made one. The only cargo he cared about was his golf clubs. As long as they could fit into the trunk, the vehicle was big enough. Anything more was a waste of space.

I stared out the window and listened to Anna's CDs on my headphones. She had ended the first CD with a song by Bauhaus, "Bela Lugosi's Dead." It was almost ten minutes long. It started with a tapping sound, drumsticks against the metal rim of the drum, and then that sound became distorted, echoing and repeating over itself. A slow bass came in, droning along until the guitar snarled around the rhythm; it was almost two minutes before there was any singing. The chorus was basically the title repeated again and again, and another phrase along with it. I had always thought the phrase was "I'm dead," but when I listened to it on headphones it sounded like "undead," which made a lot more sense, I guess.

Anna had always laughed when she played that song. "Are they serious?" she'd said. "It's so campy—high drama and tragedy." She thought it was hilarious. "Do you think they thought it was funny?" she'd asked.

"Does anybody else?" I'd said.

"People take it very seriously. My father said it was like the Goth anthem."

"It's a little creepy."

"But fake creepy, like vomiting-pea-soup creepy. You have to laugh."

I listened to it over and over. It was funny, but I wasn't laughing.

My father looked over at me and lifted his chin. I took my headphones off.

"When you went to that TV show," he said, "did you sign anything?"

"A release form, I think."

He nodded and looked back toward the road. "I think I know what they wanted with the photograph." When he was sure that he had my complete attention, he said, "They wanted to do a show about you, using the taped stuff they didn't use before, and then the picture."

"And?"

"When they found out the release form wasn't binding, that you lied about your age, it ruined their plans."

"How do you know this?"

"Your old man isn't a complete idiot," he said.

"You ruined my chance to be on TV." He knew I was joking.

"You're young, you'll have plenty of better chances."

It took us about three hours to get to the stadium. We had to wait on line at the will-call window for tickets. I had brought along a pair of binoculars, even though my father had kept insisting that I leave them at home. "We have good seats," he'd said. "You're not going to need them." When he finally got the tickets, he noticed that they were in the upper deck. He didn't say anything about it until we got all the way there.

We were in the first row of the upper deck, about halfway between third base and the left-field wall. "These aren't bad," he said as we sat down. It was a cool, gray day, threatening to rain any minute. Every now and again a strong wind would gust into the stadium and hit me in the back. I felt that if I stood up the wind would blow me over the railing and down into the seats below. I had never really thought of myself as afraid of heights, but I couldn't look straight down from our seats. Yet there was something inviting about the height; it made me want to jump. It was a physical urge, an impulse or temptation that had to be resisted. There was no way I would jump, but I had a feeling in my gut, in my muscles, that made me think that I might jump despite my own will. I wanted to move away from the railing, but then what would I tell my father? That I was afraid? I kept the binoculars to my face and concentrated on the players on the field or scanned the crowd.

My father was eating oyster crackers out of a bag he'd brought inside his coat, and drinking a beer. He was trying to keep score, but he kept getting distracted, or else he was just making conversation. Or maybe he was trying to make me focus on the game. He kept asking, "What happened?" I had to pay attention to the game and help him out with the plays. "Was that three-six-three?" he'd ask. "No, the pitcher covered first," I'd answer. We almost had a conversation.

Around the fourth or fifth inning I noticed a group of Goth kids sitting across the diamond, near the top, in right field. I hadn't noticed them before. There were eight or nine of them, and I thought of how there might be a group of them at every sporting event, huddled together in their black uniforms. Then I saw her. It was Anna, in the middle of the group, calmly watching the game. With her blond hair she was like a piece of hay in a stack of needles.

I told my father that I would be right back. I rushed up the aisle and out of the stands. I had to make my way around the entire stadium, running through lines of people at the concession stands and bathrooms. I ran as fast as I could, but kept getting slowed down. It took me more than ten minutes to get to the right-field seats. I could hear the game on the field, and from the televisions at the conces- sion stands. Something had happened in the game; a big roar went up from the crowd. Everyone was standing when I came out into the seats. I hurried up the steps—there had to be more than a hundred to the top row—and waited for the crowd to sit down so I could see. I was out of breath. I was still one section away from the Goth group; I would have to go down the steps, across another section, and then up again. I looked frantically for Anna once I got to the right section. The group was sitting at the end of three rows, close to the aisle. I looked for her, right in the spot where I had seen her, but she wasn't there. The spot was empty.

"What do you want?" one of the Goths asked me.

"Nothing. I was just looking for somebody."

"She's not here," another one said. It was Bryce Druitt.

"Where is she?"

"You should know."

"Why's that?"

"Your buddy almost killed her."

"I don't know what you're talking about," I said.

"Claire OD'ed on shit she bought from your friend."

His words barely registered. I must have been talking like a robot or a zombie. "I didn't know," I mumbled. I looked around furiously, hoping that Anna would show up and stop everything, that she would show up and say that Bryce was lying and that everything was all right.

"What are you trying to do? Get rid of all the girls in school?" Bryce said.

I had to leave. I couldn't talk to them anymore. Something on the field made people jump to their feet again. The Goths stayed in their seats; I could feel them looking at me. The crowd was roaring, and the Goths were silent, staring at me. I felt I might pass out or throw up, maybe just fall down the aisle and roll onto the field. My legs ached and were weak. I turned and walked slowly down the stairs. I heard Bryce say to the rest of them: "That's the boyfriend of that bitch who almost killed me." I wanted to run back and scream in his face, I wanted to punch his teeth out, but I had nothing. I was suddenly exhausted. I could barely move down the stairs. Adrenaline was coursing through me so strongly I was almost shaking, but I had no energy. I made my way down the stairs and into the walkway that led to the concession stands. I waited there, knowing that Anna would never be returning to where I had seen her, but still I waited.

When I eventually made it back to my seat, my father asked me where I'd gone.

"I just took a walk around."

"I saw you way over there." He pointed across the stadium.

"I saw Bryce Druitt."

"And you had to rush over there?" I didn't answer. "What did he have to say?"

"Nothing."

"What's he doing here?"

"I don't know."

"What a coincidence."

It started to rain, a cold drizzle, and no one moved. Only a few umbrellas opened. The rain felt good at first, but then it'started raining harder. People moved out of the lower seats and gathered under the overhangs; some left the stadium. We were stuck in the rain.

"Do you want to go?" my father asked.

"There's only a couple of innings left." It was a close game. My father was keeping score. He'd be disappointed if he had to leave with an incomplete scorecard. He seemed more intent in putting all of the plays on paper than relaxing and watching the game. He dutifully filled in all of the boxes with numbers that didn't mean anything to me; he kept track of everything, the number of pitches each pitcher threw, the time of the game, the temperature, the names of the umpires. The whole story was there in pencil on his program, neatly detailed and accounted for.

I sat through the rest of the game thinking about Claire and Carl, and Bryce, and Anna. I kept looking over at the spot. It was empty. I had imagined her. I knew that I had, but the thought kept creeping into my brain that she had been there, and had left when she noticed me coming over. I fantasized that she was still alive, that she was tormenting me, haunting me, playing with me on purpose. Every time this thought went on, I tried to push it out and consider what Bryce had said. Questions kept piling up, ping-ponging through my head, colliding so quickly and so hard that they became blurred, dented, and damaged. I clutched the binoculars and stared across the field. I'm sure my father had noticed that I wasn't watching the game, because he asked me what happened on almost every play. "Was that a called third strike, or did he swing?" "Was that a wild pitch or a passed ball? You have to look at the scoreboard—they'll put the official decision up there." "What was that? Come on now, help me out." I was moving the binoculars back and forth from the pitcher to home plate to the upper deck where Bryce was still sitting, until I became dizzy, disoriented. I had to put them down and take a few deep breaths.

My head was aching so badly that I thought it would split open. I wished it would split open and release everything in it, all the thoughts that were boiling and building up steam, and then maybe I could calm down. I looked down again. It was hard not to jump. I just wanted some relief. I thought I was going to cry. I could feel the tears building up in my eyes. I had to close them and lean way back in my seat. The crowd roared again. A walk-off home run. The game was over.

"Are you okay?" my father said.

I opened my eyes. "I got dizzy all of a sudden."

"Maybe you got up too fast. Just sit there a second and relax." He sat down and went back to writing on his score-card. The cool breeze felt good. I sat and let it stream across my face until I didn't feel so clammy. We stood and joined the crowd making its way down the cramped rampways to the bottom of the stadium. It took us almost an hour to get to the car, and then we sat in traffic for almost another hour. My father didn't seem to mind. In fact, I think he was enjoying himself.

"We should try to go to more games," he said. "When it gets warmer."

"Can we take the train next time?" I said.

"Why? This isn't so bad."

As we passed the exit to Ellroy, about an hour and a half from home, the rain turned to snow. Large, wet flakes rushed toward us out of the black night. They were dying stars, or tiny white fists, crashing down on us. My father had to slow to about twenty miles an hour, just to see. "April snows are the worst," he muttered.

We didn't get home until almost ten. The ground was covered with snow. There must have been a foot of it. I had to get out and shovel a path for the car. I moved as quickly as I could and then called the hospital.

Claire was there, all right. I thought I should go and check myself in. Maybe they would give me some pills or something to stop me from thinking so much. Maybe they'd drill holes in my brain and steam would come hissing out. Maybe they'd just slice part of it away, scrape away mold and crust, and I could spend the rest of my life sitting in a chair with a stupid smile on my face, happy and oblivious of the world.

The next morning I had my mother drive me to the hospital in Shearing. They wouldn't let me see Claire. They wouldn't let my mother see her either. Claire was in the ICU. They would let only immediate family members in there. My mother talked to one of the nurses but no one would even tell her why Claire was in the hospital. We drove back home.

I went over to Carl's.

"I didn't sell anything to her," he said. "I don't sell that shit."

"Who did?"

"I don't know."

"You know."

"You don't even know why she's in the hospital," he said.

"All I know is what Bryce told me."

"That's right."

"What do you know?" I said.

"The same as you. I don't know anything."

Claire was in the hospital for three days. My mother drove me there again after school one day. She stayed in the waiting area while I went to Claire's room. As I turned the corner toward her room, I thought I saw Carl at the end of the hallway. Whoever it was, he moved quickly; I couldn't be sure that it was Carl, and I almost followed to see whether it was. I couldn't think of any reason why he'd be in the hospital; he didn't know Claire well enough to visit her, unless what Bryce had said was true.

I entered Claire's room. It had the same sterile smell that I remembered from the train, only with more plastic. Claire was sitting up in bed, but her eyes were shut. The other bed in the room was empty. The dividing curtain was pulled all the way back against the wall, and the bed was precisely made, with sharp creases and perfect pillows. It looked rigid, fake, a little scary, like the inside of a coffin. I had expected to see tubes coming out of Claire's nose and arms, but there was nothing. She could have been taking a nap in the hospital, perfectly fine and ready to leave when she opened her eyes. Her hair was a mess, tangled at the back of her head, and she didn't have any makeup. She was wearing a hospital gown with a robe over it. This was the first time I'd seen her without her Goth gear. She looked healthier. Without makeup, her face had color; it was friend-lier without the black circles that usually surrounded her eyes. She appeared too healthy to be in a hospital bed; it didn't look right. I stood in the doorway, wondering whether I should leave, but she turned, opened her eyes, and smiled. It was a tired, forced smile.

"I won't stay long," I said. "I just wanted to see how you're doing."

"Stay awhile. It's so boring in here."

"When do you get to go home?"

"They said that if I'm not out of here by five tonight, it will be first thing tomorrow morning."

"Why is that?"

"I don't know. Paperwork or something. It's like a restau-rant, you're meal isn't over until the check comes."

"Where are your folks?"

"My mom had to go pick up my sister from school. I don't know where my dad is. He hasn't been here that much."

"I'm sorry."

"He's just mad."

"Your mom's not mad?"

"That will be later."

"There's a rumor around school about the whole thing," I said. "Well, actually a couple of them." I waited to see if she wanted to hear them. She gave me another tired smile. "One of them is that this was deliberate, and the other is that my friend Carl is responsible."

"Responsible how?"

"That he sold you some bad stuff."

"Who is saying that?"

"A lot of people now, but I heard it from Bryce." The first part wasn't true. I had heard only it from Bryce.

"Bryce is an asshole." She hadn't really answered the question. I waited, but she didn't go any further.

"How'd you get here?" she asked.

"My mom. She's in the waiting room."

"Oh, I'm sorry. You shouldn't keep her out there."

"It's all right, she's good at sitting around doing nothing. I don't think it's possible for her to get bored. Or else she's so bored all the time, it seems natural to her."

We were silent for a little while.

"At least you don't have a roommate," I said.

"There was one, but she left."

"She got better?"

"I don't know. They just wheeled her out last night and she never came back. I was kind of out of it anyway, but they never tell you anything."

"It sounds kind of creepy."

"Hospitals are like that. You should be here at night. You hear all sorts of strange, horrible noises, and people are coming in and looking at you, waking you up and taking your temperature or blood pressure or whatever, and half the time you don't know what's going on or why. And then during the day, you don't see anybody and there doesn't seem to be anything going on. They're like vampires, only coming out at night."

"With any luck you'll get out of here before it gets dark again, before the vampires come back."

"I hope so. My mom should be back soon to check on it."

"I'd better go, then. Or we could wait around to see if you need a ride or something."

"That's all right. I'll be fine."

"I hope so," I said, and got up to leave.

"Come here." Claire held out her arms. I went over and gave her a hug. "Don't worry about me. It was an accident. Just an accident."

I had hoped that she would tell me more than that, but she didn't and I didn't want to press her. I smiled at her and lightly grabbed the sleeve of her white gown. "It's too bad they don't have this stuff in your color," I said.

She laughed. "Can you imagine, patients dressed all in black? This place would really give you the creeps." An image of Anna jumped into my head—she was laid out in the other bed. Both she and Claire were dressed in funeral clothes, stretched out in hospital beds, the sheets pulled tightly to their shoulders, their lifeless faces heavy with makeup, but their eyes were wide open, staring straight ahead.

"Call me when you get home," I told Claire.

"I will."

As my mother drove us home, I began to think of Anna as a bad force in my life. I had never thought that way before, but nothing seemed to be going right. Instead, the days kept getting stranger and stranger. She was somehow controlling events, tampering with the world in ways that only confused me. I wondered whether she was responsible for Claire. We had kissed, and then something bad had happened. Bryce claimed that Anna had wrecked his car on purpose. I didn't know whether to completely believe him or not, but if it was true, what did that mean about Anna? If she could drive a car into the steel edge of a bridge, what else was she capable of doing? Even if she wasn't responsible for all the bad things that were happening, they were still happening. They could be coincidences—that was the word my father had used at the baseball game—but there were an awful lot of them. Here I had been desperately trying to reach Anna, trying every way to receive a message from her, make contact with her, and maybe all this time I should have been trying to get away from her, refusing any contact she tried to make. Isn't that why we were told to avoid Mumler, because it caused bad things to happen? And now they were happening.

Bryce drove a new black Dodge Ram truck. It replaced the black Intrigue he had driven until the accident. It was said that someone had written, "Bryce Druitt is Ram tough," in the girls' bathroom on the first floor at school. It was rumored that Anna had written it. The only thing she ever said about it was, "If I wrote it, it was meant to be sarcastic. The problem is, there are a lot of girls who like Bryce but would never say so because he's a Goth." Claire had once said pretty much the same thing, that if he looked like the rest of us, he'd be one of the most popular guys in school. Instead, he was a scary guy. He was the type of guy who could wear black eyeliner and still look like a badass.

A few days after Bryce got his new truck, someone stuck a "Got Jesus?" bumper sticker on the back. He found out who did it and beat the guy up, but left the sticker. He thought it was funny. "I would have put it on myself," he told the guy, "but don't fuck with my vehicle." Bryce always used the word "vehicle" whenever he referred to his own ride, but never when he talked about anyone else's.

I had been trying to meet Bryce after school ever since I saw him at the baseball game, but he was always gone before I could find him. I would see where he had parked before school, but when I came out at the end of the day, his truck would be gone. I knew that sometimes he would drive away for lunch and park in a different spot when he returned, so after school I would walk around the parking lot down the hill, or down by the football field, where there was more parking, but I wouldn't see it. Finally, near the end of the week, I got to his "vehicle" before he did. It was a cool spring day, but the sun was trying to do its job. I could feel the warmth reflect off the black paint, and every few minutes I got close to the dark metal and tried to warm up, like it was a radiator or the last embers of a fire. A lot of snow had melted, but there were still piles along the street, where it had been plowed repeatedly over the course of the winter and been pushed into larger and larger mounds, and in the shadows of buildings and underneath trees, hiding from the sun.

I'd been waiting more than twenty minutes when I started thinking that maybe Bryce had had to serve detention. I didn't want to wait another forty minutes.

"You weren't leaning on my vehicle," he said. He had come up from behind, and startled me. He wasn't that much bigger than I was, maybe a few inches all the way around, but he always seemed to tower over me. He had on his usual gear: black stocking cap pulled down over his shaved head, close to his eyes; long black double-breasted coat, something you would imagine Napoleon's soldiers trudging around in; black jeans; big black army boots. He had snow all over him, as though he'd been rolling in it. Obviously he hadn't come directly from school; he'd been somewhere else. He might have come out of the woods across the street, then seen me near his truck. I didn't know.

"You weren't touching it." It wasn't a question.

"No," I said. "I wasn't even near touching your truck. I was wondering if I could talk to you."

"Let's find out."

"I overheard you say something at the game."

He gave me a hard look and seemed to grow in size. I thought about dropping the whole thing, but it was too late.

"I heard you say something about how it was Anna that almost killed you in your accident."

"She caused the accident," he said, matter-of-factly.

"You mean like with a spell or a curse?"

"No," he said. "She was driving."

"I didn't know that."

He shrugged.

"She wasn't hurt."

"Not a scratch."

"She didn't get in trouble with the cops or anything."

"She wasn't there when they came. She left the scene, and I told them I was alone in the car."

I didn't say anything.

"She did it on purpose, I think. Because of the notes I left in your locker."

I still didn't say anything. My mind was trying to catch up with what he was saying.

"I've got a box full of letters and art and books, just like you," he said.

"Yeah."

"You can have it all if you want."

I started to leave.

"How about an obituary?" he asked.

"What?"

"You got one in the mail, right?"

"I don't know what you're talking about."

"Ask Claire who sent it to you."

I should have asked to see the box of things Bryce claimed he had. It was a mistake. I should have looked at them; it might have answered some questions. At the time, I didn't want to listen to anything he had to say, and I didn't want anything he had to offer. Preen was right, I wasn't trying hard enough.

schooled

I tried to forget about what Bryce had told me, but I knew that sooner or later I would have to ask Claire about it. Maybe it was Bryce who had sent the obituary and was trying to blame Claire, or maybe he was trying to drive us apart. I looked at the walls of my room and wondered how many of the postcards and pictures matched those Bryce had received. I wondered whether his walls had once replicated Anna's. I studied each piece taped to my walls, writing down when it was sent and what information was on the back. I put a Post-it on each item. I had deleted most of her e-mails, but I printed out the ones I had kept, and put

them in a notebook. Everything was tagged and put in order; if Anna had left only puzzles, I was determined to
solve them. I worked on this at school, writing the connec-
tions, references, and allusions in my notebook during
class. My grades tanked. I started getting D's on tests and
assignments. The only class I was interested in, the only
one where I paid attention, was Mr. Devon's. And interesting things happened there.

   I was sitting in his class, making a collage. There were
ten or so of us in the room, and before anyone noticed or
said anything, Carl's dad had walked in, and was sitting at
one of the tables, watching us work. Everybody knew right
away that he was drunk. His face was slack and flushed,
and his eyes struggled to fix on anything and take it in.
Mr. Devon watched him for a few minutes and then approached him.

   "I can get you some materials if you want to join us,"
he said.

   Carl's dad swung his head around and looked up at Mr.
Devon with a curious expression. "No, I don't think so. I'll
just sit here a minute if that's okay with you."

   "If you're going to sit, then why don't you go sit at my
desk." He motioned toward his office, hoping that Mr.
Hathorne would move away from us.

   Carl's dad didn't even look up. "Right here is good for me."
He looked at the students working near him, studying them
with apparent confusion. "What kind of schoolwork is this?"

"This is art class," Mr. Devon said.

"I was looking for my son."

"He's not in this class this period," Mr. Devon said. "If you want, we can go to the principal's office and find out where he is."

"That's all right, I'll hook up with him later." He looked at Mr. Devon again, but with a steady, hard gaze this time. "You ever shot anybody?" (Later, some people claimed he had said "killed," while others thought they'd heard him say "caught.")

"I've been shot once."

"By a camera? You've got a lot of cameras around here, right?"

"I've still got the bullet in my neck."

"Let's take a look at that."

"All right, let's go outside and I'll show it to you."

Mr. Hathorne got up to follow Mr. Devon, and as he turned he noticed Mr. Devon's sculpture in the corner. Suddenly he ran toward it, grabbed a chair, and smashed the chair against the sculpture. Some of the girls screamed. Mr. Devon ran over and tackled Carl's dad, forcing the chair out of his hands and knocking them both to the floor. He pinned the drunken man's arms behind his back and marched him out of the room. He was gone ten minutes or so.

You don't get to see a teacher rolling around on the floor too often, and probably have even fewer opportunities to see him fighting somebody while he's down there. You would have thought that more than half the school had been in Mr. Devon's classroom that hour and had that opportunity, to judge from the number of people who claimed to have witnessed it. The whole school was impressed with how Mr. Devon had handled Mr. Hathorne. Some people said Mr. Devon had destroyed him; others said that if Mr. Hathorne had been sober, he probably would have taken Mr. Devon. Of course, if he had been sober, he probably would have never come into the school. But Mr. Devon's actions ranked second in most-talked-about subjects—everyone was debating whether or not Mr. Devon really had a bullet in his neck, and how it had gotten there. Some people maintained Mr. Hathorne had put it there, and that was why they were fighting. It's funny, but the whole episode actually made Carl more popular, if that could be possible; people sympathized with him, wondered how he could be such a nice guy with a father like that. It made me wish my dad would wreck the school in a drunken fit. But I was never that lucky.

then carl

You can have too many conversations. I might have had the fewest conversations in history, and still I had one too many. I asked too many questions, or said the wrong thing too many times. All people have a line they don't want you to cross, or a breaking point on a particular subject. Unfortunately for me, I reached my limit with Carl.

. . .

"What's going on with you and Claire?"

"What do you mean?"

"Is there something going on with the two of you?"

"It's true," Carl said.

"How long has that been going on?"

"For a while," he said. "It kind of started on Valentine's Day."

I was embarrassed. "Did she tell you that I kissed her?"

"She told me," he said. I could tell by his expression that she hadn't.

"I would never have done anything, if I'd known."

"That's all right. We just didn't want to make a big deal out of it. It started real slow anyway, and we didn't want to jump up and down about it with all that you were going through."

"I'm still going through it," I said.

"Why did you give that picture of Anna to Gerald Preen?" I asked. I didn't know that he had, but I was working on an obvious hunch—Carl was the only connection uniting Anna, Mr. Devon, and *The Channel.* I had to guess whether he had introduced Mr. Devon to Preen's people, or had gotten the photo from Mr. Devon. It was a fifty-fifty shot, and I figured that if Preen would go to elaborate lengths to fake his psychic readings, why wouldn't he fake a photo as well?

"I sold it to them," Carl said. "It was strictly business."

"Does everything have to be business with you?"

"I didn't know what they were going to do with it."

"Did Mr. Devon give you the picture of me?"

"You should ask him."

"And how about the picture of Anna?"

"She gave it to me." I guess that was supposed to be his payback for my kissing Claire. "She kissed me back," I wanted to tell him, but I didn't. I didn't say anything. I walked away and thought that I would never talk to Carl again. I couldn't talk to him, not after what he had done. I imagined I would just walk past whenever I saw him, treat him like wallpaper, something I wouldn't notice. Then, after we graduated, he'd move on to Alaska or wherever, like we had talked about when we were kids. I wouldn't go, even if he still wanted me to. Maybe he'd changed his mind; he was full of secrets. He kept Claire a secret from me, and then he sold that picture simply because he could, and didn't say anything about it. What kind of friend is that?

I still talked to Claire, but it wasn't the same. She said that Carl was sorry for what had happened. "You should talk to him," she said. "He wants to talk."

"Then he should talk to me."

I was done with Carl, and I saw Claire less and less. She stopped coming by in the morning to talk to Billy and me, and with no news to discuss, Billy and I had nothing to talk about. If I wasn't called on in class, I could pass the entire schoolday in silence. It was almost the way it had been before I met Anna. I would see Carl in the hall or outside school, shaking hands and talking with people, and think that maybe he didn't even notice that he and I hadn't said one word to each other in more than a week. Why would he? Nothing had changed for him, he was still friends with everybody else in town, and he was with Claire now anyway, the two of them together, so what did they need me for? In a few days he did need me, though, and I wish that he hadn't.

I was walking down Valley View Road after school, and was almost home, when Carl emerged between two houses, sneaking along like a cat in an alley. "Hey," he said in almost a whisper.

"What are you doing?"

"I need to talk to you. Can we go to your house?"

Carl was nervous. I don't think I'd ever seen him nervous before. It didn't suit him. We went into the house through the front door, avoiding my mother, and up to my room. Carl closed the door and unzipped his backpack. He took out a package, a little larger than a shoe box, wrapped in brown butcher paper, and a yellow envelope that was stuffed with cash.

"I need you to hang on to this for a while," he said.

"What for?"

"I have to go away."

"Where?"

"Just hold on to this."

"Tell me what's going on, Carl."

"I can't. There's no point anyway."

"When are you coming back? Does Claire know?"

"I can't tell her. She wouldn't approve. You're the only one, and I can't even tell you the whole thing. It's going to be all right, though. I'll be back as soon as I can. If not, you've made yourself a tidy sum there." He opened the envelope and handed it to me. I counted it.

It was almost $5,000.

"This doesn't make any sense," I said. "Tell me what's going on, and we can figure out another way."

"This is the best thing. I'm sorry about before. Thanks for helping me."

"I'm not helping you. I'm just taking your money. Let me help you."

"You are," he said, and then he was gone.

Two days later Carl's mother reported him missing to the police, and a few days after that Mr. Hathorne wandered into the police station and confessed to Carl's murder. "I killed that boy," he shouted when he came through the doors. "I'm telling you, and you can go tell his mother—I killed that boy." He told the police a detailed story about how he had taken Carl across the river into the woods of Mumler and killed him, and then dumped his body into the river. He described the exact spot in the woods and the precise place in the river. He went on to confess to the murder of Anna Cayne. He wrote out his confession and signed it. There was, of course, only one problem. He was drunk at the time.

When he sobered up, he denied everything. "I'll say anything when I've been drinking," he claimed, and there wasn't anyone in town who wouldn't have attested to that. The police kept him locked up all the same. Walking to school, you could see the yellow boats in the river, and on them men in red jackets dragging long poles through the water, or peering down into the darkness, looking for Carl. I hated the sight of those boats. Day after day they sat there, moving a few yards up the river or a few yards down, the crews looking where the old drunk had told them his son was. He couldn't be in that water, I thought, but what did I know? I wished they would drain the damn river and leave it dry.

Every day I wondered whether I should go tell the police about my conversation with Carl just before he disappeared. They should know about it, but what did I really have to say? All he'd said was that he was going away—well, the police already knew he was gone. He hadn't told me where he was going, or why, or anything else. And I couldn't tell them about the money. And how would my story stack up with Mr. Hathorne's? He'd given the police pages of information, plenty of details, two murders, exact directions and locations. He'd led them somewhere. I had only one sentence, and it didn't take them anywhere. There was nothing for me to say.

How is it that the truth can seem so flimsy, so scant, and that lies can be so detailed and solid? It was obvious that

Carl's father had been lying in some drunken rant—he kept telling the police that from his sober cell—but they continued to comb the woods and sit in their boats on the river. "It's a waste of taxpayer money," my father said, "keeping those boats out there and those guys in the woods. A lot of good money thrown after the bad words of a drunk."

"They have to look for the boy, anyway," my mother said. She had refused to acknowledge that it was Carl, my oldest and only friend.

"It's Carl," I said. "Not 'the boy.'"

"They would have to do the same thing for any boy," she said, meaning it was the same thing.

the difficulty
of forgetting

I had a dream that they found a body. Their search finally yielded something. The rumors had been swirling around school, and when I caught up with Billy Godley he told me it was true. "The body's in bad shape," he said. "They have to send it out for tests."

In the dream there was some confusion and arguing about whose body it was, between those who insisted it was Anna and those who were equally convinced it was Carl. The question was put to a vote. Everybody showed up at the town hall; people came with signs and buttons, and some of the people who thought that it was Anna who'd been found in the woods insisted that Carl was responsible for her body's being there in the first place. Before anyone could vote, however, Carl walked calmly into the hall where people were assembled, his blue visor pushed back casually on his forehead. He smiled and waved and shook hands, like a politician. He went to the front of the hall and spoke into a microphone at the lectern there.

"This is what I want to know," he said. "Did she know she was naked in the woods? Did she know that they found her in a shallow cup of earth, and could she have told us if it was an unfinished grave or just an indentation she laid in or was laid in? Did she know that her black coat was folded on the ground nearby, her ten-eyelet Doc Martens placed side by side, with the socks rolled and tucked neatly into the places where her feet should have been? Did she know that she had been there for months, just patiently lying there, waiting for someone to find her?" He held up a photograph of the frozen river, the hole, and her empty dress left on the ice, the last remains of a melted witch. It hadn't fallen to the ice haphazardly, however, but had been arranged carefully, the arms pointing down, the body straight behind, a black arrow pointing to the hole, or somewhere else.

When I woke up I called Billy Godley and asked him whether he knew anything about the dress. Had his father said whether the police considered it a clue, an arrow? I asked him whether there were any photos from the scene that I could see, showing which direction the dress was pointing. He said he would check on it.

By the time I got to school, Billy was already there. On a map, his father had drawn where he thought the dress had been. The police hadn't thought about the dress as an arrow. "He said that was an interesting take on it," Billy told me. Just a few months too late, I thought.

I took a ruler and drew a line across the map, starting at the dress. It was guesswork; it may not have meant anything, and if I was off by even a degree, it would change everything, and if you followed the line from the ruler out far enough, you'd wind up somewhere in Alaska, but the line went right through Mumler. I felt stupid for not thinking about Mumler before. I should have gone out there; I should have been thinking harder, working harder at trying to find Anna, or what had happened to her. Mumler meant something; it seemed so obvious.

Between classes I spotted Claire, and told her about Mumler and asked if she would go there with me.

"I didn't know you guys went there," she said.

"She wanted me to see a ghost."

"Did you?"

"We just got cold. It's not cold now, at least."

"This is going to sound stupid," she said, "but I don't want to go there until Carl gets back."

"I understand. He's going to come back, Claire. Don't worry about that."

"Okay."

"Besides, nothing happens over there, all the bad stuff is on this side of the river."

At the end of classes, Claire was waiting for me at my locker. "When are you going over there?"

"You're going with me?"

"It's a stupid superstition, right?"

"I'm not the best person to say, but I think so. I'm going back, anyway."

"Then I'll go with you," she said. "It's the least I can do."

We went the next day, Saturday. The last time I had seen Mumler, the trees were bare and the ground was covered with snow. You could hardly see the "No Trespassing" sign now because of the brush and tall grass, and the trees filling with new leaves. Nothing looked the same. We walked past the sign and deeper into the woods as I tried to locate where Anna and I had been.

There were bugs everywhere, small black flies that flew into my mouth as I breathed hard trudging through the tangled brush. Claire was wearing black jeans and a black long-sleeved shirt, and an old beekeeper's hat that her father had found on one of his daily searches. ("Maybe we should bring your dad," I had said. "Even he won't go into Mumler," she replied.) I had made fun of the hat before, but I wished I had one now. The bugs were annoying, filling the air at my eyes and nose and ears. Besides, who would see me out here anyway?

"What are we looking for?" Claire asked.

"We were by a chimney," I said, "but I think we walked along here. I don't know. It's hard to tell. We have to do it like this. I saw it in a movie." I took her hand, and we stretched out and walked together in a line.

"Does it work with only two people?"

"That's all we've got."

We walked intently, looking for something I could recognize, anything that might announce the place where I'd been with Anna. For a moment I imagined we could have been out on a beautiful day, holding hands and carrying a picnic basket, looking for a nice spot to have lunch and wait for the dark and the ghosts. I wondered . . . If Carl didn't come back, if Claire and I might . . . and then the thought was gone. I wanted Carl to come back. I wanted Anna to come back. I wanted everything to be covered in snow again, to be the way it was the last time I had been in these woods, not searching for clues and signs and a ghost that might not even be there.

We wandered in the woods for another twenty minutes or so. Claire would look through the trees, trying to find the chimney, and then down at the ground in front of us, her netted head bobbing around like some anxious, exotic hunter's. Suddenly she stopped and bent at the waist, peering at something on the ground that I couldn't see because of the tall grass. She pulled me over. Nestled in the grass was a black cell phone. I went to pick it up and she grabbed my arm. "Don't touch it," she said.

"We should see if it's Anna's." It looked like her phone. I wanted to pick it up.

Claire shook her head. "Fingerprints. We should leave it right there and go call the police. She was right, but I wanted to know right then. I wanted to know whether it was her phone, and if it was hers, when it was last used and who it was she had called and who had called her. With Claire's reasoning, I would have to wait.

I stood and stared at the phone in the grass. I was convinced it was Anna's. I grabbed my phone and dialed her number, looking at the ground to see if anything would happen. I couldn't get a signal in the middle of the woods.

I continued to stare at the object on the ground. It was an answer, lying a few feet from us, but we shouldn't pick it up, so it was just another question, another riddle. Finally Claire pulled me away, afraid that I was going to give in and pick up the phone.

"We'll call them as soon as we get to your house," she said. "Then we'll bring the cops right back here. It will only take a little while."

We were driving back to my house, the warm air blowing in through the open windows of Claire's car. The sun was bright and fuzzed at the edges, a dandelion floating in a blue pond. For someone else it was probably a perfect day. It should have been. Claire was nothing like Anna, I thought. She was timid and quiet and safe compared with Anna. Whatever feelings I had for Claire—and I did like her—were gone. They had disappeared as quickly and as unexpectedly as they had first struck me. It was just as it had been with Melissa, except those feelings had come and gone faster. There was no reason for it, the attraction simply passed. Did that mean that the feelings I had once had for her weren't real, or that they weren't strong enough?

I turned from the window to Claire. I would ask her about something I'd been keeping to myself.

"Did you know that somebody sent me Anna's obituary in the mail?"

"From the paper?"

"No. It was a personalized one, just for me."

"I didn't know that." Claire's voice shook. She knew what was coming, and I didn't want to have the conversation any more than she did, but I kept talking.

"Bryce told me about it. He said I should talk to you." I looked at her. Her face was red, caught red; she was ready to cry.

"I sent it," she said.

"Why?"

"Look . . . it wasn't my idea." She was crying now. "Anastasia asked me to send it, so I did."

"When did she ask you?"

"A couple of weeks before she was gone. She said that you'd been helping her with her obituaries and this was the last one and she wanted me to send it to you. She told me when to send it."

"She wrote it?"

"She wrote it."

"That's not what her dad said."

She shrugged. "I don't know. Maybe she didn't write it. I just sent it like she asked me to."

"Did you read it?"

"I read it."

"Is it true?"

"Some of it, maybe. I don't know, I asked her and she wouldn't give me a straight answer. I just figured it was another puzzle."

"And the end? You let her write that about me?"

She looked at me as if I should know better, and I did know better. You weren't going to stop Anna from doing what she wanted. "You didn't take that seriously, did you? She said that you would laugh, that you'd know she was joking, teasing you about never calling her Anastasia. You were the only one she ever let get away with that."

"But why did you send it, even after she was gone?"

"What do you mean, why? She asked me to send it, and I did. Didn't she have all of us do stuff like that all the time, make stuff and cut up crap and send it around to each other or put things places? I hate all of that now. It's so stupid." Claire was yelling. I should have been the one yelling.

Instead, I said quietly, "Let me out here."

She pulled over to the side of the road and I got out. I walked up ahead and she sat in the car. I wasn't that far from home, maybe ten minutes. I kept looking back and the car was always there the side of the road, even when I made the turn onto Brook.

I called the police once I got home. They drove me to Mumler, and I showed them where Claire and I had found the phone. They photographed the area, and retrieved the phone and put it in a clear plastic bag. They weren't going to touch the phone right now, one officer told me; it had to be checked for fingerprints. He had picked it up with rubber gloves, so I didn't see why he couldn't turn it on right then and tell me. The police probably wouldn't have told me then anyway; they would have had another excuse to keep information from me. I had done the right thing—I could have picked it up and turned it on when I was there with Claire. I didn't even have to call them. And what did I get for doing the right thing? Nothing. They said they'd let me know as soon as they could. They would let me know anything else they found too. And they did search the area more, but found nothing.

I went home and lay on my bed and called Anna's cell. I didn't expect anything, and I got nothing in return. It rang and rang. My mother came to tell me that dinner was ready, and sat beside me on the bed. She turned off the phone and put her arm on my shoulder. I didn't move. She ran her hand across my back and shoulder. I didn't move. I didn't even open my eyes. I didn't want to cry again. She ran her hand across my back and shoulder, quietly and calmly.

"You should eat something," she told me.

"I should," I agreed. I didn't move and she didn't leave; she remained beside me on the bed, lightly rubbing my shoulder the way she used to after tucking me in at night when I was little. I wished she would stay there forever, and then I was asleep.

. . .

The past is a river. It flows. It winds around, coursing through my memory until it arrives in the present. It looks the same, but everything has changed, different waves making up the same water. At times it is frozen, stagnant and still, and other times it rushes at you with a strong current, washing over everything. It is always moving, changing from second to second, as unstable as those elements at the end of the periodic table that Mr. Devon had talked about. I wanted to have control over it, but things I wanted to forget kept flooding back, and things I wanted to remember, letters and e-mails I threw away, passages from Anna's notebooks, drifted away.

If I could, I would choose to forget everything, to forget Anna entirely, but that would mean becoming a completely different person. I would gladly do that, don't get me wrong, but I know it can't happen. In some ways I am different already, changing into someone I never planned to be, changing and moving downstream, but still remaining.

Billy Godley was waiting for me Monday morning at school. He had news. It wasn't Anna's phone after all. It was Mr. Hathorne's. "And this is the part you should know before everyone starts talking about it," he said. The last call Mr. Hathorne had made was to my mother. Billy wasn't going to say anything to anybody about it, but it was only a matter of time before everyone knew. People weren't going to think anything that wasn't already racing around in my head about that phone call. I didn't know whether to run home and confront my mother about it immediately or call my dad at his office and let him know. Maybe he already did know. I prepared myself for the rumors and the questions, but made it through the day without having anyone say anything.

I went straight home after school, and there was a squad car in the driveway, next to my father's car. I hoped I hadn't missed anything. When I entered the kitchen I saw the same officers who had talked to me months before, sitting in the same chairs they had sat in months before. My father was sitting at the table, and it was obvious that they had just started talking. My father glanced up at me with a look that said, "Hold it right there," so I stayed where I was, off to the side, intrigued and taking some satisfaction that my mother was now the one having to explain herself. I never thought that she would be mixed up in anything illegal or wrong; I never thought she'd be mixed up in anything at all. I expected her to collapse or come apart in front of the cops. This wasn't the smooth, uncomplicated day she always tried to maintain; this was a mess she couldn't run to the neighbors to solve. Surprisingly, there were no hysterics; she was composed and answered the officers' questions directly, in a confident, calm voice.

She said that when Mr. Hathorne had called her, he was drunk and wanted her help, wanted her to take him back to rehab. "My wife is responsible for him getting to rehab the first time," my father explained. "He's been something of a project of hers."

"Where was he when he phoned you?" the policeman asked.

"He wouldn't say," my mother replied. "I told him that I would come and get him, but he wouldn't tell me where he was." He then went and turned himself in to the police and confessed himself a murderer.

The officer closed his notepad and said that he didn't have any more questions. In my head I kept shouting, "Ask her about coffee, ask her about dinner"—I wanted to show them where Mr. Hathorne had sat and eaten, but they had finished. Maybe my mother *was* just trying to help. Maybe Mr. Hathorne *was* something of a project. She'd never had a project before, as far as I knew. It's what my father had told the police, and I remembered him lecturing me on telling them the truth. It could have been true. I'd like to think that my mother had more sense than to get mixed up with the town drunk—sexually, I mean. She was already mixed up with him in some way, that's for sure, but I wasn't sure she had more sense than that.

waiting for a whale

I felt the way Jonah must have felt right before he got swallowed by the whale. All sorts of bad things were happening on the ship where he was hiding from God, and Jonah knew that he was the cause of the trouble. After the ship was caught in a violent storm, Jonah told the crew to throw him into the sea so the ship could be saved. "I know it is because of me that this great tempest has come upon you," he said. And once they'd thrown him into the sea, where he was swallowed by a great fish, the storm ended and the ship and the sailors were safe again.

Was I as responsible as Jonah, I wondered. If I left, would Carl come back? If I threw myself into the river, would that bring Anna back? They were the ones who had left, and look what had happened to the rest of us. If I were gone, would everyone else be safe?

f l i g h t

The final bell of the year rang, sounding better and brighter than any other bell of the year, and the school was filled with people running as fast as they could to clear out their lockers and start the summer. I took my time. I almost dreaded the vacation. What would I do all day, every day? There were too many days, too many hours to fill. It was like a trap waiting to be sprung, why should I rush into it? I stood in front of my locker, wondering whether the few notebooks and pens were worth taking home. There was a book on Diane Arbus that Mr. Devon had given me to read right after Christmas, shoved way in the back. I grabbed everything from the locker and headed to his room. The halls were quiet, with almost everyone gone. Some teachers remained, cleaning up their classrooms.

I found Mr. Devon busily packing.

"I didn't steal it," I said, and handed him the book.

"Did you read it?"

"I think so," I said. "She lived happily ever after."

"Do you have a few minutes?"

"Plenty of them."

"Can you help me with some of these?" Together we carried about a half-dozen boxes out to his truck. "You wouldn't want to help me with that again, would you?" he asked me back in the classroom. He nodded toward the sculpture in the corner. I shrugged and helped him crate the creepy thing. He got a handtruck and we rolled the crate outside.

"What are you doing this summer?" he said when we walked back into the building.

"I don't have a clue. How about you?"

"I'm going up to a cabin in Alaska. No TV, no electricity, just me, some books, and a lot of fish, I hope."

"Where in Alaska?"

"This place called Slocum," he said. "I've been going up there for a couple of years. I'll be back in time for football, though. I expect you to come out again."

I nodded. "I always thought about going to Alaska."

"It's beautiful up there. You should go sometime. I highly recommend it."

He directed me to a few boxes in his office. "That's all trash." Can you put it in the hall? They won't know it's trash if I leave it in here."

I grabbed the first box and was sorry that I'd lifted it. It seemed even heavier than the sculpture. I made it out to the hallway and went back for a second box. This one I just kicked on the floor, getting a good few feet with every push from my leg. As I turned into the hallway, one side of the box gave way and papers spilled onto the floor. I bent down and was throwing them into the box when I noticed an envelope. It looked like Anna's handwriting on it. It looked like one of her homemade stamps. It was Mr. Devon's face, smiling from one edge of the tiny square to the other.

Inside the envelope was a piece of notebook paper with some writing—"How do you draw a bunny?"—and a drawing. At the bottom of the page, in small, loopy letters, was written, "the new york correspondence school did not die," and "June 5, 1973." That date was crossed out and underneath was "January 13, 1995." The drawing looked nothing like a bunny. I couldn't tell what it was. The handwriting looked like Anna's, but trying to look like someone else's. It was the same notebook paper she used. There was nothing to tell me when it was written, no date, no postmark, nothing. It seemed that it should mean something, a coded message between the two of them. I thought that maybe it was Mr. Devon she had contacted after all, and not me. I imagined that she was still alive, that the letter had come from Alaska and she was up there waiting for him. He would go there and be with her and they would live happily ever after. I actually thought this.

I went back into Mr. Devon's office and held the letter out to him, confronting him. "What is this?"

He took it from me and looked at it. He could tell that I

was upset, but he was as calm as anything. Smiling, he said, "She slipped a folder under my door one day, early in the year, maybe September. It had a few drawings in it, and a note about what she was trying to do. She wanted my opinion on them, I guess, but she never came by to talk about them, and I forgot about them. Then when she was . . . when she disappeared, I found the black heart and put it in your locker. I found this today, and I put it in the trash. I'm sorry, I should have given it to you."

That was all he was going to say about it. I didn't know whether to believe him or not. It seemed too simple. I put the letter in my back pocket and carried the last box out to the hallway. I sat on the floor and started going through the boxes, digging through old contact sheets and unclaimed art projects and scraps of paper and magazines and official school stuff, looking for the note Anna had left for Mr. Devon, or the folder she had put it in. I wondered whether the folder was the one I had seen in that book the first time I went to her house, the same book I later saw in his office. I was filled with a nervous anger, and started taking the items out of the boxes one by one and throwing them on the floor. After a while Mr. Devon came out and locked the door to his classroom. He was leaving. He stood near me and casually looked at the mess I had created.

"Can I give you a ride home?" he asked.

"No." I didn't bother looking up. He stood there a minute and I imagined that he was thinking about helping me, but he didn't. Finally he just left.

"Have a good summer," he said. "And I'll see you at the first practice. August fifteenth."

I didn't respond. You'd think that after all I had done to help him out, he could have helped me this once. Would it have killed him to kneel down and look through a box for a second? He knew how important it was to me, and still he just left.

I finished searching through the boxes and didn't find anything. Maybe Mr. Devon hadn't bothered to help me because he knew there was nothing to find. He could have been lying about the whole thing, for all I knew. Anna had never liked him, and now I didn't either.

There was no one left at school, so I went home. I took the letter out of my pocket as I was walking and looked at it again. It had to mean something. The dates seemed an obvious place to start deciphering, and 4s came up again: June = 6, 6 + 5 = 11, 1 + 9 = 10, 7 + 3 = 10, 11 + 10 + 10 = 31, 3 + 1 = 4; 1995 − 1973 = 22, 2 + 2 = 4. But that didn't tell me anything, except that I could add and subtract. It answered nothing. If there was a code, I wasn't going to break it. The letter might have been nothing but a joke or game between the two of them. Or it might have been everything, it might have been their secret, some-thing Anna had never discussed with me. It was the proof of a lie she had told me, or had never told me. She had said that she disliked Mr. Devon, but here was this stupid draw-ing. I hated the letter. I hated them both.

I imagined following Mr. Devon up to Slocum, Alaska, and finding her there, waiting for him. I looked at a map of Alaska when I got home. There was no Slocum, not even anything that sounded like it. There was a Slana, and a Sleetmute. I tried to remember whether Mr. Devon had said either of those names, but all I could remember was Slocum. Maybe it was too small to be on a map, or maybe I hadn't heard him right. I thought about calling him and asking, but if he had lied about it the first time he certainly wouldn't tell the truth now. Maybe he wasn't even going to Alaska.

I threw the letter on my bed and began taking down everything on the walls of my room. I removed things in large swipes, tearing pictures and postcards, knocking off Post-its I had painstakingly attached not too long before. I should have been more careful. I wanted it all gone in a hurry, and I had a thought to throw everything away, but I went and found a box in the garage and piled everything into it. I went to my closet, retrieved the package Carl had given me, and put the box over the spot where I had hidden the package. I took Carl's package to my desk and opened it.

I had thought I would find Carl's ledgers inside, but I didn't. Under the brown paper was a box with a note from Anna, to Claire.

Keep these in a safe spot. Protect them as if they were your own skin and bone. Protect them as if they were your heart. Don't tell anyone that you have them, but after two months give them to someone you trust and have them follow the same instructions. You are responsible. You must know where they are going, where they will wind up. These are dangerous, you cannot let them fall into the wrong hands. Keep them safe. Pass them on. But keep them safe.

I lifted the box lid slowly, and there they were, Anna's notebooks, the complete set, fourteen volumes of her obituaries. They were tied together with black twine, and on the top volume was taped a note with big block letters: I KNEW YOU WOULD READ THIS.

I leafed through two of the volumes, but soon realized that without the master list I wouldn't be able to find any particular obituary or keep track of the ones I had read. Anna had been right, the notebooks were chaotic without the master list. I decided to start reading from the first volume, all 1,516 obituaries. I stayed up most of the night, reading about the deaths of everyone who had helped the Caynes move in, or seen them move in, then other neighbors, people on her street. Her classmates and teachers started dying next. It seemed that people appeared in the notebooks not long after she came into contact with them. I jumped ahead, and found the obituaries of people I knew she had met after she met me, but my death was not in the spot where it should have been. I went back to where I had left off in the first volume and read until I fell asleep.

I spent the next five days reading Anna's notebooks at every opportunity. I could hear her voice talking about every person, how each one lived and died. I had read some of the obituaries before, but never so many, and never so many at one time. Her caustic humor was still fresh and funny, but now I noticed another, less satisfying element in her writing. While she dutifully recounted the achievements and highlights of each person's life, the real achievement was the person's death. Almost without exception, Anna spent the most space describing the precise details of a person's demise. The deaths contained more drama and importance than the lives. I could hear Anna defending herself, arguing that the facts of everyone's life were accurate and well represented, and if the lives seemed inconsequential or diminished, so be it. Besides, she would say, you wrote a few yourself; are they any different from mine? They weren't, but I found myself, for maybe the first time, wanting to stick up for people and their lives, to defend the whole town. They couldn't be as pointless and insignificant as they seemed, these small lifetimes one after another.

I was sitting in the backyard with the tenth volume when I heard someone whisper my name. I closed the notebook and turned to see Carl standing at the corner of the house, his blue visor pulled low across his forehead, wearing his usual blazer, looking as he always did. He looked at me with a hint of a grin.

"Are you hiding?" I put the notebook under the lawn chair.

"I didn't want your mom to see me."

"She's out," I said. "Are you back?"

"I'm back," he said. "I just got back and wanted to see you."

"Where were you? The whole town's gone crazy since you left."

"I know. I just had some things to take care of. I told you I'd come back. I've got something for you," he said.

"Do you want to go inside? I need to give back your stuff."

"I'll get it later. I just wanted to bring you something."
He slipped his backpack off his shoulders and opened it.
He took out a manila envelope and handed it to me. "It
doesn't change anything, I know, but I wanted to apologize
and try to make things right."

I opened the envelope. Inside was the photograph of
Anna and me, and a negative.

"How did you get this?" I asked.

He shrugged. "It was just business." I knew better than
to ask anything else. "I've got to go," he said. "I don't want
anyone else to see me before my mother does."

"Hey, Carl, about that package you gave me."

"It's Claire's package," he said. "She wanted me to give
it to you." My mother's car pulled into the front driveway
and Carl ran across the backyard, toward the woods at the
top of Brook Road. It would take him twice as long to go
that way, but he probably wouldn't be seen. Carl knew what
he was doing. I was glad he was back, glad he had come to
see me, and glad he had done something for me. For a moment I thought that things were going to get better. If Carl
could come back, why couldn't Anna? Why couldn't everything keep getting better? I returned to my chair, put the
envelope in the notebook, and continued reading.

Near the end of the last volume, I saw my own name. I
had resigned myself to the idea that she had not written
one for me, and was glad for every page where I was absent.
I didn't want to see my own life belittled and demeaned. At
the top of the page she had written, "Something as simple

as snow," and then crossed out the first word. I won't repeat
the entire thing here, but most of it:

> One of the most important writers of the past century
> died in his sleep at the age of eighty-eight, at his home in
> Baton Rouge, Louisiana, where he had lived for nearly
> seventy-two years. . . . His first novel, published two weeks
> after his eighteenth birthday, was a modest success, but
> two years later, his next novel established him as one of
> the most important contemporary ghost story writers.
> Four more novels and a collection of short stories followed,
> all published before he turned forty, and then there was
> nothing. Rumors circulated that he had disappeared into
> the bayous of Louisiana, that he had suffered a collapse
> from exhaustion or mental breakdown, or that he had
> drowned in the Mississippi River. His readers found clues
> and explanations in his writings, but none of the stories
> and theories was true. He was living quietly in his house at
> the end of Glasgow Avenue in Baton Rouge, down the
> street from his brother, raising a family of his own.
>
> A chance encounter with an old high school friend,
> Anastasia Cayne, at Ichabod's bar had changed his life.
> They were quickly married and had two children, Erich
> and Bess. She wrote obituaries for the Baton Rouge *Ad-
> vocate*, while he raised the family. After a fourteen-year
> absence, he returned with *The Casualty of Obituaries*, a
> collaboration with his wife. "Everyone could benefit
> from being silent for a while," he was quoted as saying.
> "You have to pay attention, take the world in before you
> can accurately let it out again. There's something to be

said for silence, exile, and cunning." While the novel was an immediate critical and popular success, it was his last work. The writing kept him away from his family, and he devoted his remaining time to them. . . . He is survived by his wife and two children.

I called my brother and asked him if I could come and stay for the summer, or longer. "Absolutely," he said. "Getting out of there might be just what you need. Mom and Dad could drive anybody crazy. They're fine with you coming down?"

"They won't even notice I'm gone," I said. I didn't tell him that I hadn't talked to them about it. With any luck I'd be there before he could say anything.

"There's a ton of stuff to do here, and all of us want you to come. You can stay as long as you like."

It was easy. Why should I stay? My parents didn't seem to care whether I was around or not; the whole town didn't seem to care. If by some miracle Anna came back, I could come back then too. But what were the chances of that? Maybe she was somewhere else, living a different life as a different person, filling in her notebooks with the names and dates and deaths of a whole other town. Maybe she was in Louisiana right now, recording the deaths of one person after another. Maybe when she was done, our paths would cross or she would contact me. It was a fantasy, but there was nothing left for me here anyway, and who knows what was waiting for me in Louisiana? All I had to do was step on and off a plane and everything might be different. It was easy.

I left. I was gone.

. . .

I didn't pack that much, only a small suitcase of clothes and a backpack with a few books and Anna's notebooks. If I decided to stay, my parents could ship the rest of my stuff. There was nothing I needed, even the shortwave could wait. I could use my brother's computer. Or just do without it. Now that I was leaving, it seemed so easy. Maybe that's why Anna had left, because it was the easy thing to do.

I took the photograph Carl had given me—it was the only photo of Anna and me together, and it wasn't even real, me with a dumbfounded look on my face, and the ghostly image of Anna hovering over my shoulder—and the first postcard she had given me, the one with the photo of Pancho Villa on the front and the Ambrose Bierce quotation on the back. After writing those lines he had disappeared, vanished into the thin air of Mexico or who knows where. I could vanish too, step off the plane and disappear into the crowd.

I fantasized about stealing a car, to get me to the airport, or taking my mom's car and driving all the way to Louisiana. I wanted to disappear, leave without anyone's knowing. But I also wanted to leave something behind, to keep everyone guessing. I thought about taking a canoe down the river about sixty miles, where I could walk to a train station. Then I'd get the train to the city and go to the airport. I still had the money Carl had left me. I would leave the canoe on the shore and be gone. I would defy gravity and fall off the face of the earth, just as Anna had done. It wasn't as dramatic as an empty dress and a hole in the ice, but it was the wrong season for that, and I would still get out of here. People could still wonder what had happened; they could worry and look for me. They might think I had drowned in the river, or been kidnapped, taken against my will. Or they might think I had simply run off. Maybe they would think that I'd met up with Anna and we were finally together again, that it had been planned all along. She and I would be forever linked, both of us mysteriously disappearing into the river, or not. There would be questions and doubt. They would remember us both forever.

In the end, I simply told my parents that I was going. I came down for breakfast, and they were both sitting over their empty grapefruit halves and full cups of coffee, just sitting quietly, waiting for something to happen. "I'm going to spend the summer with Paul," I said.

My father said he couldn't afford it, and when I told him he didn't have to worry about it, he was fine with the idea. That was the only obstacle. My mother came over and gave me a hug, but she didn't protest. It was easy. It was certainly easier than some scheme of sneaking out of town on a canoe like Huck Finn. All I had to do was get in the backseat of the Volvo, and my parents drove me out of town.

"Anything you want to see before we leave?" my father asked.

I had to think about it. What was there left to see? Finally I said, "Gurney's."

We drove by on the way out of town, even though it wasn't on the way at all. Derek and Erick were there, one of them pumping gas and the other sitting on a folding chair next to Mr. Hathorne in the dim coolness of the garage. Both of them were drinking Cokes and watching the road, waiting for traffic. They all waved as we drove past; my father slowed, and he and my mother waved back. A second later we were out of town, and even though they were out of sight, I could still see them waving, their arms raised high and happy, a shiny excitement on their faces, glad to see somebody they knew.

My brother is going to pick me up at the airport. He'll be surprised when he sees me in my black jeans and black T-shirt. I'm a completely different person, more like Bryce than myself. Maybe I'll shave my head; maybe I'll dye my hair blond. No one knows me, so no one knows what to expect. I can have whatever past I want; I can forget how I used to be. It seems like it's all just remembering and forgetting. Things happen so fast, and then they're gone before you notice them. Events ambush you from out of nowhere, blindside you, and then you have to spend the time afterward trying to remember or forget what the hell it all was to begin with. The more you think about it, the more the events crumble, crack, break down, or refuse to change at all. They're either pieces of ice in your hand, changing shape and melting away until they're nothing like what they were to begin with, or pieces of glass, sharp and irritating, unchanging, reminders of pain and unpleasantness— or happiness.

I know absolutely nothing about where I'm going. I'm fine with that. I'm happy about it. Before, I had nothing. I had no life, no friends, and no family really, and I didn't really care. I had nothing, and nothing to lose, and then I knew loss. What I cared about was gone; it was all lost. Now I have everything to gain; everything is a clean slate. It's all blank pages waiting to be written on. It's all about going forward. It's all about uncertainty and possibilities. I have Anna to thank for that. I wouldn't be here, flying into the future, unafraid, if it hadn't been for her. Whether she meant to or not, she prepared me for this. I will be like her—the two of us gone wandering.

Back home they'll be wondering whether I ran off to find her; some will say that I did. Others will have nothing good to say; let them say it. In a few hours I'll be the new kid in town, with the neighbors lined up along the street, waiting for me as I arrive at my new home. I'll be the new kid in school. Who knows, I might even be popular for a change. I could be. I could be a question, just like Anna— open-ended, curling around the answer without ever delivering it. I could be whoever I want to be. I could go out for the football team, I could become a drug dealer, or I could be the new kid all dressed in black. I could be mysterious and have secrets. I could send out letters and postcards and art. I could take people down to the basement and let them listen to the secrets coming over the shortwave. There's a lot that I know. Anna didn't teach me everything, but she gave me a good start. There's a lot I can use. I could play games. I have the very last song she put on the last CD running through my head. Is that what she wanted to leave me with? My life is meant for joy? She always knew what she was doing. Maybe I will too, finally. This could be the best thing that's ever happened.

ACKNOWLEDGMENTS

(with apologies to Harry and Bess)

Now tell answer answer-be quick, speak pray-quickly pray answer-be quick look answer-be quick answer-pray now tell, pray please please tell say answer-be quick look pray-tell pray-now, pray-answer pray-tell answer-answer tell answer-be quick pray-tell answer-be quick quickly tell please pray-tell pray-answer pray-answer pray-tell answer-say look pray-now speak: Pray look pray-say tell tell, Pray pray-now pray-now pray, Now pray answer-answer look now pray pray-now now answer-be quick quickly tell Pray-quickly pray-tell answer answer look pray-now pray-look Pray-tell please please look say tell, Speak look pray-now pray.

Answer-be quick quickly pray pray-now pray-pray pray-look answer-be quick pray-tell Answer Pray-say Answer-say pray pray-now now answer-be quick quickly tell now pray-quickly look answer-answer tell answer pray say pray-pray pray pray-now now please pray-tell pray-quickly answer-be quick quickly answer-be quick pray-tell Say pray-tell pray-quickly pray-now answer-say pray pray-answer pray-answer.

www.assimpleassnow.com